NOTHING VAST

NOTHING

A NOVEL

VAST

MOSHE ZVI MARVIT

ACRE

CINCINNATI 2024

Acre Books is made possible by the support of the Robert and Adele Schiff Foundation
and the Department of English at the University of Cincinnati.

Designed by Barbara Neely Bourgoyne
Cover art: *Mountains*, painting by Mat Daly, reproduced with permission of the artist.

ISBN-13 (pbk): 978-1-946724-79-3
ISBN-13 (ebook): 978-1-946724-81-6

This is a work of fiction. Unless otherwise indicated, names, characters, businesses, places,
events, and incidents are either products of the author's imagination or used in a fictitious
manner. Any resemblance to actual persons, living or dead, is purely coincidental.

The press is based at the University of Cincinnati, Department of English and Comparative
Literature, Arts & Sciences Hall, Room 248, PO Box 210069, Cincinnati, OH, 45221–0069.
www.acre-books.com

Acre Books titles may be purchased at a discount for educational use. For information
please email business@acre-books.com.

For Imma and Abba, Danielle and Mardoche

Exactly like me: by the power of my yearnings
I am in the family.
And if I will not yearn,
I am not in the family.

—AVOT YESHURUN, from "Memories Are a House"

CONTENTS

PREFACE

Zionism began with a meditation on the fear of ghosts. In 1882, the Russian Jewish physician Leon Pinsker wrote perhaps the first Zionist tract, titled "Auto-Emancipation." In it, he rejected the historical charges and traditional bases of antisemitism—"[the Jews] are said to have crucified Jesus, to have drunk the blood of Christians, to have poisoned wells, to have taken usury, to have exploited peasants"—and argued the root cause of "Judeophobia" was much more primal. The world had witnessed the destruction of the Jewish nation two thousand years earlier when Jerusalem fell and the temple at the heart of Judaism ceased to exist—and yet Jews remained. "The world saw in this people the uncanny form of one of the dead walking among the living," Pinsker wrote:

> The Ghostlike apparition of a living corpse, of a people without unity or organization, without land or other bonds of unity, no longer alive, and yet walking among the living—this spectral form without precedence in history, unlike anything that preceded or followed it, could but strangely affect the imagination of the nations. And if the fear of ghosts is something inborn, and has a certain justification in the psychic life of mankind, why be surprised at the effect produced by this dead but still living nation.

Pinsker concluded: "A fear of the Jewish ghost has passed down the generations and the centuries." And for centuries, attempts to rid mankind of its fear had been fruitless. His solution was to clothe the ghost in flesh, give it a body; the spectral nation needed a material host.

Leon Pinsker is rarely talked of as a father of Zionism; instead that honorific goes to Theodor Herzl. And when Pinsker is discussed, the focus is usually his proposed solution—a Jewish state—rather than his diagnosis of the problem. Perhaps this is because we have no good way to talk of ghosts, which evoke either horror or sentimentality, on occasion eroticism. Ghost stories are almost always told from the perspective of the person visited by the apparition, and this person discerns the specter's temperament and intent. But there is something that rings false about such conceptions. They reify and personify the ghost, when the ghost is marked most by what it is missing.

We have no language to speak of profound absence, of things inchoate. This too is the problem in talking or writing about families, which in many ways are also ghost stories, marked as much by their negative spaces as they are by their tangible ones. The past can be a specter hanging over one's family. It is in mine—a discomfiting thing many relatives have explained away with neat narratives and silences that defy depth. In questioning these easy answers, I uncovered far more complicated questions, and I learned that if everything came together well, it was the mark of a lie. Silence and lies: these became motivations for me writing this novel, which is in many ways the story of my family, perhaps all families as they construct their collective identities and mythologies. In mine, however, the silences were compounded with the traumas—the Holocaust on one side, and struggle and superstition on the other (the jinn is always waiting to be summoned). Uncovering the stories, then, was an iterative act of returning over and over to the still-living elders in my family—those who still had access to the ghosts—and piecing facts together from the fragments offered. But it felt important, because Judaism is the metaphor of a family becoming a nation, and one can only understand Israel by seeing how its national mythology—replete with silences and lies—was constructed through the stories of early individual families that moved and migrated, resurrected an ancient language used only for ritual and prayer, and created a new self/identity to give flesh to Pinsker's spectral form.

How does one tell a different kind of ghost story? One in which the subject is not the subject, and what is hidden feels more real than what is visible? Who is qualified to serve as the narrator of such a story? For when it comes to ghosts and families, one cannot stare directly or speak explicitly.

There are rules—because superstition governs the supernatural—and these rules are the ones often passed on as commands, the ones most strictly enforced. They require that we remain silent, for an invoked ghost is always more terrifying and mischievous than an invited one.

Picture the Passover Seder. The family sits at the table ordered around the metaphors of the Seder plate: saltwater for the tears of slaves, horseradish for the bitterness of bondage, a paste of dried fruit and nuts for the mortar used in their forced labor, and so on. The table is crowded with food and people, rife with ritual and conversation; and yet there is one conspicuously empty chair, with a plate setting before it, and a full cup of wine. This is the seat for the prophet Elijah, should his ghost choose to join. The door to the room is open to allow Elijah in to dine with the family. In his absence, everyone can feel his enduring presence (just as in a piece of music, the notes are oriented around the rests; the silence defines them). Whether he ever shows up is irrelevant.

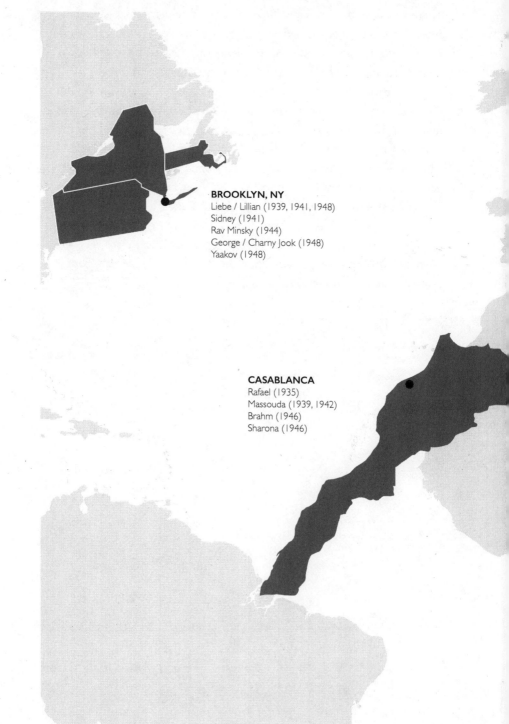

BROOKLYN, NY
Liebe / Lillian (1939, 1941, 1948)
Sidney (1941)
Rav Minsky (1944)
George / Charny Jook (1948)
Yaakov (1948)

CASABLANCA
Rafael (1935)
Massouda (1939, 1942)
Brahm (1946)
Sharona (1946)

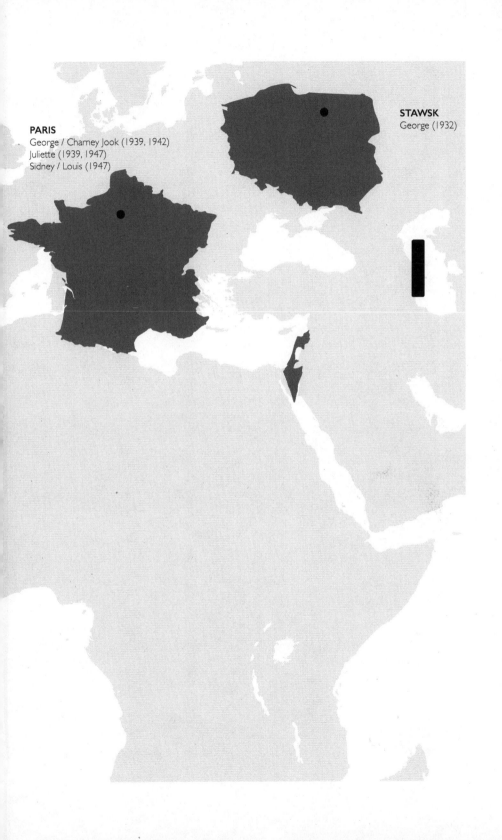

PARIS
George / Charney Jook (1939, 1942)
Juliette (1939, 1947)
Sidney / Louis (1947)

STAWSK
George (1932)

GEORGE

On February 26, 1932, George Mazar was coming home late from his work as a tailor's apprentice on the edge of Stawsk, Poland. He had spent his day tearing pieces of fabric, stitching them together, creating unseen wholes from former scraps. On this night, there was a dark but clear sky, with a moon at half full that gave off more light on the path than one would expect from its moiety. Though he'd walked this way home hundreds of times, George noted the streets looked different under this light. It was probably the long winter nights, he thought. His eyes had become so adjusted to the season's darkness, the sudden illumination was surprising. Houses seemed larger, turned at odd angles, and cast long shadows onto the dirt road. Some houses seemed to fade away, while others inexplicably appeared to push into view. He thought he remembered this area having more wooden homes, the type common among the poor and Jewish, but all of these were of stone. They were squat and modest, with the surnames of the current or former families carved into the stonework, supplemented by what looked like years of construction or dates of residence. George squinted to read them, but even in this bright moonlight, he couldn't see clearly enough.

While he was looking around with new curiosity, a man emerged from one of the small homes. The street was otherwise empty, and George immediately noticed the presence of a sudden other. The man looked old to George as he ran toward him, though George was at an age when he judged most men over forty with full beards to be old. Despite the man's seeming stage of life, he moved quickly and not at all stiffly, appearing to glide along the snowy path.

"George, George!" the old man yelled.

George stopped and examined the man but could not place him. "Good evening. Are you talking to me?"

"You are George, right?"

"I'm sorry to say I don't recognize you. Have we met?"

"Zerach's grandson George?"

"Yes, but he passed some time ago—may his memory be a shield unto us. Did you know him?"

"I know him well. We are old friends."

The man grasped George's bicep in that manner men do when they want to ensure you stay in place. George's arm tensed, his muscle contracting to free him, but the man's long, surprisingly strong fingers wrapped around the bicep and squeezed tightly.

"We are davening the Shacharit prayers, but we are only nine. Will you join us to make a minyan? It would be a mitzvah."

"Where?" George asked, unaware that there was a synagogue on the street.

"Over there." The man pointed with his other hand, the finger seeming exceedingly long. "From where I just ran."

George looked at the small stone structure. He had never noticed it before; it appeared old, humble, but was ornate in its stonework. It had a name etched into it, either the family name or perhaps that of the synagogue; George couldn't make it out. "I didn't know that was a synagogue. Might I ask what type of congregation it is?"

"Of course. It is a congregation of the mason."

"Stone masons?" George asked, not knowing the trade had its own house of worship.

"Will you help us make a minyan? We are stuck at a point in the service and cannot continue without you. Not until we make ten. It would be a great mitzvah."

George was confused as to why they were davening the morning Shacharit so late at night, but he felt he'd asked enough questions. He agreed and followed the old man, who retraced the footsteps in the snow to the synagogue. The man let George in first, then stepped in closely behind him and quickly locked the door. A wise precaution, George thought; in such places there was always a danger of violence from the state or the citizenry.

Once inside, George reverted to his habit of making sure there was a minyan according to the rule of never counting Jews. Instead of using numbers, he began mouthing the ten words of Psalm 28:9, with one word for each man he saw: *Hoshia et amecha, uvarech et nachlatecha, ur'em v'nas'em—Save your people, and bless your inheritance, and tend them and carry them.* At eight words, he stopped, then included the old man and himself, mouthing the final two: *ad ha'olam—until forever.*

George grabbed a tallis off the rack, but hesitated. He usually just hung the tallis over his back and shoulders, as he was taught at bar mitzvah, but these seemed especially large, meant to cover the body, and the eight other men who were swaying and rocking in their prayers all had their tallises draped as hoods. It seemed their custom, so George followed suit. The old man did likewise. With everyone covered in black-and-white cloth, George took a position behind the pews, joining the group at the outer edges, the tallis now obscuring most of his body, arms, and head.

There was no rabbi at the bima to guide them, though in a small congregation such as this one, at a weekday prayer, that was not uncommon. Every thirty seconds or so, one man close to the bima would say a fragment of a prayer to set pace, but George struggled to identify it and find his place. Since they were standing and had been in need of a minyan, George began reciting the Shemoneh Esrei. After several minutes of silent prayer, punctuated by the barely audible fragments, the old man grabbed George by the arm again, squeezing him harder this time. The man looked so different with the tallis as a hood—gaunt and pallid. Outside, his beard had seemed his most striking feature, but in here, where it was dim, with windows near the ceiling that brought in little light, his enormous teeth were what stood out. They looked like a horse's, long and narrow, powerful, but barely anchored, seeming ready to fall out at any moment.

"Will you do the first Aliyah?" he asked in a grave tone, pointing toward the front of the room.

George stared at the man, confused. "Aliyah?" It was Friday. There would not be a Torah reading, even at night. Why would there be an Aliyah, then, if there was no Torah reading?

"Please," the man said. "Go up. It would be a great mitzvah."

George was suddenly unsure of the day, of himself. Disoriented, he agreed and kissed his siddur, which he had picked up and held even though he knew the prayers by heart. Laying down the book, he walked up to the bima, put his hands on the sides of the wide podium, and turned to face the congregation. They each looked dark under the hoods of their tallises, shadows obscuring their features. Not one of them looked up as they rocked and prayed, but George could see their mouths moving. Or less their mouths than their teeth. They each seemed to have the same long gaunt teeth as the old man. Were these the teeth of masons? he wondered, not quite certain what that meant. As they muttered the prayers, he could hear their teeth chattering. It was a sharp and hollow sound, reverberating through the small space. He had not heard it when he stood in the back, but at the front of the room, it was overwhelming.

George tried to focus on the faces to see if he recognized any of the men— Stawsk having a large but tight-knit Jewish community—but they were a blur. He peered at the man closest to him, who'd set the group's pace with fragments of the prayer George could not place, but all he could see was a broad brow hanging over gray teeth, a mouth full of them, all coming together in a percussive rhythm. The sight made George queasy. He felt like he could smell the hot, sour breath from their mouths, but it must have been a mingled memory of all the old men who had held his arm tight and talked closely to his face. A childhood of hot breath from mouths beginning to rot had embedded the odor in his nostrils. It never really left. Old cabbage soup with turned herring, cured meat that had gone bad, agitated mothballs on long-resting fabric. Sometimes simply seeing an old mouth brought the smell back into his nose. These men were too far away for George to actually detect the rot, so it must be his imagination, but still his stomach turned, which caused his body to seize, because it also brought forth the memory of the old men always holding tight to his arm while they breathed their ancient sickness into him. George's own teeth began to feel soft and furry, unclean and fungal.

Realizing the Torah was not on the bima for his Aliyah, he wondered why it had not been brought out from the aron kodesh. He turned to see if the ark was open and if there was a specific Torah designated for the day, but it was empty—no Torahs, no brackets to hold the Torahs. George looked at the aron kodesh more carefully and realized it was unlike any he had seen before. It was narrow rather than wide, tall rather than squat. Instead of having two doors that opened out to reveal the grandeur of the scrolls, it had only one door that was hinged open on the left, revealing its entire empty space. Though the shape seemed familiar, George could not place it.

He turned again toward the congregation, feeling much time had passed with him alone at the bima, with no attempts by anyone to retrieve the Torah. The men still rocked and muttered with teeth chattering, not in unison, but in rhythm. Then it struck George—the shape of the aron kodesh. He knew it. It had eluded him because it seemed so out of place—like an unusual spice in a cake. It was shaped like a coffin. Now that he'd seen it, it was unmistakable. Behind the bima, in place of the aron kodesh, stood a large but simple pine box in the shape of a coffin, open and empty. Was it possible that this small synagogue appropriated such a box, using it as the holy ark? An aron kodesh was essentially just a wooden box, but was such a substitution allowed? Did the masons treat all wood as fungible, to be exchanged without meaning?

Disgusted, George pushed away from the bima and suddenly felt unsteady. His balance disappeared, and as his legs began to fail him, he grabbed the bima for support, but his arms felt weak, unable to hold up the weight of his increasingly heavy body. The light in the room felt evasive, the dimness tricking his eyes into seeing shapes and colors around him, but everything was blurry, making it impossible to focus. He felt dizzy and nauseous, trembly and cold, all the individual sensations from the evening mixing and remixing.

George moved forward, hoping the motion would keep him on his feet. He didn't want to fall in this place, increasingly unsure of where he was and how he would get home. George rushed the hooded figure closest to him, grabbing his arms in the way of old men, and the arms felt boney and frail. Is this how it felt to seize another in this manner? Concerned that he might pass out, he looked at the man beneath the tallis and yelled, "What is this place?"

Though he was creating a commotion, no one turned to look; the congregants remained engrossed in their prayers.

George ran to the door, but it gave nothing at his push and pull. It was locked by an absent key. The windows, high above, were sealed and out of reach. The room was a stone box, and he struggled to understand how he could get out.

When George was a child, a rabbi had scared him into doing his prayers by warning him that every prayer George missed or left unfinished in this lifetime, he would have to complete before he could go to Shamayim in the Olem Habah. But since Shamayim too is filled with prayer and study, in which one also has to keep on pace, any prayer you left unsaid in life would leave you struggling to catch up, always behind, dead but stuck, unable to fully ascend.

The old man who'd invited George in began to walk over to him, slowly but with intent, as if indicating that something needed to be done. The congregants turned their heads to look, straining their necks as the man moved closer to George in the back of the room. Suddenly afraid, George darted around the pews. He circled the room, touching the walls and books and anything that might move to reveal a gap. Nothing opened or moved. After circling several times, making himself dizzy from the rotations, George stopped at the bima, standing again in front of the empty aron kodesh, panting and struggling to breathe deeply, letting his arms support the full weight of his body.

Though George was no longer at the door, the old man had continued to walk toward it, turning to watch as George went round and round. Catching George's eye now, he opened a clenched fist and revealed something that George could not make sense of—a metal metacarpal, straight but ending in a hook—holding it in his open palm for what felt too long. Finally, he took the object and inserted it into the lock, turning it with little effort, and pulled open the door. He looked at George as if inviting him to leave, giving him so easily what he'd tried so hard to get.

George hesitated, his body simultaneously weak and seized in fear, not knowing if he would make it to the door. Pushing off the bima, he rocked backward first, and then forward, using the force of momentum to run straight through the center of the room. Though it was a small room, it took all of his strength to keep his balance and maintain his movement. Once he was within a few feet of the door, he could see outside and feel the cold night air.

Before reaching it, however, George tripped. Not on anything in particular, but simply from his feet not lifting as he intended. He began to fall, past the point where he could right himself, but before he hit the floor, the old man grabbed George's bicep, catching him and pulling him back up. As George regained his feet, his eyes met the old man's for a long moment. Still holding George's arm tight, the man said, "You have done a great mitzvah here. May your memory be a blessing." He released George's arm, and George lunged through the door, running into the night.

Somehow the moon had set, and the streets were dark as George hurried home. He felt as if it took hours, going down wrong streets and switchback alleys, shadows shifting, spinning him around.

Exhausted, he finally found himself at home. He went to the kitchen and opened a cabinet, noting the names of dry goods. Flour. Kasha. Beans. Oats. Honey. Rye. Seeing and repeating the words gave him momentary comfort. He entered the other room and tore a piece of blank paper from the back of a book. On it he wrote a note to himself so that he would know in the morning that what had occurred was not a dream, a terrible nightmare, and folded it into his pocket.

When he woke, George read the note and then found his mother and father in their usual places. He hesitated but then told them all that had happened, in detail, waiting for them to interrupt and provide an explanation. But they didn't; they stood in silence and listened carefully. His father, in particular, paled at the story, staring at George as if he were a different person. His parents agreed without discussion that he should depart as soon as possible, go far away. They went to their hiding place in the kitchen and pulled out a small stack of zlotych—a good portion of their savings— and told George that he must leave Stawsk, leave Poland.

Three days later, George arrived in Paris.

RAFAEL

On the morning of May 8, 1935, Rafael AbuHazar approached his aunt with a request.

Several months earlier, the twenty-three-year-old cobbler had married, and now his wife was pregnant with their first child. Though only thirteen and illiterate, Massouda, the soon-to-be mother, was an ardent Zionist. Rafael didn't know where she got her ideas, where her convictions came from, but she was intent on moving to Palestine as soon as possible. Rafael argued—in the most gentle and conciliatory way so as not to invite a fight— that they had family and friends in Casablanca, and he had a good job and a nice house on Sidi Fatah. Their lives were within the walls of this ancient city; it was where they were born and where they'd played in the streets as children. But Massouda would respond that they'd make a new life within the walls of a new city, and what cities are older than those in Palestine? She would then remind him that the move had been a precondition of her agreeing to marry him, and she had no intention of dropping it.

Rafael said he understood, and that he would continue to try. So on this day, he went to visit his aunt Miriam—his mother's sister—with a small gift of significance: a chamsa his friend had crafted to hang in her kitchen, to help ward off al-ain, the evil eye. It was a right hand with tin and silver fingers and a palm inlaid with colored stones creating a single eye. The jinn were everywhere, lurking, searching, demons hiding in plain sight as people and animals, and one had to remain vigilant to ensure they stayed at arm's length. Rafael knew Miriam would not welcome his request, but he hoped that a surprise visit, a gift, and a description of Massouda's continued insistence, might cause her to acquiesce.

Upon his entry, his aunt kissed his cheeks and ushered him into the salon, where she stuffed the ornate silver teapot with handfuls of fresh mint leaves, squeezing and breaking them to release their oils. Then she weighed down the leaves with several overflowing scoops of white sugar before pouring boiling water over the whole concoction and shutting the lid so that the magic could take place beyond their gaze, in the darkness of the pot.

Rafael knew better than to speak during this ritual.

While the tea steeped, his aunt rushed back and forth from the kitchen, bringing out small platters of cookies covered in sesame seeds, as well as figs, dates, and oranges. Rafael always marveled at the efficiency with which she served food. It was fast, pleasingly arranged, and felt as if she'd prepared it just for him. As if he'd been expected. She also brought in three small clear glasses encircled with gold floral designs. Always an extra glass, he knew, in case of another visitor or a wayward prophet. It also helped to balance the tray, Rafael thought, but no one ever mentioned that reason.

After a few minutes, his aunt stood and lifted the teapot far above the table, pouring a stream of sweet tea straight into the delicate vessels without a drop wasted, creating a large frothy foam above each half glass.

This was the Amazigh way with tea, a holdover from the family's days in the high Atlas Mountains. The foam created by the oils and sugar, the height and angle of the pour, would protect the tea from the sand. The red sand of the Sahara mixed with the gray sand of the mountains, finding its way everywhere. It would be in your food, in your water, in your tobacco, in the corners of your eyes, in your underwear. But the Amazigh had found a way to keep it out of their tea. They measured their respite from the sands, not in moments, but in glasses—and for a dozen brief glasses a day, they shared a communal escape.

It took patience and practice, skill developed over years, to properly execute the simple task his aunt had just performed. In his glass was the result of generations of tradition and decades of experience. Rafael knew that moving to Palestine might mean losing all of it, not just the connections to family and friends, not just the job and maybe his trade, but even the seemingly small things that punctuated the day. The tea, the food. Did they even have the tomatoes necessary to make matbucha in Palestine? Wasn't it a swamp in the north and a desert in the south?

Rafael picked up the glass carefully, three fingers on the bottom and his thumb on the rim to balance it and prevent a burn. He began to sip and suck—

never blowing—to temper the heat and take in the tea without scalding his tongue.

His aunt picked up her glass and held it similarly, every part of the ritual a shibboleth.

"How are you, habibi? How is your lovely bride?"

"We are good, thank God. Massouda sends her love. And did Mmee tell you that she is pregnant?"

"Tfoot, tfoot, tfoot!" Miriam shot back to silence Rafael—a warning not to invite the evil eye.

"Oh, I have something for you. My friend Moussa from Rissani made it specifically for you."

Rafael hoped she caught his emphasis on the town, since it was the home of the Abuhatzeira family of rabbis, whose tombs were temples for his family. Reaching into his bag, he pulled out a small piece of folded canvas, which he gently opened to reveal the chamsa. He held it in his right palm— a hand inside of a hand—for his aunt's inspection and acceptance.

Miriam took the chamsa and walked away, into the kitchen. She hid it quickly and quietly, then returned, kissing Rafael on the hand and then forehead, thanking him.

He felt the moment was right. "Khaala Mari," he asked, "you know that my Massouda wants to go to Palestine, yes?"

"Yes, I've heard. She is a lovely child."

"But she wants to go now. It's important. She feels a connection to the land that I can't explain, and she feels that we should be there now, as a family."

"She is young. We all felt that way. Palestine calls out from the stories we grow up with. But they are just stories. Your life is here, with all your family. She will move past it as we've all moved past it."

"Maybe we should all go," Rafael suggested, not believing she would agree, but hoping she would see that his suggestion was more about the promise of Palestine than the curse of family.

"One day, God willing, we will." Miriam kissed three fingers cinched together, and raised them toward the ceiling.

"Yes. Yes. Until then . . ." Rafael took the last sip of his tea. ". . . I was hoping that you could give me your brother's address in Tsfat. Or maybe some way to contact him. He lives there, right? Near Yerushalayim?"

Miriam poured Rafael another glass of tea, again with a height-defying froth. She didn't answer. Though usually a loud woman, Miriam was a master of silences. When she was present but not speaking, you could feel it more than words. The silence swelled in the room, making it difficult to stay still and not fidget and scratch. She would sit motionless, with eyes that watched your every uncomfortable move, every agitated twitch, until you understood any further words of yours would come out as dust and hers the wind.

Rafael sucked and sipped at his tea, filling the air with whatever sounds he could. But it didn't help; the superfluous noises only gave the silence strength. Finally, he conceded and continued, "We just think it would make it easier to eventually go if we know someone, family who could help with introductions and tell us where to go, what to do."

"Rafi, habibi, I have no brother," she said finally, clutching and rubbing a small stone between her fingers.

Rafael didn't know how to respond to this. He had heard it before in some manner, in conversations among others, but he'd never had a reason to challenge it. He took another sip of tea, trying to use the pause to his advantage, before quickly realizing that the silence gave him no strength. He modulated his voice to respond calmly. "Khala, I know that you do. I remember him from when I was a boy." Then, losing control of the tempo, he let the words tumble out: "And I remember when he moved to Palestine, and there was even talk of visiting. He used to send letters and little gifts. We still have some of them. Olivewood trinkets. And then a few years ago, everyone stopped talking about him, like he never existed. I don't know if you two had a fight, or it was a fight with the family. I'm sure it was serious, but this is serious too. I made a promise to Massouda that we would go. We have to go."

"Rafi, why do you involve yourself in matters that are none of your business?" Miriam snapped, annoyed at being repeatedly challenged.

"But Khala, it is my business now. I left it alone for years. Did you ever hear me ask a question about him, to you or anyone else? Did you ever hear me speak his name? But now it's important for me to get in contact. I've told Massouda about him, and she has been bothering me for more. I have to give her answers, and I don't know where to find them except through the family."

"You should both leave it alone. Get this nonsense out of your head," she said in a softer tone, but still holding firm.

"What happened? Please, just tell me that," Rafael pleaded.

"Why? Why is it so important that you know everything? There are certain things we shouldn't know."

"Because maybe then I can understand. And if I understand that it is *really* impossible, then I can be honest with Massouda and we can look for another way. But I do not want to lie to her, so I am asking you for the truth."

"Fine. Enough!" Miriam exhaled loudly, her body deflating. Grabbing the teapot, she poured from a seated position, without flair or foam. She took a breath in, sipped, and began: "Let me tell you, God was everywhere. And as you know, Amram moved to Palestine, to Tsfat, years ago. He was a true Zionist, God bless him, and it was his dream to go." She paused and drank from the glass. "Things were hard, but they were good for him for years. He made it work over there. He married a Moroccan woman—from Rissani, like your friend Moussa—and they had a beautiful daughter. They named her after one of the seven blessings of Palestine. Tamar.

"Then Amram did something, looked at something, said something he shouldn't have. He was always an idiot in that way. Many men are." She looked at him accusingly, as a man and not a beloved nephew. "His wife and young child soon died in an accident. He buried them, and it nearly broke him, but he tried to continue on. He focused on his work, the little meat restaurant he ran, on building a home, and thought of maybe getting remarried.

"One night, Amram got out of bed and walked to the bathroom. Someone was waiting for him in the dark, and they put their fingers in his eyes. Deep, deep inside. He was blind after." Miriam's voice became louder as she held up two stiff fingers like a snake's fangs. "And we don't talk about him. We don't speak his name."

Rafael waited a moment, not knowing what to say. "That is terrible. I never knew of this tragedy. But I don't understand, what does his blindness have to do with us no longer talking about him?"

"Please, habibi, leave this alone. You now know the story. It's not possible to contact him. We shouldn't be talking about him. We have already spoken about him too much." Miriam looked around the ceiling and into corners of the room, showing more fear than Rafael had ever seen her exhibit.

"Who blinded Amram?" Rafael asked.

"We cannot know. Why do you ask such nonsense?"

"Please?" Rafael pleaded. "Who do you think put their fingers in his eyes?"

Again Miriam's gaze darted around the room. "We don't talk about it." She put her head in her open palms and began muttering a prayer, sinking into the words and low rhythm of the phrases. He recognized the prayer, the same one his mother would retreat to, calling out to God and the people of Israel: Shema Yisrael, adonei eloheinu, adonei echad. He heard her add the word damdama. *Damdama.* She then continued inaudibly before jumping to her feet, going to the kitchen, and returning with a burning bundle of rue. Smoke streamed off the tip, filling the space.

Rafael knew it was time to stop. He had his answer. It would not be possible to contact his uncle; he'd have to find another route to the Holy Land. He could not tell Massouda about the blinding, as he did not understand it fully himself, but he had to tell her something so she would stop asking. He decided to say his uncle had died, that the accident which had taken his uncle's wife and daughter had taken him too. It was all very tragic. But these things happen in foreign lands far away from home. It seemed the easiest way to make Massouda move past the idea, and to give Rafael time to find another path—though he also wondered if his uncle's mysterious death might scare Massouda away from the idea of moving to an unknown place, where someone could die and even their family did not know of it.

Rafael considered his glass; it was empty. His aunt Miriam continued to burn rue and move the smoke around the room, fumigating the air and mumbling an incantation in the tone of an interrogation. He could not understand half the words, but some were ones he had heard before. *Damdama. Eyes. Askara. Dead and drooling. Hatifa. Screaming. Sahita. Crying. Sahaba. Sight. Kavkava. Lying.*

LIEBE

On December 9, 1938, Lillian Minsky sat in a room in the Bedford-Stuyvesant neighborhood of Brooklyn, unable to concentrate. At the front of the make-shift New York City classroom, the teacher stood at the slate board, making trees of words: action trunks growing from subject seeds and shooting off predicate branches.

The man is going to the store to buy a ham.
The dog is barking at the cat.
The wife holds the child.

Lillian stared out the window at the advancing clouds. Though it was not yet noon, the clouds made the sky look gloomy, and the early win-ter darkness agitated Lillian. Doubly so on this day because the darkness brought the Shabbos, and she still had to find a way home, finish cooking and cleaning, and generally help prepare the house, all before sunset.

Lillian could not keep still, shifting in her chair, surrounded by other new immigrants learning English. The class was for women under eigh-teen from middle and eastern Europe, and she appeared to be the oldest in the room. No one asked her age, however; nothing good came from ask-ing questions or speaking answers. This was the rule that every immigrant knew. As long as you kept your mouth shut, you could be anyone from any-where. Some days, when leaving the house, her mother would hold one fin-ger vertically across her lips to communicate both *goodbye* and *say nothing*. The moment you spoke, you were a Litvak, a Vilniak, a Kulak, an other. And that information would be used against you, to exclude you, and once out, there was no way to recontain it. Lillian liked that no one asked questions, no one talked, because she lived in fear that she'd be found out. She knew that her voice, or her word choice, or her opinion, or some other detail that she could not control despite her constant state of vigilance, would accidentally reveal who she was, what she was doing here.

One of the officials in one of the many offices she had to visit—Naturalization, Public Welfare, Mental Hygiene, Social Hygiene; they all became as one in their administrative demands and oversight—told her about the *American reset*. She forgot how he described it, and wasn't really listening closely when he discussed it, but she held on to the concept and repeated the words in her head, where they grew in importance. She took the term to mean that she could be a different person here, that since no one knew her, she was only the parts of Poland that she'd brought with her and held out for others to see. Otherwise, she could be a new woman, in a new place, and take back the years she had lost.

Liebe left Poland at age twenty-four and traveled back in time, arriving at Ellis Island as seventeen-year-old Lillian. The years disappeared in the fog of the Atlantic when no one was paying attention. Those years had been taken from her originally, so she felt no shame in stealing them back on the journey. Liebe didn't tell anyone her plan; not her mother or father, sister or brother. On the boat, when the English speakers talked, she listened closely to learn the number—*seventee, sewenteen, seventeen*—and repeated it over and over to learn the pronunciation. Before she knew what a word tree was, she planted simple saplings throughout the decks and common spaces of the ship.

I have seventeen breads.
I have seventeen zlotych.
I have seventeen years.
My name is Lillian, and I have seventeen years.

When she announced to the customs official that she—Lillian—had seventeen years, no one corrected her. Her father appeared deep in thought, either considering the large folder of documents he carried or a scholarly matter or both, balancing the sacred and profane simultaneously. Her mother merely turned to look at Lillian's siblings. Her younger sister seemed nervous, waiting for her turn to say her words to the customs official. Lillian's brother—the youngest—was transfixed by the city, unable to turn his gaze away since it first became visible from the boat. If her parents noticed, they said nothing.

Lillian tried to forget through silence, and though she could hide the facts from herself, she didn't know how to keep the fears away. Especially fear of the night; specifically, the streets at night. She could no longer feel a love of the dark, but she knew it used to excite her. She knew that she used to look out at the stars, counting the days when the moon grew and then counting down until it disappeared. She was the oldest child by a few years, and she spent hours weaving intricate fantastical tales for her brother and sister about how the moon watched over each of them and knew their names. She knew she had played in the streets at night because she could picture all those dark corners beside her father's yeshiva, near the market, in narrow alleys where she'd hide as a game with her girlfriends. Though she could still recall how her eyes would adjust to the dark, running from place to place, she could no longer experience the joys and mysteries of the night.

Now, thoughts of unpopulated streets when dusk stole twilight, of growing shadows as the sun slowly set, brought only anxiety. The sky was darkening outside the classroom, and though Lillian understood it was only the result of moving gray clouds, knowing the reason did not calm her. It was getting darker, and she was getting increasingly nervous. The class was supposed to break at noon for lunch, but it was running over, already 12:15, and Lillian was trying to control her breathing. She inhaled deeply and then exhaled slowly. Realizing she was making a sound others could hear, she tried to silence her breath. She didn't want anyone to notice her panic, because then they might ask her a question, and nothing good came of questions. Better to wait until the break and then quietly slip away like the twilight, with the Shabbos as her excuse.

When the streets were numbers, Lillian counted them by their number names so she felt she was advancing at a fast pace. Flatbush Avenue, 21st Street, Ocean Avenue, St. Paul's Place, 18th Avenue, 17th Avenue, the British streets whose names she could never pronounce, and then magically, 10th Street. The walk was long—almost two hours—but each day she only had enough money for either the subway or a bialy, and she still had never ridden the subway.

As she rushed home on the long avenues, she thought of her father's long journey from Stawsk to Radin to see his old teacher, the Chofetz Chaim, on her behalf. She'd never asked her father to go; in fact, she didn't want him to go. Liebe had wanted him to stay in Stawsk and do what she asked of him.

Her father, Rav Moishe Minsky, was the head of the town's yeshiva, a well-regarded Musar scholar whom countless constantly visited, seeking his advice and wisdom. Some even called him, despite his deep protestations, one of the Tzadikim Nistarim. But if he were actually one of these mythical thirty-six righteous humans, meant to justify the continued existence of man, how was it that when Liebe told him what had happened to her, he didn't respond with what she thought was both the easy thing and the right thing. He'd hesitated. He hadn't acted. Instead, he'd locked himself in his study for days, thinking and reading. When he could not reach a conclusion, he said he would travel to Radin to ask the advice of the Chofetz Chaim. Liebe urged her father to stay, to do something *now*, to speak up for her. She explained that she would see the young man walking around the town, near the market, beside the yeshiva, all with impunity, as if he had done nothing wrong. Outside, there was nowhere for her to escape him, and it wasn't right that she should have to hide indoors. Her father explained that it was not so simple to accuse the town rabbi's son. The rabbi was a great man, from a long lineage of great rabbis, with his son studying to continue the tradition. Confronting the son, exposing him, bringing charges before the beit din courts, would tear the community apart. What if the beit din were to convict the son? What would that do to people's beliefs in Hashem and the teachings? Or what if they did not convict him? What would that do to their beliefs in truth and justice? And though the rabbi himself had done nothing wrong, his reputation would be stained, which he did not deserve. Liebe cried as she repeated how she did not deserve any of it either; she was innocent when the rabbi's son approached her on the street. In the creeping moments between twilight and dusk, when the new moon meant no moon.

Her father said that he understood and didn't put any blame on her, but he needed guidance before he could do more. Who better to advise him than the greatest living rabbi in the entire Pale of Settlement? He asked that she be patient as he traveled the long road to Radin.

Lillian's walk to Borough Park always took longer than it should have, because she avoided parks and streets that had public stairways or subway entrances at blind corners. In her head she kept a detailed map unlike the sort found in any books, one that promised safe passage to all her usual destinations. As she made her way home now after leaving the classroom, Lillian tried to focus on the street and maintain a level of awareness, but she began thinking of that night's dinner. She would probably be too late to help cook, but she wondered if her mother was making a cholent, mixing the potatoes, barley, beef and bones, eggs and vegetables into the giant roasting pan to cook and fill the house with a smell that carried her back to Poland. Since it was kept on a low flame throughout the Shabbos to avoid the act of lighting a fire, the cholent, overwhelming all other senses, permeated Lillian's life for twenty-four hours.

The mere thought brought the body of the stew into her nose and mouth. Lillian remembered helping her mother cook when her father returned from Radin. Liebe had been worried all week, and had wanted to find a way to ask her mother sensitive questions about the lateness of her yom hachodesh, what she should do. In passing, she raised the issue, but received only silence in response, and she didn't know if her mother had heard or understood. She let the matter go, hoping that the Chofetz Chaim would provide a divine and elegant solution to the mess. Following routine, she left on the usual day of the month as if to go cleanse herself at the mikvah, but instead went to the forest on the edge of Stawsk for several hours, where she knew she'd be alone. It was then she first realized the shadows felt different.

Her father had rushed to make it home before sunset, not wanting to spend Shabbos in a foreign town. Her mother lit the candles, and the family sat for dinner and discussed the week's Torah portion, all while Liebe waited for her father to talk about the trip. Her sister and brother debated the differences in the two tellings of the twelve spies sent to the Land of Canaan, her sister arguing that the people sent the spies, her brother that God sent them. They looked to their father to settle the dispute between the Book of Numbers and the Book of Deuteronomy. He responded with a summary of Rashi's interpretation as compared to the Rambam's interpretation. Then his eyes became bright as he talked about the joy in seeing Rav Kagan in Radin, using the rabbi's name rather than title, as he had when serving as the great man's student and scribe. He told stories about the work that Rav Kagan was doing as a teacher and a scholar, and posited that he was truly one of the Tzadikim Nistarim—a designation he adamantly rejected for himself.

Liebe's throat felt unable to open, and she choked on her cholent. She'd been patient for the weeks her father had been gone, despite glimpsing the rabbi's son on several occasions. One day, from across the street, he'd even had the nerve to wish her a good Shabbos. He had gone from avoiding her eyes to a greeting in such a short time. Soon he would be speaking to her again, in public and in private, and all of it felt too much.

Her father was a thoughtful and sensitive man; people would visit with problems and questions, and he would draw from his encyclopedic knowledge of the Talmud to bring the wisdom of ancient teachings to an individual's modern and unique issues. He would listen for long periods, then retreat to his books and his mind before delivering concise and elegantly composed answers. Visitors would leave their visits with clear direction from a great rabbi who had weighed all considerations, balanced them, and delivered his judgment with certitude. They would tell her she was lucky to have such a tzadik as a father. She could not understand why in her case he exhibited no apparent urgency. It made her sick to her stomach.

Liebe had been feeling ill for weeks, the entire time her father was gone. She hoped it was due to the anxiousness over the wait, and her disgust over him carrying her story like a gangrenous limb across the Litvak region. She'd had a hard enough time trying to explain to her father what had been done to her—going into his study, sitting on the footstool as he sat at his desk. It brought bile to her throat to think of her father sitting similarly in the Chofetz Chaim's study, holy books between them, surrounded by the great rabbis of the region who clung to Rav Kagan's ankles. All those thirsty men who drank his waters and cleaved to the dust of his feet. And he, her father, describing what one great rabbi's child had done to another great rabbi's child. All of them nodding and stroking their beards as if they were being presented with some halachic riddle to be debated, considering this and considering that, revisiting aloud the words of the Rambam, delivered with a thumb for emphasis, then weighing them against the teachings of Rav Hillel and Rabbi Akiva—all to come to a reasoned conclusion they could all agree upon. Nodding and harrumphing, finding consensus and satisfaction at having solved the puzzle. It made her sick. After what happened, she had gone to her father as a father, and he had responded as Rav Minsky.

In their town, Liebe knew a woman she'd heard had lost a child not by accident. While her father was gone, Liebe wondered how the woman had done it. Was it something the woman ate or drank, a scalding liquid or bitter root from the forest? Did she put something inside herself or suffer a fall? Before the rumors, the woman had been a friend of her mother's, and after her father returned and Liebe's sickness did not subside, she resolved to visit her. Liebe imagined different paths their conversation could take. Would she be offered tea and cake? Would gossip be exchanged before talking of what was not to be talked about? Would the woman refuse to give Liebe help or tell her what had to be done?

Liebe picked a market day so she had an excuse to be gone. She plotted her route, the shops she would go to before the visit and those she would stop in after dropping by the woman's house with small sweets and cakes.

The visit was not as she'd imagined it—there was little conversation—but the woman said she would help, warning Liebe this might make it difficult or impossible to have children, and pointing to her own empty house as an example. When it was finished, she said Liebe would know if it had worked within a day or two by what came out of her. She explained there would be pain and cramps, and Liebe might feel peculiar around others. She cautioned Leibe not to tell anyone, because what she'd done wasn't done, and if others learned of it, Liebe would always be known for this deed.

Liebe thought about how her father would counsel women who suffered stillbirths and miscarriages. According to the Talmud, if they had discharged something like hair or a shell that dissolved in water, it was to be considered the same as blood, and they had to go immediately to the mikvah to purify. If it looked like a fish or grasshopper, they would remain impure for seven days. If it looked like an animal or bird, and the sex could be determined, then they were impure for fourteen days and pure for sixty-six days. In no case, her father explained, might the unborn child be mourned if it did not live for thirty-one days after birth. Liebe thought about these numbers, wondering how many weeks or months she had to further sacrifice until she could return to normal.

When she'd arrived home that evening, she unfolded the skirt she had worn the night of the encounter with the rabbi's son. It had a small tear along the seam and was stained from the ground. She held the skirt and, at the tear, rent it completely along the seam until it was a piece of flat fabric.

On her long walk home to Borough Park, Lillian got lost in that night of her father's return from Radin. She remembered waiting during dinner for some sign that everything would be rectified, that the greatest rabbis in the region had reached the right answer. The meal went late into the evening, with songs and prayers, all the festivities that ushered in the Shabbos. At each transition, when song turned to another course, and prayers turned to lessons, and one story that had been repeated a hundred times became another story that had been repeated a hundred times, she waited for her mention. The routine, which she knew by heart and which used to bring comfort in its repetition, now induced anxiety as she waited for something different. After dinner, Liebe stood in the kitchen, cleaning and putting away food while her father retired to his study. She looked over her shoulder every few moments, expecting an invitation in—for perhaps that is where this conversation must take place, she thought, among the ancient books and holy words. She would sense a shadow in the kitchen and think it her father come to talk to her, but it was nothing. A tree branch in the wind, a moving curtain. At points she would count down in her head—drey, tsvey, eyner—and then spin suddenly, imagining the fortuitousness of her turning just as her father came to stand in the doorway, about to say "Liebe." But he did not appear. And as days passed, then weeks, he said nothing.

Now Lillian walked into the apartment in Borough Park, and immediately the Shabbos entered her and stopped her at the doorway. She could hear the quiet sounds of preparation, each person doing what was required before they all congregated at the table. Tonight there would be singing and laughter, and her father raising questions about the week's Torah portion. This week's was Vayeshev—meaning "and he lived"—which told of Jacob and his family settling in Hebron, and Jacob avoiding death twice. She'd always wondered why the *he* in the title referred to Jacob, when Joseph was the survivor. And she knew if she raised the question, her father would excitedly deliver his thoughts and the thoughts of the rabbis who had come before him.

The family gathered around the table. By the dim glow of the small lamp left lit throughout the Shabbos, Lillian stood before the candles, ready to strike a match. She and her mother alternated the candle lighting by week. Tonight, it was Lillian's turn to light them and lead the prayer. It was a hushed meditation performed in a whisper, with two inward facing palms that covered the candles' flames. Her hands moved from over her eyes to the candles, obscuring the light, fluttering sideways as murmured prayers were recited by all. This was a private prayer that women controlled. It was customary to use the moment to pray for children, health, and happiness.

Instead of doing so, Lillian thought about the time following her visit to her mother's former friend. She had carried herself differently, yet no one in the family had noticed she was weak. The words from her English class came into her head: *The man is going to the store to buy a ham. The dog is barking at the cat. The wife holds the child.* Back and forth her palms moved, casting and controlling the shadows flitting across her family's faces. And each time she brought her hands too close and the flame skipped sideways and bit her, the singe of pain snapped Lillian into the moment, if only for an instant.

JULIETTE

On August 5, 1939, Juliette sat in her usual spot in her usual café in the 5th arrondissement for her late-morning snack when she saw something unusual: there was a tarte aux abricots available.

It was rare for this café, this time of year, especially with the difficulty getting certain foods the last few months, particularly those from the east. She wanted to go to the counter to order the tarte—maybe another coffee as well—but she spied George sitting alone at a table near the pastry case. He was wearing fashionable glasses and a scarf that allowed him to blend in with the academic modernist crowd, but to Juliette he still looked Polish or Lithuanian, someone from the Old World. Juliette was in graduate classes with George at the nearby Sorbonne, where they both studied linguistics, so it wasn't a surprise to see him. They were on friendly terms, and each time they saw each other they talked in one of the several languages they were focusing on, sometimes for hours. But there was something she didn't like about George, and she couldn't quite put her finger on what it was. As Juliette turned her coffee cup upside down over her mouth to get the last drops of espresso mixed with sugar—her favorite part of the coffee and the morning—she weighed whether the tarte was worth the very real likelihood that she'd be eating it at George's table. The Germans had a perfect word for this mix of emotions, and she chuckled slightly at its imagery.

"Je voudrais un café et une tarte aux abricots," she said softly at the pastry counter, hoping to keep the exchange quick and quiet. George looked over his shoulder—among his many oddities, she'd noticed, was a continuous looking around rooms and behind him, like a thief—and saw her.

"Bonjour, Juliette. Comment ça va?"

"Ça va." She paused. "Et vous?" Juliette insisted on using the second person formal with George, even though they were approximately the same age and apparent friends. She liked how language could create and maintain distance in a single syllable.

"I am good," George responded in heavily accented English, indicating that he wanted to practice English conversation with her.

George's French was good—with his semi-polished accent and ruddy look, he could easily pass for a Marseillais—but when he spoke English, he sounded like an eastern European Jew. Juliette, whose English was soft and melodic, hated George's English accent with its hard stops, throaty sounds, and extra-long vowels.

"Would you care to sit?" George asked as he touched a chair at his table.

Juliette placed her coffee and tarte on the table and sat. "Bien sûr—of course." She went through her usual ritual of mixing a small spoonful of sugar into her coffee, stirring with the contradictory hope that it would both dissolve and remain as bittersweet remnants for the end. "How is everything? How is your family?" she asked before taking a bite of tarte, thinking that by simultaneously eating and listening, she could keep their time together short.

George looked nervously to his left and right, then behind him, his eyes resting briefly at the door. Juliette wondered if the gendarmerie would rush in and arrest him, and if so, she was curious what it would be for. Theft, assault, conspiracy, perhaps some crime against children?

"I have not heard from them in a while, but I think they are good."

"Where are they again?" Juliette asked, using the opportunity to get more information about George's past.

"They are in Tunis," he responded curtly.

"They are in Tunis *now*?" Juliette asked. "Or they are from Tunis?"

"They are in Tunis now," George replied, mimicking her accent. "But they are originally from Djerba."

"Djerba? Your family is Tunisian?" Juliette tried to hide her disbelief.

"Yes. Tunisian." George gave nothing more.

Juliette took another bite of the tarte, seeing if he would stick with his answers or if he would try to modify them to something more plausible. He looked a little dark, but still light for a Tunisian. It was possible his family was part Circassian, maybe intermarried with crypto-Jews from Iberia, she thought, trying to work out the migration patterns. No, she decided. He had the unpleasant hand gestures of a Maghrebi Jew, always pawing at his cheeks and lips, and his Arabic was good, much better than hers, and even his Tunisian dialect sounded authentic—but he was clearly a Polish Jew. She could feel it in her bones. A Litvak from the Pale of Settlement. It came out in little ways beyond his accent when he attempted English. He refused to practice Polish with her, saying he didn't speak it and had no interest in learning it. But every Jew knew some Polish, or at least had an interest in it, and this would be true especially of one who spoke so many other languages. Juliette had also noticed his occasional use of Yiddish when he got frustrated, or when all other languages failed him in expressing something specific.

Juliette did not especially care for Jews from the east or the Maghreb—she found them loud, queer, and dirty—but she prided herself on being able to distinguish the races. Though George's face and tongue could pass for Maghrebi, his mannerisms were not those of an Arab. She wondered why he lied about himself, his family, and his past. She wondered why he was in France, whether he was perhaps a Bolshevik agitator. Or perhaps he was a follower of Bakunin or Kropotkin and their Russian collectivist-anarchist nonsense. She had heard George advocate passionately for the Republicans in Spain and warn about the dangers of Franco and his Falangists. Though Juliette didn't disagree about Spain, she didn't want France led into another great war, especially not because of the worries of some troublemaking Jews. All of it was trouble. Trouble followed Jews—it was a fact of history—and if George was lying, he must be in the thick of it. Scooping the sugary coffee sludge from the bottom of her cup, Juliette put the spoon in her mouth as she considered how to change the subject.

"How is your research coming along?" she asked. They shared a doctoral advisor, but she knew little of his research. Her advisor and others in their program described it as *important work, groundbreaking insight*, but she had her doubts.

"It is very well. I am hoping to be done soon. There are some papers I still await from Marseille, but they should be here soon, and then I think my research will be finished."

"I know you are studying the change in the French language between the Ancien Régime and the First Republic, during the Revolution, but I realize I do not know much about your work."

"It is very boring." George waved his hand dismissively.

"Please, I am interested. And I have a high tolerance for ennui. Don't forget, I too am a graduate student. And a French-born one, no less."

"No, no, no," George responded, sounding particularly Yiddish. "It is not for a café. Perhaps when it is written you can read it and tell me your thoughts. Now please, tell me, have you been hearing the rumors from the east, from Niemcy, uhm, Deutsch . . . Allemagne?"

Juliette realized she wasn't going to get more from George, so she went along. She had heard stories from friends in Germany about new rules, new policies, a new direction for the country, but things had been problematic there since the war and Weimar. And though her German friends complained because Germans loved to complain, they also seemed to think that the National Socialists were taking their country in the right direction. She assumed George was asking because of the Nuremberg Laws and how Jews were being treated. Juliette was against the Leggi Razziali in Italy and the way that racial classifications were used under those laws, but she thought the Nuremberg Laws and similar ones in Hungary were adequate responses to what no one could deny was a Jewish problem in those countries.

"I have not heard anything in particular," she answered. "What is it you have been hearing?"

George switched to French, this no longer being an exercise for him. He wanted to be clear and to clearly understand anything Juliette might know. "They say that things are getting bad, worse than when Franco and Mola occupied Madrid. I have heard people worry about the spread of Fascism, with El Caudillo, Il Duce, and Der Führer surrounding France."

Juliette responded in English. "Who is saying this? Communists? And have not things been quite bad for Allemagne, and Italie, and Espagne for many years? Is it not perhaps better that they should have stability in their economies and pride in their cultures? Is this not simply people prone to worrying, worrying?"

"I don't think that is what the Fascists and the Falangists and National Socialists are bringing. I have friends who fought in Spain because they saw the danger in Franco and the other generals."

George had in fact left Paris to volunteer with the Abraham Lincoln Brigade. It was where he'd learned English and had seen the nastiness of the fight. In Poland, George had experienced sporadic violence—usually the result of bored or angry goyim—had seen people bloodied and windows smashed, but the violence in Spain made him more scared than any time since he had left Stawsk.

After a few months, he'd come back to Paris, not able to leave his studies indefinitely and not able to stomach staying and watching a massacre. "France will soon be surrounded by militaristic Fascists," he said, again in French. "I admit that I'm worried."

Juliette remembered one night some time ago, when they were both out with fellow students. George had been drinking, and he said he'd begun to feel like the east and west were closing in on him like nine masons. It had stuck with her because she didn't understand the idiom.

"You are always so worried, George," she said now. "France is strong, and we do not want another war. I don't know what will happen over there, but the Republic will be fine. And, if you are so worried—" Juliette lifted her cup to look for any sugar remnants, but it was empty. "—you can always return to Tunisia. You said your research is almost complete. Maybe there's no reason for you to be in France any longer." This last comment came out colder and crueler than Juliette intended. "I mean, to be with your family, of course, to care for your parents, in the case something does happen."

Though Juliette continued to speak in English, George understood precisely what she was saying and thought she might be right, not about Spain or Germany, but about his parents. "Perhaps," he replied. He thought about Stawsk often, the tight-knit community, the comforts of tradition, the Great Synagogue. He thought about his parents there, elderly and alone, with little money or connections outside of Lite. On some days, he wished they had all left Poland together. But on most days—he'd be ashamed to admit to anyone—he was glad they hadn't come with him, that they sent him away alone. Though he wanted them to be well cared for, and to be a part of that care, he couldn't imagine living in Paris with them. Only a few days' journey, Stawsk felt ancient compared with Paris, a throwback to a time that was dying or dead. Paris was alive with people and new ideas, whereas Stawsk was filled with ghosts, and you couldn't bring one world into the other. And not only could one not bring Stawsk to Paris, George knew his parents couldn't leave Stawsk behind. Still, he worried about them, as he worried about everything these days.

He'd been studying the last days of the Ancien Régime in classrooms and in archives, analyzing the changing patterns in the French language as pressure had built and a new order pushed out the old. And he'd started to detect similarities with the world around him, locating instances in which various ideological groups would stretch the meaning of well-known words and phrases for political purposes, also inventing words to describe a new power structure rooted in otherhood. He'd found the greatest occurrences in Germany, and to a lesser extent in Italy, Spain, and Hungary. But he didn't know if what he saw was real and pressing or if his natural inclination to worry made the connections feel urgent. This was why he talked with Juliette and others at every opportunity. She had been born in France and raised in Paris; certainly she would be sensitive to serious changes. Her own research was on the intersection and development of languages in border communities, especially in the Alsace and Basque regions. She was highly attuned to minor changes and deviations, in the ways that reality was reflected in language. If she'd detected any important shifts, she'd surely tell him.

"At least we have apricots." Juliette remarked, uncomfortable with a silence that she felt responsible for. "Things can never be that bad with stone fruit."

"Mm-hmm." George sighed in passive agreement.

If he wasn't going to try, Juliette thought, neither would she. Her cup still in her hand, she lifted it to drink, though it was completely empty. She thought to make a joke about this but stopped herself. She was now determined to sit in silence with George until one of them had had enough.

MASSOUDA

In the early afternoon of September 21, 1939, Massouda AbuHazar left her house in the Mellah in the old city of Casablanca to do her weekly shopping for the family. Her usual days in the market had become routine—a seemingly bizarre traversal through narrow alleyways to shops and stalls in an order that took into account limited stock that would run out early, weight loads and distances, the separation of milk from meat, and the need to keep certain items cool. There were no straight lines to her movements, and from above, it may have resembled a bee's erratic dance. It was the repetition that made it possible, because she used no lists, Darija being only a spoken language and Massouda not knowing how to read or write in Classical Arabic.

On this day, she would have to create a new routine, however, because instead of preparing for a feast on Shabbat, she was preparing for a fast on Shabbat with a feast to follow, for tomorrow would be the eve of Yom Kippur. This confluence of holy days—Yom Tov upon Yom Tov, Shabbat shabbaton atop Shabbat—not only meant preparing different meals with different rules, it also required one to seek forgiveness from those one may have wronged during the year, all before God sealed the verdict in the book of life, where one's name and forever fate were inscribed.

Standing in front of her home, Massouda was unsure of herself for the first time in a while. She knew that she'd go to the butcher last, because she didn't want to carry freshly slaughtered animals through the souk, and she knew better than to watch him slaughter the animals and then return later, after he'd dressed and wrapped them. Plus, he was the last person she wanted to talk to about apologies before Yom Kippur.

Massouda was already late getting started because the wet nurse would not let her leave without first having her dreams interpreted. Massouda didn't like hearing and interpreting peoples' dreams, but some auntie in the Mellah who read dreams had marked her as possessing her jinn, saying that she had been born clutching a coin. Ever since, she had heard dream on top of dream and tried to give them meaning. Though Massouda was only sixteen and had not seen the world, her days were filled with disjointed images of spiders crawling and teeth falling and infidelity and people who didn't look like who they were in real life but were who the dreamer said they were. And her nights were filled with an uncontrolled replaying of these images with the narratives that she provided. Massouda's name meant *happy* and *lucky* in Arabic, but it had grown increasingly hard for her to believe that what others said was a gift was really lucky, and for her to remain happy when constantly exposed to the rawness of peoples' innermost thoughts.

Massouda decided to wind her way to the vegetable vendor first. She needed tomatoes, peppers, and garlic to make matbucha, and the apology she needed to convey was fairly straightforward. She moved through the market at an inconsistent pace, walking quickly through some areas, while slowing to almost a complete stop at others because one person negotiated a cart at a snail's pace or another blocked an alley while arguing with a vendor. She hated pushing her way through the backups that resulted from such disagreements, and she also hated moving slowly because the flies would quickly gather and the street cats emerge with their shrill demands. They seemed always to be waiting at the edges, ready to appear whenever a commotion caused the market-goers to stop. It amazed her how quickly the streets were taken over by nature when people became still.

If she were indeed lucky, some old alaguz would appear behind her, pushing her way through, swinging her breasts from side to side, clearing a passage. As soon as Massouda was shoved out of the way, she would follow closely, not yet willing to become that impatient old woman, but perfectly willing to benefit from her.

Massouda had hoped there would be a line at Abbas's vegetable stand so she'd have an excuse to keep things short. But it was empty, past the morning rush. And as soon as the smiling Abbas saw her, he called her over excitedly.

Abbas had always been kind to her, and she felt terrible for what she had done. So after selecting the produce for weighing and pricing, Massouda handed Abbas two coins for payment. The first coin more than covered the cost, and Abbas looked down at his open palm, confused as to why she'd given him the second. The additional coin was Massouda's favorite of all Moroccan currency, the twenty-five centimes piece from 1924, with a hole in the middle and a large Seal of Sulaiman on the back side. She would collect these coins when they were given as change and never spend them, even when she needed the money, instead filling a small purse with her collection. Some days, as she prepared to go to market, she would open this purse, filled with a dozen or so coins engraved with the star, and would pretend that she was preparing to go to the Jerusalem shuk. Massouda didn't know much about Palestine, but these coins allowed her to close her eyes, rub her fingertips along the ridges of the stars, and pretend that she was there. As apology to Abbas and penance, she felt she should give one of her precious coins to him.

"Habibti, this is too much," Abbas said, extending his half-open hand, which the arthritis made difficult to fully close or open.

"Hajji, it is for peppers from months ago that I never paid for."

"When? I don't think you owe me anything." He looked around half-heartedly, probably for his book of debts.

"I apologize, but I did it behind your back. It was during a period when Rafi had little work. I took without asking or paying. Will you forgive me?"

"It's fine. I didn't know about it. I don't remember it. I don't think it made any difference at all." Abbas again offered his palm with the coins.

"No," Massouda shot back. "You have to take it. And please forgive me."

There was a brief window when the veil between worlds would open, and the book of life would be sealed within the week, so she needed him to accept the apology. To say that it meant nothing, or that it was as if it never happened, was not an acceptance; it was an attempt to erase it. Massouda had heard it said that man could forgive, but only God could erase.

"Okay. Okay. Habibti, you are forgiven." Abbas brought his stiff hand back behind the stall and, without moving a finger, tipped his still-open palm sideways. The coin dropped down, and when it landed, Massouda could hear that it fell into a pouch full of other coins—the sound of a penance she hoped would reverberate to the heavens.

Walking away from Abbas's stall, even with several kilos of vegetables in a sack tossed over her back, Massouda felt lighter. She believed that the first apology, even if relatively straightforward, would set the tone for future ones.

Though she had known he wouldn't, Abbas could have refused the apology. He could have said that trust was broken and he could not accept payment or her words of contrition this late. However, if she made three genuine attempts to apologize, and each one was rejected, then the sin would have transferred to him. As young children, Massouda and her brothers exploited this loophole, apologizing three times in quick succession, as if it were an incantation, and then imagining the sin leaving through their noses and entering the person who refused to accept. But she was no longer a child and no longer played such games. If Abbas had refused, she would have had to return several times that day to apologize and hope he eventually conceded. He also could have called the police, but Massouda was less concerned about that.

From Abbas's stall, she walked down the alley where small metal parts were sold, mostly assorted replacement pieces for household items, interspersed with random parts from large machines. The metal pieces were always arranged on rugs on the ground, with the vendors sitting or squatting beside their wares. The wiry men were sometimes twisted into odd shapes from crouching on rugs for years, thin limbs splaying in all directions. As she passed, they turned the sides of their faces toward her, but wasted no effort raising their heads or trying to draw her attention to their collections.

From there, she went through a part of the market devoted to the French. The foods and ingredients were mostly imported from Europe, kept in closed containers and crates to protect them from the market air and Moroccan hands. They'd always intrigued Massouda, but they were too expensive to even consider. As she walked by these stalls, she couldn't help but give the food curious side glances, then felt compelled to display her disgust by whispering "khara" in a harsh but barely audible tone.

Massouda arrived at Hassan's stall and immediately filled her bag with fruit and paid. Business first, she thought.

"Hassan," she said, calling his attention. He turned toward her, smiling in the manner of a fruit vendor, all teeth and no trust. "I want to apologize for anything I did this year that may have hurt you."

Hassan's smile dropped.."Why? What did you do?" he asked, his natural suspicion coming through.

Massouda realized she would not get away with a generic apology and would have to explain herself. "I heard that you were sleeping around, so I blessed you, and for that I am sorry."

"I am not sleeping around," he shot back loudly, and too quickly, as if prepared for the accusation. "From whom did you hear that? Was it Amina? Does my Amina suspect me of something?"

Massouda had listened to many dreams and had heard many worries of infidelity that crept into people's midnight thoughts. But when she heard Amina's repeating dream about her husband, Hassan, sleeping with a woman from the restaurant, it felt different. Amina's dream didn't need interpretation because it wasn't a spiritual intervention or a shadowy glimpse into the other world; it was what Amina knew to be true but couldn't admit. Massouda grasped this in an instant, and as soon as Amina left, she'd blessed Hassan in anger.

"No one told me," she replied. "One just hears things."

"Well, I don't want you going around repeating it." He straightened his body so that he loomed over her. Then, as if he'd heard a detail he wasn't expecting, he demanded, "And what do you mean you *blessed* me? You mean you *cursed* me? Is that it? With what?"

"Tfoot, tfoot, tfoot." Massouda looked around for any demons he might have accidentally invoked. "Why do you say such ugly words? I don't know exactly what I blessed you with. Probably something fitting the act. Maybe impotence and boils, that your eggs should hatch inside you, aches and an infection that won't heal, a bone that protrudes on the spot where you walk. But I apologize. It was not my place. And I am here seeking your forgiveness."

"Why don't you just take back the curse?" he asked, shrinking, genuinely asking, his voice getting quieter with each word. "I have heard that you are close with the jinn." By the time he reached the end of the sentence, it was almost a whisper.

"What are you, stupid, Hassan? Stop saying that word!" Massouda snapped. "I can't. I only bless. Only God can erase a blessing."

"This is ridiculous!" He stiffened. "I do not accept your apology. Take your fruit and go."

"Please, Hassan, it is sincere," Massouda said, aware that this was technically her second ask.

"Child! Leave! Go back to the Mellah."

Massouda became annoyed at Hassan's stubbornness and decided to ask a third time now, rather than return. "Hassan, I am sorry. Will you please forgive me?"

Hassan barked a word and waved at Massouda with the back of his hand. "Go sit on a stick!"

Massouda stood for a moment. She took a deep breath, her breast filling with air, and then exhaled slowly and fully—stomach tight to push out all the cleansing breath, to give the sin time to float between the space separating them and migrate to Hassan—before walking away.

All that was left now was a visit to the butcher, for some chickens and an apology.

Yosef's shop smelled of death. Behind his stall, Yosef kept a makeshift menagerie, with chickens, turkeys, lambs, and goats living their final days in cages and pens. Some people would just ask for a generic animal, leave while it was slaughtered, drained, and dressed, then come back later to pick up the meat. Indeed, Massouda herself used to do so—but she now insisted on being present for the entire process.

She needed two chickens for the feast following Yom Kippur, so she walked behind the stall without saying a word to Yosef and looked over each caged bird. Massouda couldn't describe precisely what she was looking for: some mixture of size, weight, activity, alertness of eyes—general signs of health that she knew when she saw. Today, she spotted her birds quickly, both striped and speckled, maybe sisters, agitated and fully aware of their circumstances. She called to Yosef with a short shout, loud enough to reach over the sounds of the animals, and pointed out her choices with both hands.

Yosef came to the back, grabbed the birds from their cages, held both under one arm, and told Massouda that she should return in half an hour, after they were slaughtered, drained of blood, and stripped of their feathers. Massouda replied she'd stay and watch, steadying her small body to show that it was not a negotiation. Yosef seemed annoyed, as butchers often were, but still proceeded. Grabbing his short blade, he pumped a floor paddle several times to get the whet wheel spinning, then pushed the knife hard against it, sliding it back and forth as the caged animals squirmed and screamed, nearly drowning out the sharp metallic tones. Yosef put down one chicken and placed a box over it. He held the other chicken on the table with his left hand, mumbled a Hebrew prayer, pulled the chicken's head back, brushed aside the neck feathers, and slit the bird's throat. Then quickly, he lifted the box, repeated the prayer, repeated the embrace, and killed the second chicken, placing them both upside-down in a pot—their legs hooked onto metal rods while the blood still pumped—to empty out the birds. Almost immediately, a swarm of flies appeared from nowhere, surrounding and then entering the blood-filled pot.

Yosef wiped the blade on his dappled smock, put it down, and asked Massouda if she wanted a cup of tea. When Massouda nodded, he stuffed small handfuls of mint leaves in two glasses, grabbed a vessel sitting on a small fire, and poured, placing the tea on a small crate that was one of the few surfaces free of blood or bile. Yosef pointed to a small stool and said, "Sit! You wanted to stay and watch, so *please* sit."

Massouda sat and put the glass of tea to her face, mostly to allow the fog of sugar and mint to cover the smell.

Pulling a crate near, Yosef sat beside her. "So, tell me, booba, why do you insist on being here for the slaughter and the draining? It's not normal, especially for a girl so young."

Massouda waited to answer, sipping her tea and staring at Yosef. She had known him since she was a child, when she'd play in these alleyways with friends. Yosef would often give them small bags of entrails and other pieces to feed to the street cats, and Massouda and her friends would run through the alleys with an army of cats following, pretending they were leading a feline force against the French invaders. Even then, Massouda had thought of Yosef as an old man, with his browned teeth that separated at the gums and appeared as bones filling a hollow mouth. Looking at him now, Massouda wondered how he had not continued to age, still appearing the same old man she had always known.

"I am sorry to say that I feel I must verify my purchase with you," she told him, using the most formal words and tone she possessed.

"Why?" The wrinkles on his face drooped, showing sudden sadness. "What have I done?"

"Do you remember on Pesach, I chose one of your lambs?"

"Yes, of course." His eyes grew distant, retreating to the catalog of kills he kept in his head at all times. "It was a fine lamb."

"I believe you switched it for another. When I began preparing the lamb, I saw that it was different from the one I had chosen."

"Booba, I did not do that," he said without defensiveness, sounding sincere. "Why should I do such a thing?"

"I don't know the reason, but I am certain it happened."

"I am sorry you feel that way." Yosef looked down, sullen.

Massouda had no time for pity or self-pity. "That is not a proper apology," she said, certain this did not count as her first refusal.

"For what should I apologize?" Yosef replied. "I did nothing wrong."

"I told you what you did."

"Child," he said. "Each day I come here and I slaughter animals for everyone. For you to feed your husband and your children." His voice grew louder. "I live in a world of blood and flies for you. I come home and my grandchildren cannot look at me or hug me. They see me as the harbinger of pain and death. I bring them kumquats and plums so that they'll enter the room while I am there. And you want I should apologize to you?"

"God knows what you did, and so do I. Tomorrow is the eve of Yom Kippur."

With a fierce frown, Yosef drank the remainder of his tea, set down his empty glass on the crate. "Booba, you are welcome to stay here and guard your chickens. I have other people to help. A good final sealing to you on Yom Kippur."

Massouda took her time finishing her own tea, looking around the back room, one half filled with animals braying and cackling, the other with recently slaughtered animals, their blood draining into pots and buckets. Sitting in the middle on her low stool, she tried to block out the surroundings, concentrating on whether there were any other apologies she needed to give or solicit.

Even after she left Yosef's stall, Massouda could not stop smelling death. The odor was trapped in her nostrils. She would call the phenomenon "stink nose" when she tried to describe it to others and asked if they too experienced it. She would explain that the stench of the moment of death was unique, that it would enter your nostrils and sit there, reminding you of darkness and tickling your nose like a fly's putrid wings, beating backward at every breath. She found it strange that she could never get used to the smell—that when it was there, she never forgot it was there, even for an instant. When she spoke about it, people were confused, so she stopped speaking about it, even though the stench remained.

For her return to the Mellah, Massouda took the long route so she could stop at Patisserie Belkabir for some sweets. Belkabir stood on a pedestal with all the sweets arrayed around him in a horseshoe pattern. She imagined that he smelled of pistachio and honey. A quiet man she had never spoken with except to place her order, he always smiled warmly at her. Today Massouda approached the raised counter to ask for a small bag of assorted items. For the children, she explained. Belkabir nodded, understanding, and created a story in a bag. When she put forward two coins, he pushed them away. "For the children," he said, winking. She smiled.

As soon as Massouda turned the corner, she found a spot to sit, tore open the bag of sweets, and ate them secretly.

SIDNEY

On the hot afternoon of August 5, 1941, Sidney Kleinmann wore his finest suit and prepared to spend part of the day strolling through Gimbel Brothers in Midtown Manhattan. Sidney didn't want to stand out, but he knew that he would, considering most of the clientele were upscale ladies and that he planned to shop in the women's sections of the store. Sidney also had a limp that caused him to bounce as he walked—a strut of sorts gifted to him by a policeman's club during the Communist-led street protests several years earlier. No, Sidney did not want to stand out, but knowing he would, he had found ways of embracing it. He had grown up in a Lower East Side tenement, and in those crowded streets filled with ragpickers and hockers, Sidney dreamed of becoming a Broadway actor. On some days he pretended he had made it and that his job was just a rehearsal, replete with costumes and supporting characters. August 5 was one of those days.

Sidney had studied the way the wealthy dressed, trying to distinguish the different categories of affluence. With many men, prosperity was displayed through the subtle details of appearance and manner. Often these indicators became apparent only when the wealthy man engaged you, which he did only if you were worthy and had access to his semiotics. You had to speak the language to speak the language with someone who spoke the language. When an old-money man put out his hand to shake, you could see cufflinks of silver or gold peek out of his sleeve, but just slightly and without apparent design. When he touched your shoulder in approval, you could see the watch, held by soft, supple leather, and hear its staccato movement with twenty-one gems marching in unison in your ear. When he offered you a pen, he would screw off its top, and still the weight of the bottom half would bring your signature to bear. And when he sat, you could see that the suit he wore was recently tailored for his present physique, with consideration for the multiple moments of the day of a man of leisure.

Sidney knew that he could not mimic a man of old money, so for his visits to Gimbels, he approximated the arriviste. This other species made demands for attention and led with his assets. Sidney's limp was not a problem because it allowed him to use a monogrammed silver-handled cane that counted his steps in clacks, which rang throughout the high-ceilinged spaces of the building. The cane was also useful for pointing and demanding, a trait of the nouveau riche, and if necessary for self-defense, which was always on Sidney's mind. His less-than-perfectly-tailored suit could be obscured by the loud blue pinstripes, the display of a fat wallet, and by fully embracing the character of a man of appetites rather than taste.

Sidney always entered at the corner beneath the clock, so he could see the entirety of the expansive floor without having to turn his head to surveil it and risk looking out of place. By entering at the corner, Sidney was also able to walk straight through the diagonal of the room and get a sense for which workers were in which departments. He knew many of them by name, so it was easy to strategize an approach, once he saw where they'd been stationed on a given day.

Today, upon taking only a few steps into the building, Sidney was greeted by a woman he'd never seen before—a floorwalker—who asked if he needed help. Sidney generally didn't trust the floorwalkers because they worked directly for the superintendent of the store, rather than being in the usual ranks of workers. In his experience, the easiest way to avoid conversation in these situations was to begin with frustration and annoyance. So in response to the woman's question, Sidney displayed exasperation as he explained that his wife, Clarina—stated loudly, with contempt—was in need of a satchel and hosiery, gloves, and other such notions.

In labor argot, Clarina was used when speaking to working women—to determine if someone was trustworthy. If they were in the know, then they'd know what Clarina really meant, and if not, it was a meaningless name. Sidney had a set of code words and phrases to determine who was safe, and he deployed them in a variety of places and circumstances. In approaching men on the streets or trains, he would casually ask if they knew of any good restaurants close by, emphasizing that he *adored seafood, but hated fish*. At night, in the Bowery, he might ask if a man knew of a good *gay* club that was open, *a place where a man could have fun*. Most would simply direct him to a crab shack or local jazz club, but a few grasped the significance of these everyday words. Almost every word Sidney spoke cast a shadow in which the real meaning often hid.

The floorwalker didn't seem to take notice of the name Clarina, guiding Sidney to the section where handbags were sold. Behind the counter, a young woman was arranging bags on the shelf, her back to them as Sidney and the floorwalker walked up.

"Lillian, this gentleman needs assistance in choosing a handbag for his wife."

"Yes, I need a good. Strong. Everyday bag. For my wife, Clarina." Sidney emphasized every word for effect.

The woman turned, and he saw it was the Lillian he knew. "Price is not a consideration," he said, then dismissed the floorwalker with a flip of his wrist. "I can handle it from here. I don't need an audience to watch me shop." Sidney hoped that if he was curt, she would keep her distance.

As the floorwalker sped away, Lillian met his eyes, her mouth twitching with the effort to hold back a smile. "Would you like a suggestion, sir? Or do you already know what you want?"

The floorwalker out of view, Sidney smiled and responded, "You know I always want to hear what those on the front lines are thinking."

"How are you, Sidney?" Lillian asked in a whisper, leaning forward.

"Don't whisper, Lillian," Sidney snapped. "It looks like you've got something to hide. And don't lean in; it looks too familiar. Always assume that someone is watching, because someone is always watching."

Lillian appeared shocked by Sidney's cold tone, and seeing her face seize, he tempered his annoyance, continuing more playfully. "And I will act like a bourgeois customer, for appearances, while you ape a scissorbill."

Lillian's expression eased, and she let out a slight smile, as if it were all a game.

"May I see that one there?" Sidney pointed to a large handbag, and when Lillian placed it on the counter and released its clasps and flaps, he pretended to inspect it. Instead, Sidney looked to his sides. No one was paying particular attention to him, so he slipped a stack of papers from the inner pocket of his suit jacket and stuffed it into a compartment in the bag.

"These are flyers for you and some of your sisters here," he said. "We're having a meeting at the Labor Lyceum off Bushwick Avenue on August seventh. It's important that you and some of the other shop leaders show up."

Lillian's eyebrows lifted. "That's the day after tomorrow. So soon. I don't know all the schedules, and I might not even be able to make it. What happened that there is so much of a rush?"

"It's not so much what happened, but what needs to happen," he said with excitement, then worked to temper his tone. "The International sold us out to the boss for pennies on the contract. We didn't get forty hours, we didn't get protections, and we didn't get a voice. All we got was a dollar fifty more a day. And that was their first offer. Accepted. No counteroffer. Just accepted. It's time to show the boss *and* the International that this local is not a pussycat; it's a wildcat."

Lillian grew excited, knowing this was talk of striking. She had come to relish union culture, especially in the largely ladies-led union at Gimbels. She quickly took to the language of solidarity, with its brothers and its sisters, and secretly carried with her everywhere an old Knights of Labor pin Sidney had given her, which read *An Injury to One is the Concern of All*. When she got nervous, she would rub her thumb along the smooth face of the pin, seven times, clockwise; when she got very nervous, she would push her thumb against the sharp needle in the back, sometimes until she drew blood. The pin was smoothed almost beyond recognition on its face and encrusted with her dried brown release on its hidden side.

"This doesn't give me a lot of time to get the word out," she said, worried it would all fail on her account. Sneaking her hand into her pocket, she began rubbing the pin.

"I know, but you can do it," said Sidney. "Hide flyers in the common spaces. Sneak them in the sales ledgers at the end of the day, so when someone flips through them, flyers fall out. Put them in toilet paper dispensers in the stalls. . . ."

Lillian chuckled quietly.

"Don't laugh. You know as well as I do that all workplace disputes run through the bathroom. Use the store chutes when you send down merchandise; they'll scatter on the back floor without anyone even noticing. The spies and fancy ladies can watch you out here under that big clock, but they don't have a way to watch the hidden common spaces."

"But the bosses," Lillian said, putting the point of the pin to her thumb. "Will they not find them too?"

"Yes, exactly. Now you're thinking like an agitator. That's entirely the point," Sidney explained. "The bosses will find them, because the flyers will be everywhere. Keep an eye on who turns them in, because that will show you who you can't trust, those lumpenproletariat bastards. But maybe even get a few of your sisters to turn some in. We want the bosses to know, and we want them to be scared we're coming for them, that the contract won't keep us docile. And we want them to overreact—because they always overreact—and call a meeting. We want them to try to root out the instigators and agitators. Make threats. Try to act tough, and in doing so they will show how scared they are. That will get the word out in ways we could never do on our own. Remember, the boss is the best organizer; we just have to trick him into doing our work."

Lillian smiled at the lovely simplicity of it all. "We all know how often they trick *us* into doing *their* work."

Sidney returned her smile.

"All right," Lillian said, pulling her hands out of her pockets. "I can do that. I'll make sure we get to the meeting. Are you thinking we might strike?"

"We might have to. We'll definitely have to organize and act as if we're prepared to strike."

"Do you think it will be like Woolworth's?" Lillian asked, terrified and fascinated by the prospect of the direct confrontation that would come with a sit-in. She wanted to feel the power of using the body as a form of protest, a weapon, simply by sitting.

"I don't know," said Sidney. "We may have to occupy the store to put the fear of God in the bosses, but we'll try other means. I'm not sure the feds wouldn't try to break us now, because of the war in Europe or some other excuse."

"I'll tell you this, Sidney, I don't know how much support we'll get from the ladies that shop here. It is not like the five-and-dimes, where the girls who work there live down the street. These wealthy ladies are different; they are like a bunch of szlachta." Lillian made a sashaying motion with her hips. "They like to pretend there are no problems here, that there's no such thing as class, that it's a fantasy world where everything is pretty and perfect. I've seen some of these ladies weekly for over a year, and they know nothing about me beyond my name. And even that they forget."

"If we strike, it'll be a different kind of strike. I don't know who, if anyone, will support us, maybe not even the International. But you remember the songs we sang at the last meeting? 'We Shall Not Be Moved' and 'Solidarity Forever'? If we have solidarity and class consciousness, we shall not be moved." Sidney's voice had risen, seemingly in spite of himself.

"I liked the other ones more," Lillian said, and when Sidney furrowed his brow, she winked. "Remember 'Mademoiselle from Armentiéres'?"

"Barbara Hutton has the dough, parlez-vous.
Where she gets it, sure we know, parlez-vous."

Sidney chuckled.

"Barbara Hutton, she gets mutton; .
Woolworth's workers, they get nuttin'!
Hinky dinky parlez-vous."

Sidney tapped his cane to regain control of himself. "Oh, Lillian . . ." he started, then cleared his throat. "But the first thing we have to do is get the word out about the meeting, and then gather and make some difficult decisions. Get the stack I gave you out there and start telling those you trust about it quietly. I'll hit a few other departments. Who is working in hosiery today?" Sidney thought he could slip a pile in some hosiery tubes.

"I think it's Frances," Lillian said.

"Oh good. She's good. I'll go talk to her. You might want to put that bag aside with my name on it," Sidney suggested. "That way, no one will accidentally stumble upon the flyers. Plus, it'll make it look like you made a potential sale to a very difficult customer." He grinned.

Lillian lifted the handbag from the counter. "What name should I put on it? Not Sidney, right?"

"No. Just make one up. I'm not actually going to buy it. Turns out I don't need another handbag." First putting his hands on his hips, Sidney then quickly moved them to his face, raising his index fingers to make his eyebrows disappear: his impersonation of a fairy. Smiling, he tapped the counter hard and began to walk away.

*　*　*

Listening to the rhythm of Sidney's cane echoing across the floor in two-four time, Lillian picked up a Gimbels' purchase card and paused for a moment, trying to think of a fake name. She then wrote on the front: *Hold For Mr. Cohen*. It was the highest order name that she could think of.

NISSIM

In the spring of 1942, Massouda AbuHazar took her children on their first trip that year to the beach. When they set out, it was the late afternoon and an unseasonably hot day, the kind that usually came with the full weight of summer, when the souk developed a putrid smell and the thick of the market air settled in every alley. For everyone inside the walls, the knowledge that the Atlantic Ocean sat there, waving just beyond the souk, offering the promise of bathing and feeling the cool wind, was nearly unbearable.

Massouda had tried to wake Rafael to persuade him to spend his day at the beach with the children, but he'd arrived home in the early hours, after another late night. A new world had opened up in Casablanca since 1940, a world underground, and Rafael had seized an opportunity to make secret money. He repeatedly explained to Massouda that the extra income—hidden and tax-free—was necessary to fund their move to Palestine. He reminded her that she'd recently turned twenty, and if she wanted to make it to Palestine before she was an old auntie, he needed the extra work—that without family there to help, everything about setting up a new life would be expensive. Massouda said that she feared he was being tricked by Mama Ghula, who was fattening him up in the night, preparing to feast on his flesh, like in the stories. He brushed aside her concern as the nonsense his mother and aunts used to say.

When Rafael had started working in the dark economy, he first made military boots and bootleg uniforms for militias and resistance fighters, then dabbled in forgeries and the occasional illegal metalwork. Lately, he had also been participating in a card game to increase his fortunes, everyone being flush with the influx of illicit work. The card game, Massouda knew, was usually what kept him out the latest—and ruined him for most of the next day.

Massouda continued trying to rouse him throughout the morning, because she wanted help taking four children and supplies on the buses to the beach. She told him he could sleep on the sand just as he could sleep at home, that the sun would be good for him. He said he was sick, but since he'd had a good night, they should take a taxi. He then handed her a small wad of bills and a satchel of coins.

Massouda quickly rifled through the coins to see if there were any of her favorites within; there were not. Spying the money, Nissim had asked if they could have sfenj at the beach, and Massouda was surprised. A year earlier, when Nissim was only two, the family had been walking in the hills high above the ocean when they'd come across a small sfenj bakery and stopped to eat the fried dough sweetened with honey. As the waves of the Atlantic beat against the cliffs, the family sat on the sidewalk in the sun, making themselves simultaneously sticky and oily.

Massouda hadn't imagined the memory would stay with Nissim, or that he'd come to associate the ocean with doughnuts, but it shouldn't have come as a surprise. Nissim created a rich world of associations, categories, and rules that he was forceful in imposing on everyone around him. He referred to himself only in the third person, but since he couldn't pronounce *Nissim*, he renamed himself *Bazja*, emphasizing the soft Moroccan *zzhh*. The street dogs were all girls, and the street cats were all boys. Certain zones in the house and the souk were *safe*, which meant that all game rules were suspended the moment someone entered those areas. Some wall hangings had to be at child eye-level, and some had to be at adult eye-level, according to a mysterious aesthetic principle understood only by him. He told jokes that were one sentence or one word long, with the setup and the punchline merged, and then laughed uncontrollably at his wit. He would point to random people and objects and describe them as *good* or *bad*, without any further explanation. And the ocean meant sfenj. Such was Nissim's world.

Though she disliked the port, it was where taxi drivers congregated, so Massouda decided to walk there rather than getting a taxi from the neighborhood. The walk was not too far, even in the late-afternoon heat with four children in tow, and she'd be able to negotiate a lower fare there, leaving enough money for both sfenj and the ride home. Though she didn't explain her rationale to the children, Nissim somehow understood, and he thanked his mother and asked if he could lug the jug of water to help.

When they arrived at the port, Massouda could see the German and French ships lined up, swastika flags flying in the Moroccan wind. The sight made her sick, made her feel unsafe, and she hastened the children into the taxi. The drive mostly hugged the coast, with nineteenth-century mansions rising up on the left and giant waves out of the Atlantic on the right. Along most of the coast, the ocean was too wild to swim in or even get near, but at what they called the beach there was a break that tempered the inherent violence of the water. In the final stretch of the drive, the taxi rose up a hill where white French villas perched on cliffs being whipped and chipped by the white-haired waves. On the edge of this hill was the small sfenj bakery they'd found the previous year, with boulders jutting from the sidewalk where they'd sat to eat while looking down at the sea. As they drove past the bakery, Nissim caught sight of it or smelled it and began crying out for sfenj. He was usually calm in his demands, so when he cried or screamed, everyone took notice. Massouda, sitting in the rear of the taxi with him, explained that they would stop on the way back, after they negotiated a fare with the return driver. Nissim seemed to accept the compromise and went quiet, putting his head out the window to feel the spray from the water colliding with the cliffs.

At the beach, Massouda opened the rug she used to carry the fruit and drink. She weighed down the rug and pointed to a nearby palm tree, telling the children where they would find her, reminding them to stay together and that Simi, the eldest at six years old, was in charge. She also told them if they needed to pee, they could find a spot on the beach away from people, or squat in the shallow waters, but if they had to kaki, they should come back to her, and she would help. They yelled their agreement as they ran off in unison.

Massouda loved watching them run and play together, and she often wondered what she'd done to be blessed with such wonderful and happy children. She knew so many who'd experienced stillbirths or children with mental or physical problems. Watching her young ones now, she smiled at her fortune, before quickly realizing that she was unnecessarily inviting the evil eye.

Sometimes Massouda felt bad that Simi had to take on so much at such a young age, but she seemed suited to it. Simi had not only been an easy baby and toddler, she'd quickly become second in command, helping with her siblings. Was it the responsibility or Simi's temperament that had made her prematurely serious, Massouda wondered. She asked herself different questions about Nissim, who played as any three-year-old would, but also spent hours each day at Massouda's side, weaving fantastical stories that went nowhere and everywhere. She marveled at how he made sense of non-sense and nonsense of sense, but sometimes he scared her with what he described—images that should have been alien to a child—and by how he lived in a dual world. Depending on the day, she wondered if he had an exceptionally strong imagination, or if something was wrong with him— if something possessed him. Her concern caused her to pay special atten-tion to Nissim, and the other children took notice. When Nissim insisted they all act according to rules he seemed to make up, Simi, in particular, would sometimes become upset. More so when Massouda played along. Nissim was Simi's charge, but when there was disagreement between them, Simi saw that her mother rarely sided with her.

Massouda watched as the children made paths in the sand, creating cir-cles on top of circles, which looked like ancient maps of the heavens the old book vendors were sometimes selling. When they reached the water, they followed its movements. As the tide receded, the children would scream and run after it; and then, as the sea grew into a mound that threatened a wave, they would scream an entirely different scream and race back to the beach—which was, Nissim had announced when they arrived, a safe zone.

Eating grapes on the rug, Massouda trained her eyes on them in the distance, their figures dancing on the beach and singing their screams. The sun reflecting off the water made it difficult to stare at the children for a long stretch, however, so Massouda closed her eyes and focused on the sounds they made. She would watch them by listening. She could picture the movements of the water by the tone of their screams: the waves bring-ing a shrill chorus, followed by a full-throated ululation at the water's re-treat. It sounded so round and perfect, the cycles—with the seabirds bark-ing and the wind whipping it all together.

On the backs of her eyelids, Massouda began to picture Jerusalem— just across the sea, she imagined. She conjured up the walls of the city, so much higher than Casablanca's walls, and the Tower of King David rising up above it all, piercing the heavens. She heard sounds of streets filled with people, rocking in Hebrew prayer in the open air, turning the city into a giant synagogue. Her mind drifted to the idea of wandering the shuk and tasting grapes from Galilee, Sabra from the Negev, and citrus from Yaffo, speaking in Hebrew that seemed so formal, and looking up at the same sky where Moshe had seen God thousands of years earlier. An endless sky. She opened her eyes and looked up past the fronds of the palm tree; the same sky, but so different.

Massouda realized that she didn't hear the children. Looking out at the beach and water, her eyes were momentarily burned by the radiance. It was all glare—the white sun, the clear water. As her vision returned, she saw Simi running toward her. And then Amram, and then Annet. The sand made them run funny, she thought, laughing at their uncontrollable little bodies and the way they swung their arms wildly, engaging everything in their movement. She squinted to peer beyond Annet, expecting to see Nissim with the others. He wasn't there. She blinked and looked at the children again, but again saw only three. She looked to their sides, to the expanse of beach, but still couldn't find him. As she studied the shore carefully, Simi came within earshot.

"Amu, amu," Simi yelled, still running. "The water took him away."

"What?" Massouda asked, exasperated. Simi's words made no sense.

Stopping in front of her mother, Simi repeated, "Amu, the water took Nissim away."

"What?" Massouda jerked to her feet, alarm snaking through her. "Where?"

Simi pointed her small arm to a spot on the beach, a spot like any other. Massouda could not see Nissim. Running in the direction of Simi's outstretched finger, she pushed her way into the shallows as a wave receded, and then looked frantically to each side. She turned in complete circles to her right and then her left. She could not see Nissim. Simi, Amram, and Annet waited by the line of sand that separated the dry from the wet, looking afraid.

Rushing back to Simi, Massouda asked, "Where is Nissim? What happened to him?"

"The water took him away," she said simply, and Massouda wanted to shake her for being so composed.

"How?" Massouda demanded. "How?"

"He had to go pee. So he went into shallow water like you said. And he pulled his pants down and sat."

"Where is he?" Massouda repeated.

"He was peeing, and a wave came. And he tried to pick up his pants. And he fell. And the water took him away. He was gone so quickly. We ran back right away."

Massouda once more turned to the water and scanned the entire expanse, the horizon, trying to take in and make sense of every detail. From this angle, the sea looked black, no longer clear and blue with white froth as it appeared from her spot under the palm. Noticing a child playing, about the size of Nissim, she felt a moment of relief. But just as quickly, the moment passed. It wasn't Nissim. She lost her breath. Suddenly everyone around her seemed to be laughing and swimming, as if nothing had happened. She wanted it all to go completely quiet so she could listen for Nissim, scream for Nissim, hear him respond. But most of the noise was from the ocean and the birds, and they could not be silenced.

Putting her hands on her remaining children, Massouda said, "Come, let's go home."

For once, Simi looked unsettled. Annet began to cry.

Averting her eyes from her children's faces, Massouda tugged them away from the water, away from the sand, toward the taxis.

"Wait!" cried Simi. "What about our stuff? The rug. And food."

"Yala!" Massouda announced loudly, as if they could not hear her over the din.

Walking away, she felt them twisting in her grip, craning over their shoulders to search the ocean. Massouda could hear the waves moving as they had before, over and back, the sand running after the water, rolling into the sea, only to be redeposited a moment later.

Massouda thought back to a childhood story about a girl who was visited by a maggid in a dream and told that the hakham's newborn son would be her future. Frustrated by having to wait for the baby to grow before she could start a family, the girl placed the infant inside a box, put his amulet around his neck, and threw him into the sea. This sea. Casablanca's sea. In Tangier, a different hakham bought a fish at market and found the boy alive inside. A boy so beautiful, the goats would not graze if they saw him. After being raised to bar mitzvah by the Tangier hakham, the boy found his way home by grasping the amulet and following its fortunes.

"Was he wearing his amulet?" Massouda asked Simi and the other children. She heard no response. She continued pulling them up the hillside, all the while listening carefully, trying to separate the myriad noises—the screaming and shrieking, the tumbling waves—for a sound she knew.

CHARNY JOOK

On September 27, 1942, in the Marais in Paris's 3rd arrondissement, Charny Jook squatted in an alley in the Tunisian fashion. If someone spoke to him, he was prepared to respond in Derja, broken French, or broken Classical Arabic. He knew that no matter his fluency with the language, one should never pretend to be French. The French were skilled at recognizing the details of accents. A mispronounced syllable, an archaic or too-formal word, an errant idiomatic expression could give you away in an instant. French was a minefield like no other, everything a shibboleth, and everyone's ear a trap in waiting.

It was much easier to be Tunisian, because even after sixty years of occupying Tunisia, the French never bothered to learn Derja or to become closely acquainted with the region's customs and culture. For some reason, squatting on the sidewalk had become the mark of a Tunisian. And in that position, Charny Jook attracted many insults—a person once yelling that he looked like a *shitting Arab*. He'd wondered what was unique about the way that Arabs shit. Didn't everyone squat? But Charny Jook was happy to be mistaken for a Tunisian on the streets of Paris, and he did everything possible to encourage that impression.

At first, Charny Jook had disliked his code name. Everyone had one in his cell, so he wasn't opposed to the concept. But *Charny Jook*? And in Russian, of all languages? All because of his dark complexion and eastern origin. They took such incidental qualities and transformed them into his essence. He'd resisted at first, but code names were like nicknames: the more you resisted, the more they stuck; and the more you objected, the more you revealed how deeply they cut. So now, around the two people George could trust most, he was Charny Jook, always the two words together, like a proper name—the Black Cockroach.

Charny Jook was growing nervous because the mandatory curfew was fast arriving, and he'd not yet seen his contact walk by. The plan was for the contact to pass by in one direction, then turn around and walk in the other direction, with Charny Jook following at a distance to their meeting point. Even squatting in the alley, with a view of the bustling street, Charny Jook felt too exposed. Any one of the various officials or collaborators might cause trouble for him. He didn't have anything incriminating on him, nothing that could be considered contraband, but someone could always find a reason to bring you in. And once you were in, it was hard to get out. Even if you hadn't done anything wrong. They could just be culling the streets in search of forced labor in the Service du Travail Obligatoire, and decide you were fit enough to help the German war effort.

Waiting, Charny Jook started to think about Charles, Juliette's younger brother. In some ways, he missed Juliette and their back-and-forths in various languages in various cafés. Though he never quite trusted her, he liked her. George had only briefly met her brother Charles a few times in social settings before the war, but recently, Charles had started to seek him out, always running up to him on the street, yelling, "George. George." Juliette had moved to Vichy to work in some capacity for the government, and George had first assumed that Charles was feeling lost or lonely. Then Charles started asking a lot of questions, like his sister used to but more pointed, less conversational, and always only in French. A few weeks ago, while Charny Jook was carrying a translation for the underground paper he secretly worked for, Charles appeared again, out of nowhere. Always out of nowhere, at inopportune moments—when Charny Jook felt especially vulnerable.

After they'd exchanged a few pleasantries, Charles started complaining about the lack of available food, saying it was all potatoes and onions all the time. Perhaps Charny Jook was being overly suspicious, but he could not understand why Charles was trying to make common cause with him. They weren't countrymen; they weren't lantsmen; they weren't comrades.

Charles then turned from complaining about not having butter and cream to praising the British. George knew the code—praise the British, never criticize the Germans—and that it was a test to see if someone was safe. But he didn't trust Charles enough to engage seriously, and he didn't think Charles could contribute anything to the cause that would make it worth the risk.

Before George could respond, Charles leaned in and whispered, "George. George."

Charles always said the name with a hard *G*, in a manner that sounded more eastern than French.

"You're Jewish, right? Juliette said something like you might be." Charles tapped his own chest. "I'm safe. You can tell me if you're Jewish."

George denied being Jewish and excused himself, saying he was in a rush to meet a friend, which was true. Charles asked if he could come, explaining that he'd lost his job and had nothing to do, and that any friend of George's was a friend of his. George politely declined, explaining that his friend was shy and a bit of a Schopenhauerian. He followed up with a joke that Charles would just be an object to his friend's subject, but Charles seemed confused. For a moment, George thought of further stating that Charles would just be a *du* to his friend's *ich*, but he quickly realized it was best not to make an oblique reference to a Jew, even if Buber was Austrian. Besides, Charles probably wouldn't get the joke.

On his haunches in the alley, Charny Jook looked at his watch and saw that there was only an hour left until curfew, and considering he'd need to get back to his flat before patrols started, he resolved to give his contact another fifteen minutes before abandoning the idea of meeting that day. Then he saw something that stood out, even on this busy street: a pair of SS officers strolled to the corner and stood there. They looked young—younger than he was—and they were talking to each other, laughing. Charny Jook felt a rush of fear and anger. He'd never had any actual interactions with the SS, but he knew if they wanted to cause problems, there was no way around it. They weren't like French police, who would often take a bribe or allow you to talk your way out of trouble.

Charny Jook lit a Tunisian cigarette—a harsh brand of tobacco that disgusted the French and Germans alike—hoping the stink would cause the officers to keep their distance. He breathed deeply to try to relax, inhaling the pungent smoke, burning his lungs and chest. He could control his fear, but he found his fury more difficult to contain. Despite his best efforts, he had been unable to make contact with his parents or any family in Stawsk for about a year. He'd heard rumors of what the SS had done there, how they'd crowded Jews into synagogues and then torched the buildings with them inside. He imagined his parents trapped, choking on burning Torahs, as their synagogue—his synagogue—filled with death, the group sanctuary becoming a mass tomb. He could hear them screaming in Yiddish, see them scratching at the walls, feel them looking for any opening. The windows were so high, they would scramble on top of one another in a vain effort to reach them, scramble until they fell. He couldn't bear the thought of the whole community, built over centuries, burning in one flame with their sacred objects as combustibles.

Charny Jook had heard that the Germans joked about the efficiency of the Polish pogrom, how they didn't have to waste a single bullet, and that the synagogues got destroyed as a bonus. The rumors reached him months ago, and at first he'd dismissed them as impossible; just another example of the general misinformation that he would hear each day. As time passed and he was unable to make contact with anyone from his hometown, however, he began to believe. Documents started coming through for him to translate—in Polish and Russian—describing the destruction in the east and showing that what the rumors suggested was indeed possible, and most likely true. They had first- and secondhand accounts of the efficient destruction of Jewish communities and great yeshivas across Litvak, with the repeated mention of fires burning.

Crouched there, watching these two SS officers laugh, Charny Jook was enraged. He simmered and hoped they wouldn't walk past him—both for fear of what they might do to him, and also for fear of what he might do first. Charny Jook remembered how his contact had warned him: *Under no circumstances can you harm a German. If we kill one of them, they'll kill a hundred of us. We only go after French collaborators; never Germans.*

The words *never Germans* sat with him now as he recalled his contact's face, the expression on it when Charny Jook told him about Charles. The contact asked for Charles's full name and any other personal information Charny Jook knew, as well as the locations and times of day when Charles had approached him. The contact wrote down every detail in tiny handwriting in his small notebook. Charny Jook couldn't remember if he added that Charles seemed lonely and pathetic, that he may have simply been trying too hard to bond, but it would have been obvious to anyone who met him. He hadn't seen Charles after that, and now he wondered what had happened. Had Charles simply disappeared, or had he *been* disappeared?

Still squatting, smoking his harsh cigarette, and watching the SS officers in side glances, Charny Jook moved his identifying papers from his front pocket to a spot on the backside of his pants. He wasn't sure why, but they felt safer there. The officers still hadn't moved, and the fifteen minutes he'd allotted to waiting for his contact had elapsed, but he didn't want to move first—afraid it might invite attention, and attention arouse suspicion. So he lit another cigarette and continued to rest on his haunches, his legs starting to burn from the position.

To keep from staring at the soldiers, he glanced around at the shops, some of which were shuttered, though the cafés were still open. He saw people inside them, drinking coffee, smoking, arguing, laughing, as if everything were normal. He marveled at the way people adjusted to new circumstances, both disgusted and envious of their abilities. He wondered why he was doing what he was doing, putting his life at risk translating words into other words. George had begun working with the resistance out of a need to help the cause, and he'd assumed everyone would do their part, but as far as he could tell, most of the French simply found a way to forget and move forward. They gathered in cafés, hung out in groups, and griped. And it wasn't clear that *his* efforts were having any effect. Half the time, he felt like a child playing, sneaking through the streets, keeping secrets and plotting intrigue, all of it a game without consequence.

Charny Jook heard someone call out in German. For a second, the voice sounded distant and hollow, carried by the wind from another reality. He looked around and saw the two SS officers walking toward him, one pointing in his direction. The other exclaimed loudly, "You there, come here," his face revealing nothing of his intentions.

Charny Jook stood, wobbled slightly, his legs weak from squatting for so long. He righted his posture and felt a tickle envelop his legs. Raising his eyebrows, Charny Jook pointed at his chest, as if to ask, *Me?*

"You, Arab. Come here. We want to talk to you," the other officer yelled as they both ambled over, the command belying their casual gait.

Charny Jook felt nothing but terror. Everything his contact had ever told him about how to deal with French or German authorities fell away. This could be nothing—just two bored soldiers looking to harass a squatting Arab—or it could be everything. He knew he should do as they said. If he approached them, he might be stuck, but if he ran he would surely be chased and, if caught, imprisoned or executed.

He was still standing at the other end of the block, and no matter his reasoning, Charny Jook could not persuade his body to move toward the officers. Their yelling grew louder as they came closer, seemingly annoyed that he did not meet them halfway to submit to his fate. Steeling himself, Charny Jook took a step toward them and then, almost involuntarily, pivoted on his front leg and ran with all his strength in the other direction. There was a brief silence that he interpreted as the SS officers being stunned—perhaps as stunned as he was by his actions—then the clatter of boots on stone as they gave chase.

Charny Jook careened around every corner, running in the general direction of the Seine. He could hear the officers behind him, their weapons and medals clanking as they ran awkwardly in dress uniforms made for posturing. Charny Jook didn't have a destination, but he thought if he kept turning down alleys and streets, he might lose them. He hadn't considered what would happen if he reached the river, and as he neared it, he realized his mistake. Neither the bridge nor the riverbank would offer much cover. As he turned another corner, Charny Jook saw a street drain—one with a concrete break big enough to fit a small man—and he knew his pursuers wouldn't follow him into the sewer; better to lose him than to dirty or tear their crisp uniforms.

At the drain, Charny Jook quickly got down on all fours and squeezed his hands and head in. He levered his arms against the inside wall, and his lower body followed without too much friction. As soon as his hips cleared the opening, he tumbled down into the sewer.

For a moment, he lay in the shallow septic water, listening. Hearing nothing, he sat up and then stood, trying not to splash for fear the ripples would resound and the echo be heard at the surface. His entire body hurt. He instinctively felt like he should limp, but neither leg demanded it. He started walking slowly in the black sewer, the darkness broken by small streams of light entering at odd angles from the street above. Quietly and deliberately, Charny Jook moved in a straight line, shuffling rather than stepping so as not to agitate the water. He didn't know where he was going, but thought it safest to stay underground until morning, when the curfew was lifted and the streets would be filled with others. He needed to create distance, so he continued to move in as straight a path as possible.

After a few hours of walking at a consistent pace, Charny Jook saw a penumbra in the middle of the tunnel ahead. Thinking his eyes might be playing tricks in the low light, which reflected off the filthy water in strange ways, he kept walking, trying to focus on what appeared to be an object and its shadow. He had become more comfortable with the shadows in Paris, fearing more and more what could be seen in the sunlight. As he drew closer, he saw a dog, or what was the right size and shape for a dog. But what would a dog be doing in the sewer? he asked himself, then chuckled at the thought of the dog wondering the same thing about him. For the first time that day, he relaxed, amused by the absurdity of it all, comforted by the feeling that he wasn't alone, even if the other being was a dog seeking refuge in a sub-terranean passage.

As he continued shuffling toward it, the dog rose on its hind legs, easily and boldly. In this posture it was tall and oddly built, with too-short fore-legs. The dog squeaked and then hissed, the sounds echoing in the tunnel. Charney Jook saw the teeth, two on top and two on bottom, all four long and slender, brown and curved. The dog was a rat. A large rat, standing erect, staring at him, with short scheming child's hands, baring its teeth in aggression. The war had created fertile feeding grounds for rats, and he had noticed them growing larger and being more brazen in the streets, but he could never have imagined a dog-sized rat. The terror returned, even greater than before.

George let out a yell to scare the rat, but it sounded scared and weak. The rat squeaked and hissed back, displaying how its bottom teeth con-joined with the top pair, opening its jaw wide enough that George could see the back of its pink throat.

George turned and bolted for the second time that day, not caring about the noise he created. He ran at full speed in the dimness of the tun-nel, reaching out to the sides so he didn't stumble and fall. In the dark stretches between the drains, he returned to the distant Stawsk night, run-ning through barely recognizable streets—the shadows trying to pull him down with long, sticky fingers. The water splashed up to his chest, and feces crawled up his pants as he wound his way through the sewers. Every noise echoed in sinister ways; water dropping and splashing mimicked the sounds of rat squeaks. George ran, trying to get to anywhere else. The dark-ness of the tunnel allowed him to dream as he pushed himself forward, and he dreamed of getting away. He dreamed of the countryside. An image of trees and open green fields expanded in his mind, and George knew that he was done with Paris, done with his cell, done with Charny Jook.

RAV MINSKY

On May 9, 1944, Lev Kagan of Bensonhurst, Brooklyn, made Aliyah to Zion, fulfilling a great mitzvah that should be commended. Unfortunately, he left behind his wife of three years, Rivka Kagan. Now, Mrs. Kagan has petitioned this beit din to order Mr. Kagan to deliver a bill of divorce in the form of a Get, essentially alleging abandonment of the marriage. Her testimony and evidence were delivered in person to this properly constituted three-rabbi panel of judges of the beit din, and it is our duty to determine whether this case constitutes one of those rare circumstances where we must bid the husband to involuntarily deliver a Get.

Rav Minsky wrote these words in his notebook as his daughter Lillian cleaned the adjoining room. He could hear her shifting back and forth from one side of the room to the other, over and over, unable to focus for too long on any one spot. Rav Minsky tried to block out the sound. He served as a judge on the Brooklyn beit din, which was among the most important Jewish courts in the world, specializing in family law. This decision had been giving him trouble for a few weeks, and this was his third attempt at drafting it. Divorces were messy affairs, and he found it was always helpful for him to foreground the central issue to reach a decision based on the Talmud, Halakha, and teachings of the rabbis.

Rav Minsky had written hundreds of decisions and Gets in his role, but the work never became easier. He'd begun in property law, but his reputation quickly grew as one of the foremost experts on the law of Jewish divorce. He was now often introduced as the Gaon of Stawsk. That title—*the Genius*—haunted him, because only a well-known center of Jewish learning could have a Gaon, and it could only have one, if it had one at all. It put him in the shadow of the great Geonim of the great Jewish centers of learning of the diaspora: the Vilna Gaon, the Rahachow Gaon, the Pinsk Gaon. Even in normal times, it was a burden to carry the title, but especially now, during this period of cultural and religious crisis. Rav Minsky had felt the emptiness from the Jewish settlements across eastern Europe, and he'd heard tales from incoming Jews about the destruction of their great yeshivas across Litvak. All that remained to the names of these towns were the Geonim—the "geniuses" whose lot it was to characterize and carry on the unique traditions and customs of these erased places, to give them continued meaning.

> *By all accounts, Lev Kagan is a man of character. He has studied Torah and Talmud. It was reported that growing up, he asked his mother what he should do as an occupation, and his mother responded that he should become whatever it was that Zion needed. Lev Kagan became an engineer, so that he could contribute to the construction of a city on a hill. In doing so, he fulfilled two great mitzvahs: he honored his mother and our collective homeland.*
>
> *Lev Kagan was introduced to Rivka by an esteemed matchmaker who had consulted with the families. When Lev Kagan first met Rivka, it was at a family dinner at the house of his future mother-in-law, Rivka's father having passed, may his memory be a blessing. The evidence shows that at the time, Lev Kagan was an engineering student who had become a vegetarian due to his sensitive nature. However, while he was at his mother-in-law's table, he ate her meat, leading her to describe him to several others as a "mensch."*
>
> *Lev Kagan and Rivka have been married for three years, but they have not been blessed with children. Neither party has alleged barrenness of womb or sterility, either of which may serve as separate halakhic grounds for divorce. Rather, it appears that they have not yet received this particular blessing from Hashem.*

As Rav Minsky wrote these words, he thought of his own children, specifically Liebe, though she went by Lillian now. In Stawsk, his wife had hinted that, though unmarried, she may have been blessed with child, and he had tried to advocate for marriage with the town rabbi's son. No matter the circumstances of conception, a marriage and family were always the preferred option. But it was not to be. When Rav Minsky had asked his wife about the end of the pregnancy, she responded curtly that it was God's will. This meant there was nothing else to say because there was nothing else to ask. But on some days, when Rav Minsky sat in judgment of others' marriages and heard the details of infidelity and abuse and babki miscarriages, he thought of Liebe and wondered whether he had made the right decision in Stawsk.

> *The only witness to step forward in this case was Rivka, but she seemed to be balanced in her testimony, a credible witness and a fine girl, displaying no hints of evasion or untruth. Furthermore, she submitted letters and other documentary evidence that helped in providing this beit din with an accurate and full picture. Lev Kagan was contacted through the beit din of Jerusalem and invited to participate, even if only to submit a letter or other written account or position, but he was unresponsive. Therefore, we must make our decision based on the evidence brought forward by Rivka, according to the Talmud and teachings of the rabbis.*
>
> *The facts of this case seem simple enough. Lev Kagan decided to make Aliyah to the Holy Land, and his wife refused to go with him. As a result of these actions, a husband is in Jerusalem, apparently unwilling to deliver a Get, while his wife is in New York, claiming to be an agunah.*

Every time that he wrote the word *agunah*, he pictured a woman chained to a post, as the term implied.

> *However simple the facts, the interworkings of a family are never so easy to discern. Families are always filled with the unspoken truths and untruths that give it definition and bind it as one.*

Rav Minsky thought of his long days and nights in Radin with the Chofetz Chaim, shortly before the great man's death. His mentor had looked so frail and weak, but his mind was as sharp as ever. He remembered the wrenching of the Chofetz Chaim's face as he told him what the town rabbi's son had done to Liebe, as if the elder personally felt the physical and emotional pain of it all. He marveled at the old man's ability to empathize, to show it on his shrunken face and trembling body, not hiding it even for an instant. Rav Minsky remembered the silence accompanying the pained expression, while the great rabbis who learned at the feet of the Chofetz

Chaim debated the merits of each course of action. In the evenings, at dinner at the home of the Chofetz Chaim, the group never discussed the matter, instead taking pleasure in each other's company and the joys of the Torah. But after the meal, discussion returned to Stawsk and the possible options between impossibilities. Rav Minsky had wanted a full airing, for Stawsk to confront its hidden demons and for the beit din to deliver justice to Liebe—yet that, also, was not to be.

On the final day, the Chofetz Chaim had spoken. After listening for days as the various rabbis argued what the Talmud commanded in such a situation, he expressed deep personal sympathy for the Minsky family, but suggested it was not just to destroy both another family and the community in order to right a wrong. And what if it was not as Liebe described it? With only two witnesses, who would likely not agree as to what occurred, one could never know for certain, yet the destruction of a good man and great rabbi would ripple out irreparably. Even if there were truth to Liebe's account, he concluded, the beit din could not dole out true justice. The reparation that was necessary was to create a family. Thus, any child born would not be a mamzer, alien to his family and community from his illegitimacy. This was the only way to ensure that what the rabbi's son may have done would not destroy generations of families. All of the rabbis fell in line, agreeing that the Chofetz Chaim had put forth a path of divine justice, which no one of them could fully understand. When Rav Minsky held the Chofetz Chaim's hand at his departure, he could feel every bone and vein and tremor, and he was thankful he'd had the opportunity to be in his mentor's presence one last time.

> Rather than delve into each detail of this marriage, it is best to begin with the words of Hashem, our God. The Torah states that "A man takes a wife and possesses her. She fails to please him because he finds something obnoxious about her and he writes her a Get of divorce, hands it to her and banishes her from his house." This commandment from the Book of Devarim teaches us several things. First, the divorce is in the hands of the husband, which he may initiate based on the conduct or actions of his wife. Next, in order to execute the divorce, he must first deliver the Get and then cast his wife from the house.

> However, the sages knew that relations between a husband and wife are complicated—indeed the entire family is unique in its troubles—so that in

some instances the final decision to deliver the Get must not be left only to the husband. For if it were so, what would happen when a man went missing at sea or war, neither proven dead nor able to be found? Should his wife be trapped and unable to remarry? There must be exceptions under which a wife can force a Get.

The Mishnah ketubot indeed sets forth specific grounds under which a husband can be forced to deliver a Get. They are when a man is stricken with boils, when he has bad breath, when he is a gatherer of handfuls of excrement, and when he is a tanner or refiner of copper. These reasons all appear to share a common theme: they are instances when the man is utterly repellent to his wife, through disease, occupation, odor, or natural tendency. The sages understood that a woman should under no circumstances be forced to sleep with a man who is objectively disgusting, even if the man is her husband.

Rav Minsky found himself getting uncharacteristically upset while thinking through this sentence, again recalling Liebe. Then a more recent memory rose—of him going to the police station in lower Manhattan to pick up his daughter and pay the fine from her arrest. All those women and girls in the cell, many of them Jewish, and his Liebe among them. They were all huddled together singing fakakta worker songs, while in the station their husbands and fathers gathered beside a pile of the women's homemade signs in Yiddish and English. They had been arrested after some meshugah girl released a swarm of bees inside Gimbels during the workers' strike. Rav Minsky thought about all those girls and women trapped in a cage and wondered what went wrong in their lives that led them there. He'd watched as Liebe had become more involved in the union—she'd even tried to discuss money and other profanities on Shabbos—but said nothing because he'd hoped it would pass of its own accord.

Rivka has not alleged that Lev has any of the explicit conditions that would be grounds for forcing a divorce, but the question should be asked if the inclusion of bad breath has opened the door to other grounds. Does bad breath lower the bar to force a husband's hand in divorce? Does the inclusion of one who gathers handfuls of excrement mean that there are other actions which, if taken by the husband, are grounds for ordering him to deliver a Get? If a man were to pick up a handful of excrement and throw it at his wife, would it be only the first action that was grounds for divorce, or would the latter constitute such an indignity such that it alone would be enough? If a man laid his hands upon his wife in violence, would that be analogous to his handling handfuls of excrement? And if one can expand these categories, what other actions and reasons should rightly be included? Though this beit din has argued on several occasions that these exceptions to divorce indicate there are other analogous exceptions, the Rosh, Rabbenu Asher ben Jehiel, already answered this question more than seven centuries ago, concluding that the list enumerated in Ketubot is not exemplary or equivocal, but rather complete. Therefore, this beit din is powerless to expand it.

However, what of the husband's responsibilities in a marriage? Must he not provide security and protection, support and cohabitation? If Lev Kagan is in Jerusalem, one could question whether he is fulfilling his husbandly duties. Before the beit din, Rivka testified that she is currently receiving financial support from her parents and in-laws, and that since she will not move to Jerusalem, she does not foresee having marital relations with Lev Kagan. This beit din rules first that Lev Kagan has fulfilled his duty to make sure that Rivka is financially secure, because his parents and hers have provided adequate resources. There is no requirement that he deliver such support directly, only that he ensures she is not without it. In this case, the obligation has been met. Similarly, Rivka has moved back home with her parents, so it appears that her protection and security have been provided, satisfying Lev Kagan's obligations in these regards.

The question of marital relations is of a more difficult nature. Though the husband has a duty to provide such, it is not this beit din's right or duty to dictate the frequency of such relations. Rivka argues that Lev Kagan's Aliyah makes it impossible that marital relations will ever occur again. However, her argument has three major flaws that are fatal to its success. First, she is presuming to know God's will. None of us knows what will transpire, and making such bald pronouncements will not succeed before this body. Second, she is presuming to know what Lev Kagan will ultimately do, but none of us can know what is in the heart of another man. Lastly, she is not accepting any personal responsibility. Rivka could have made Aliyah with her husband, and she can still do so. What Rivka is describing as a physical impossibility is in fact, in part, in her control.

This beit din sympathizes with Rivka, but it cannot order the destruction of the family on the grounds presented. The Mishnah Yevamot makes clear that "a man cannot divorce his wife except of his own free will," and this beit din does not violate the inviolable lightly. As discussed above, there are rare exceptions to this rule, but Rivka has not presented facts to warrant such an exception. She may still try to appeal this tribunal's conclusion through a Heter Me'ah Rabbanim, but we highly doubt it would be possible to convince one hundred Torah scholars, as Rivka has failed to convince even one of the three rabbis in this beit din.

We encourage Rivka instead to preserve her resources and apply them to salvaging her marriage. Lest she conclude that this decision is unfair, Lev Kagan too will suffer by not delivering a Get as requested by Rivka. For according to Rabbenu Gershom's Takkanah of the Eleventh Century, he may not take a second wife until he has divorced his first wife. Therefore, if he chooses to make her lie alone in America, he too will have to lie alone in Jerusalem.

Rav Minsky folded the notebook closed, certain that he had reached the correct conclusion. On occasion, he would ask his daughter to type a copy of his writings for his records, both because it helped him to have such a copy and because he believed it helped her to read reasoned interpretations of the Torah. He'd not yet determined whether he would ask Liebe to type this decision, but resolved to think on the matter further, hoping for clarity by morning.

BRAHM

On the night of September 25, 1946, Brahm Ibn Salah left his underground card game early, after losing all his money, and decided to walk the streets before going home. Home was a cramped hostel for day laborers on the edge of Casablanca's Mellah, where Brahm shared a room with four other men, and an outdoor bathroom with sixteen others. For several months, Brahm's rent had been cut in half because he agreed to share his mattress on the floor with Mardosheh, an old plasterer with a glass eye who always smelled of stale mud. With weak depth perception, Mardosheh would get in close to the walls he plastered, almost hugging them flatly, and then came home caked in white flaky clay. Brahm was able to use the extra money he saved on his room, along with the up-front payment he had received for work on an American's house, to partake in all his pleasures.

However, the previous night's encounter with Mardosheh made him hesitant to return to the hostel. Brahm had come home a little drunk, tired after a full day of work and then a late dinner of street meat, to find Mardosheh already in bed. He saw the glass eye open, pale blue, clear and lifeless, peering out from the sheet. He'd thought nothing of it, having become used to Mardosheh's quirks, generally ascribing them to the plasterers' guild. But when Brahm awoke that morning, he was surprised to find Mardosheh still sleeping. The plasterer was usually up before sunrise to start his day and use the bathroom before the other men. It made things easier not to have to wake up next to the old man. At night, in the dark, with the loud snores of the others in the room, Brahm could ignore Mardosheh. But in the morning, the space was well-lit, stale with the smell of the night farts of unhealthy living, and having to open one's eyes to old muddy one-eyed

Mardosheh made Brahm consider that it may not have been worth the reduction in rent.

Brahm had learned that sharing a bed meant a constant struggle for supremacy through a language of passive aggression. Observing the lumpy form and the glass eye still peering from the sheet, Brahm coughed loudly, clearing his night throat, and then shifted violently in the hope of forcing Mardosheh out of bed first. When this elicited no response, he touched Mardosheh's arm, shaking it slightly. It was covered in white plaster, which flaked off as Brahm nudged it. It felt unlike the arm of a sleeping body. Then Brahm noticed the other eye, which never received as much attention as the fake one. It was also open and glassy, though brown, and also peering out from the sheet. Brahm rolled away and jumped out of bed in one motion, disgusted. He looked around; all the other roommates were already gone for the day. Brahm leaned in to shake Mardosheh's midsection to make sure. As soon as Brahm touched the body, stiff and cold, he knew for certain that he had slept in a bed with a dead man. Quickly, Brahm shifted his hands into Mardosheh's pockets. He felt bills and coins and grabbed them in indiscriminate clumps, stuffing them immediately into his own pockets without separating the old man's spent tissues from the currency. Brahm snapped his coat and left the room and the hostel, hands balled tightly.

As he wandered that night after the card game, where he had lost all of his and Mardosheh's money, he wondered if anyone had found the corpse yet, and when his rent would increase because he now had a mattress to himself. Could he argue that the soul remained in the bed and continue to claim the discount? Let them apply to Mardosheh's spirit for the other half. Let them insult his ghost by denying its presence. Brahm didn't know what he wanted that night—the morning's experience had left him feeling odd— but he knew he could not go back to his room and his bed.

As he walked slowly, uncommitted to the direction, a voice called out from a street corner of the road that wrapped around Casablanca, dividing the city from the sea. Brahm couldn't make out the figure, but it knew his name and he knew the voice.

"Sharona!" Brahm yelled back, genuinely excited to see her. "How are you? How is your night?"

"Slow. I think the fog has kept everyone inside."

For the first time that evening, Brahm realized there was a thick fog in the air. Though he was young, his eyesight was poor, and his chain-smoking had accustomed him to seeing everything slightly obscured by a white haze. "I'm going down to the docks, see who's around, if there is anything going, if you want to join."

Approaching, Sharona agreed, appearing at once indifferent and happy to do something other than wait.

Brahm offered her one of his French cigarettes, which he kept in a silver case for special occasions. She accepted it, and they walked down the gravel truck road to the docks, adding white plumes of smoke to the fog.

"Where are you coming from this late?" Sharona asked, always curious as to what else was going on.

"From Hassan's card game."

"It's early for it to be finished, isn't it? I thought it usually went through till dawn."

"It was not a good night." Brahm smiled, showing his shining white teeth, unstained by coffee, tea, or cigarettes.

Sharona shivered at the memory of the squeak of steel wool as he brushed his teeth. "Did you lose everything?" she asked, trying to determine what kind of companion he was going to be.

"You know what they say about a rich man? Well . . ." Brahm was about to conclude that he would have no trouble sleeping, but he thought of Mardosheh and his unnaturally opened eyes. "I am free from worry."

Sharona put her hand on Brahm's shoulder to comfort him. They both knew the touch well. "I'm sorry, habibi. But some nights are good . . . and some are very good. That's what I've learned. How was the game otherwise?"

"It was fine. But I suspect that Rafi has been cheating."

"I thought Hassan was the cheater. Actually, I know Hassan is the cheater." They both laughed.

"I've wondered for a while," Brahm said. "But Rafi's always winning. Tonight, I tried to watch him closely, to see how he does it."

"Is that why you lost? You were paying more attention to Rafi's cards than to your own?"

"Maybe. Or maybe it was the will of Allah." Brahm raised his palms stiffly in the air in front of his face, impersonating a Muslim. "But I am going to figure out his tricks soon," he vowed, cigarette bobbing with his words.

"What do you care? Let it be. Rafi has a wife and young children. I heard he lost one to the sea, poor man. God bless him."

They each rubbed objects in their pockets in the familiar motion.

"He needs the money," Sharona continued. "Come on, tonight is free, because we're friends."

The docks were a strange place at night, fully lit under harsh white flood-lights in certain spots and then fully black just a few steps away. The port was its own city on the sea, with citizen sailors from around the world, speaking a multitude of languages, but finding comfort in the familiar company and routines: sitting by their ships, eating and trading in stories and schemes. They were the heirs of Odysseus, traversing the globe in their communal homes, and the activity of the docks in peace and war had always been the same.

Several large cargo ships sat at the water's edge, so Brahm knew that the tin shack where the sailors congregated would be busy. Because of his brief stint as a merchant mariner—before he was kicked out for unspecified mis-chief—Brahm was accepted in the shack. Shaped like a roadside bus stop, with three walls and a front that opened to the sea, the structure was filled with cigarette smoke and steam from a giant pot of assorted seafood stew. Brahm and Sharona came in, grabbed a bowl each, ladled large heaping spoonfuls of stew, and sat at one of the long tables. One of the sailors was in the middle of a story, and Brahm leaned toward the man next to him and asked, "Where is he talking about?"

"Napoli. They sailed from Piraeus to Napoli, and then from Napoli to Casa. They just got in this evening."

Brahm had little interest in Greece or Italy, but the landscapes of cities and countries had been changing rapidly—literally and figuratively—and this information had value. The official news could not move fast enough to supply the need for information, so well-sourced gossip filled the gaps. And sailors, though innate exaggerators, were among the best sources for such gossip.

"When you come into port, if you are carrying certain textiles or certain grains," the sailor continued, "there's a signal you have to watch for. Because the whole thing happens quickly, and it's a chance to make a lot of money, and fast. When the boat is coming into berth, keep an eye out for groups of three men wearing what look like military uniforms, but dyed different colors than usual. If you see them, then you prepare. After you dock and disembark, the air-raid siren will go off, signaling a bombing or Vesuvius blowing her top."

Brahm spoke into Sharona's ear: "Mount Vesuvius erupted last year. It killed a lot of people and destroyed a lot of homes."

Sharona smiled politely. "Yes, I know." She then saw his face develop that look she knew well—when someone didn't acknowledge the weight of his contribution—so she continued, "I've met men who were there for the eruption. They said it was really something." Her smile grew, delivering the double entendre.

"When everyone seeks shelter," said the sailor, "that's when you have some time, maybe an hour or two, to *lose* a bit of cargo and make a *lot* of money." He took a sip of his drink. "It's all quite elegant."

"And how is Napoli?" Another sailor asked.

"In ruins. Like everywhere. But not ruined for us. Everything is for sale."

One of the sailors turned to Brahm. "What about here in Casa? Anything worth anything?"

Brahm put down the large wooden spoon he'd been using to put as much stew in his mouth as quickly as possible. He coughed, sending a small piece of indeterminate fish across the table, lit a cigarette, and took a deep inhale. "It has been slow lately," he said. "There's the usual stuff, shows, card games—but they're all filled with cheats."

"Oof!" Another sailor interjected. "If it's too corrupt here for Brahm, you know it's bad."

The table erupted in laughter, but Brahm was unamused. Cooly, he continued, "There's even the belly-dancing ladyboys, if you want to see something. They're the best in the world, and I don't care how closely you look, you'll never see even a hint of the old aubergine."

"Don't ask Brahm. He's not in the know," the man on the other side of Sharona remarked with a wave of his arm, upon which was a red world of interconnected, obviously self-applied tattoos that extended beyond where the eye could see. "What about you, Sharona?" he asked. "Anything good going?"

Sharona chuckled, knowing that sailors truly valued only what was hidden, what remained obscured. "I have a couple of friends at a couple of parlors that are always fun."

"What kind of parlors?"

"That's up to you, really. It just depends on how much money you actually made in Napoli and what kind of appetite you have."

"You see!" The sailor announced, slinging his other arm around Sharona, revealing a network of blue tattoos. "I told you Sharona would be the one to talk to." He craned around her. "No offense, Brahm."

Brahm pulled in his chair and straightened. "Forget her silly parlors and the ladyboys. I know how we can make some real money. American dollars."

All heads turned to him at the mention of American currency, and the shack fell silent, with only the odd sound of flatulence breaking the tension.

The tattooed sailor spoke up. "If you could be making real money, then why are you sitting here tonight stuffing your face with our sot-l'y-laisse stew?"

Brahm took a big bite of fish and answered with a full mouth. "For the sophisticated conversation, of course." Waiting for the laughter to die down, he continued, "But I'm serious. If you want to put some of your sailing skills to work and make big money, I know how we can do it."

The table was all Brahm's, every eye fixed on his face and gestures as he explained how he had a contact in the Irgun, and how the Jewish militia desperately needed small arms to rid Palestine of the British and the Arabs. He further explained that overstocks of guns had been coming into Casablanca from France to melt down for the metal, and how the Irgun had American Jewish money to spend, millions of dollars. Each of the pieces was in place, Brahm told them. All that was needed was a man in the middle to make it all work—*him*—and some sailors who wanted to get rich.

As Brahm spoke, the plan, which he had never put together until that moment, came into focus. He really did have a contact in the Irgun, but he would have to enlist Rafael to get Moussa on board, because Moussa's metal shop was involved in the melting of guns. Moussa hated Brahm, so he would have to use all his charm. He described the operation as it took shape in his mind, withholding key information to ensure he was indispensable. As he thought about the connections of people and countries and how it would all play out, Brahm began to get excited. He realized the plan was sound, and he could make quite a bit of money, all while doing something good. He might even eventually be able to buy his own house, a nice one on Sidi Fatah, maybe even a riad, a hammam in the basement. As he laid out the schedule for the table, Brahm thought about how if it all worked as it should—and it should—he could get off that hostel floor in no time. No more dead plasterers in the night. No more thoughts of a haunted bed. And if he could get Sharona excited about the plan too, maybe she would let him stay with her in the interim.

LOUIS

On November 11, 1947, in the 3rd arrondissement of Paris, Sidney Louis Kleinmann sat in a corner desk of the cramped basement office of the Yiddish socialist newspaper *Unzer Shtime*. He'd started going by Louis when he'd moved from New York to Paris a few months earlier, feeling his middle name sounded more French. And since he barely spoke the language and was taking a job at a Yiddish paper where he wouldn't pick it up, he thought the least he could do was take on a French moniker. On his first day, the editor corrected him when he introduced himself by saying, "Je suis Louis." "You are not Louis in France," the editor informed him, "but you *call yourself* Louis in France. Je m'appelle Louis." Louis repeated the phrase over and over, and felt like a Frenchman when he said it.

Before leaving New York, Louis had had an American's romantic view of Paris, and he'd prepared himself for seeing it in ruins—but nothing had prepared him for lonely days of sitting in a small room, drowning in socialist Yiddish thought. Louis had grown up surrounded by Yiddish, had heard it being shouted and made the butt of jokes, had used it to defuse tension and point out absurdity. But it felt odd to read and write in it all day, quietly, without emphasis or gesticulation. He knew it only as a loud language, and he couldn't get used to living with it in silence.

Ever since the international conference in Belgium in May, the previously defunct Jewish Labor Bund had been reinvigorated, and with it had come a revival of its European newspaper, *Unzer Shtime*, *Our Voice*, in Yiddish. Louis's aunt and uncle had been active members of the General Bund in Poland and had brought copies of the paper with them when they came to New York. Whenever they could, they bought and argued over well-worn copies of the American edition of the newspaper, *Unzer Tsayt, Our Time*—also in Yiddish. He grew up understanding the language and sentiments of the Bund. His childhood was rife with intense debates that merged the Bund's socialist and Jewish values in everchanging ways, emphasizing culture and historical consciousness. When he thought of his aunt, Sidney could only imagine her rebutting some idea (. . . *with respect to chaver Samuel* . . .), arguing against some position on class or Europe or Palestine—always with consideration to her dissenting brother or sister, her comrade.

The Belgium conference came at the right time for Louis. Since the mid-'30s, New York City had become an increasingly difficult place for him to live. He had grown up during the Depression, and though work and food had often been scarce for the family, he'd loved the solidarity of it all. Everyone he knew bartered in labor and food and assisted each other in mutual-aid societies. It was a socialism of the poor and unemployed, and it worked. Everything was illegal, so it was all equally allowed. But after the end of Prohibition . . . that was when things began to get unbearable.

During the dry crusade, he'd gotten in the occasional fight with someone who had strong views about the third sex, but he'd felt relatively free. With the lawful sale of liquor came new strictures. Bars now needed licenses from the state, which, even when granted, could be taken away at any sign of "disorderliness"—and of course the state defined "order" and "disorder." It was quickly made clear that more than a few fairies or queens in one location were a mark of disorder. The surveillance began, getting more sophisticated and invasive through the '30s and '40s. There were rumors of plainclothes State Liquor Authority agents—who could shut a place down permanently—everywhere. Bartenders and owners tried to get ahead of them, defining "disorder" still more broadly, just to be careful, just so they wouldn't accidentally invite trouble. They became deputies of the law, and with the repeal of Prohibition, the law was serious and unavoidable.

The changes were all the more insidious because they occurred gradually, and Louis was grateful his work with the union kept him busy. He had used his organizational skills to help with the massive strike of 1946. Labor shut down the country, and it felt like workers were ascendant. Then, suddenly, just when they were winning, the Taft-Hartley Act was introduced. Louis had fought alongside other activists to defeat what they called the Slave Labor Act, and they thought they'd won when President Truman vetoed it. But then the Senate voted overwhelmingly to override the veto, bringing

Louis's worst fears to fruition. Though strikes were still technically legal, solidarity actions, which were labor's main weapons, were illegal. And every union official had to sign an oath stating *I am not a member of the Communist Party or affiliated with such party*, along with a vague oath of allegiance to the state and its political systems.

Louis could lie, of course, but getting caught in the lie led to Leavenworth. And just as the speakeasies were purging their premises of fairies, his union brothers and sisters began to roust the communists in their ranks.

When, in the early '40s, the *Unzer Tsayt* paper was revived in New York City, Louis had written a piece connecting the Jewish women garment workers' struggle with other socialist struggles throughout the world. He gave the example of a young Jewish immigrant named Lillian who, through solidarity actions, had been transformed from a semiliterate Litvak who felt subservient to men into a zealous leader for industrial democracy. He'd described how, when he'd first met Lillian, she'd had a hollow look about her, and how taking control of her future through the union had woken her up. At one rally, she'd stood on steps in front of her fellow striking workers and given an impassioned speech in her adopted tongue that culminated in the memorable lines: *If we don't stand here today, then there is no life for us. There are no certainties, and I know that we risk everything by standing firm, that we may die on this ground. But I also know that if we don't die, then we will live.* He'd witnessed how she'd found a family and was willing to risk everything for that family.

He was proud of the article, but he remembered feeling even more pride when a counter-article was published several months later that began, *With all due respect to chaver Sidney . . .*

The Taft-Hartley Act had been passed only a month after the Bund conference in Brussels, so when the possibility of moving to Paris to proofread the European edition of the Bund's organ arose, Sidney took it. He realized there was little left for him in America, and that another opportunity like this might never come. Besides, he convinced himself that his move was no different from what his family did when it immigrated to America. They were both fleeing persecution by crossing the Atlantic, just in different directions.

The Paris offices of *Unzer Shtime* were somehow even smaller than the New York City offices of *Unzer Tsayt*, which seemed a feat, even in his experience of socialists proudly showcasing their poverty and thrift. When

Louis made a comment about the cramped quarters, the editor pointed at the sole window and responded in the Yiddish intonation that Louis knew well, "You want nice digs, go edit the Zionist rag across town."

The edition of the paper that Louis was working on dealt specifically with the question of Zionism and the diaspora, a long-running debate within the Bund that had reached new urgency with so many Jews suddenly in the Displaced Persons camps, the increasing battles between Jews and Arabs, and the growing consensus for establishing a Jewish state in Palestine.

Louis sat at his corner desk surrounded by socialist newspapers from around the world. They yellowed quickly due to the damp. He had read and reread the same paragraph before him, but couldn't quite put his finger on what seemed off about it. In defending the diaspora and the traditional mobility of Jews, the author asked rhetorically:

> With whom do you feel closer? With the Irgun HaLeumi, who applauded Franco when he destroyed the "red plague" of Spain, or with the French, Spanish, German, Russian, English, and other ideological comrades of many other nationalities who gave and still give their lives in their fight against fascism? And how does this heavenly daughter, this new Zion, this divine or cosmic idea of a reborn nation with a reborn tongue look? You must ask yourself, with whom do you feel more spiritually connected—because it is after all the spiritual connection we are talking about here—with Mickiewicz, Pushkin, Goethe, Byron, and Rolland, or with a Yemenite or Abyssinian Jewish Tribe, with whom you are supposedly united in an eternal "community of collective subconscious"?

Louis generally agreed with the author. He too questioned the idea that a two-thousand-year diaspora, which had nurtured an exquisite morality and working-class consciousness, should be abandoned in order to create a new nation in Palestine. The goals should be socialist, pure and simple. States were filled with surveillance and law, moral pitfalls, and unethical choices. The first of these choices—which concerned Louis and others in the Bund—was Zionists ignoring the fact that Arabs already lived in Palestine. What of them in this new Jewish state? And shouldn't the Jewish worker have more in common with the Arab worker than with a Jewish industrialist or banker? In the last sentence of the article he was editing, Louis felt this tension. He understood the thrust that ideology was what united people, and that it should be a workers' ideology. And he understood the polemical force of comparing something known to something unknown, but the comparison to a Yemenite or Abyssinian felt intended to promulgate a racial hierarchy. Why choose the black and dark nations of Jews when it could have just as easily been a Jew from anywhere in the diaspora?

These troubling ethnic threads ran through the entire piece, and Louis pondered how to address them. He tried to pace around the room, never liking to sit for long stretches, but between his limp and the size and clutter of the space, it proved impossible. He decided to go outside and walk the few blocks to the Place des Vosges, hoping the activity would help him focus.

When he arrived at the square, Louis instinctively headed to his usual spot and could see sitting there, even from a distance, one of the few people he knew in Paris. Louis had encountered Juliette in the square soon after arriving. She had been sitting alone, smoking, and staring off at nothing in particular. Louis had noticed her first, his natural instinct as an organizer kicking in; he was trained to pay special attention to women who looked alone and broken by the system. Though Paris was filled with shattered people, lost from family, looking for work, this woman appeared in ruins. Louis's French was still quite poor, however, so he said nothing as he settled nearby and read his English-language newspaper.

After a few occasions of sitting on the square—he reading his paper and she staring off—Juliette had approached Louis and addressed him in fluent English. Since then, they'd spoken almost every day, usually the result of bumping into each other in the square. Louis was never quite sure what Juliette wanted, why she was drawn to him, but she seemed to be searching for something. And Louis appreciated the companionship. He didn't enjoy being alone, and he had felt surprisingly isolated since moving to Paris. Some days, living in his tiny rented room and working in his office crowded with paper, he spoke to no one except through the door of a shared bathroom. (He came to know the voice and the joke well. After a sharp rap at the door, the man would ask if he had *le constipation*. When Louis would yell back *Non*, the man would hit him with the Yiddish punchline, *Ahhh, kanst du kaken!* A few times a week Louis had this conversation through a door, oddly relishing the way the French word for constipation sounded like the Yiddish *kanst du pishin*.)

As Louis came closer, Juliette spied him and waved.

"Bonjour, Juliette," Louis said, realizing from the way his jaw loosened that he was smiling for the first time that day.

"Hello, Louis," Juliette replied with perfect English pronunciation. "How goes the editing?"

"Oh, it goes. But in the English sense. Not *ça va*. Do you know what I mean?"

"I am not sure I do." Juliette held out a silver case, offering one of her pre-rolled cigarettes.

Louis took one gently from the case. "You know how you say *ça va* to mean *good*, but literally it just means *it's going*? Never mind. It doesn't matter. I have to stop making jokes in French." Louis lacked the tenacity of the man on the other side of the bathroom door.

"No, no, I like your jokes. Even when they're not funny." Juliette smiled.

"I'm sure you have a word for such jokes."

"No, we have no such word. What are we, Germans?"

Louis choked on a laugh. "See, now that's a joke about language."

"So, what is wrong with the editing?"

"I don't know exactly. I'm just having a hard time making sure the articles are forceful and logical and deeply committed to an international socialism. Maybe it's the problem of editing in Yiddish."

"This is for the edition arguing against Zionism, yes?"

"Yes. Oui."

"I personally agree with your position. Maybe make the argument at me, in English. I cannot help with the Yiddish. But perhaps it will bring clarity."

"You sure?"

"For you, bien sur. Now, come on. Talk!"

Louis liked it when Juliette took charge, becoming animated. She seemed so sad most of the time, but in those moments, he saw who she'd been before, or what she could become.

"D'accord. It seems to me that the problem we are concerned with is a problem of justice, and that the Jews have suffered a grave injustice. But I don't see how the Zionist argument—of solving one injustice with another injustice—makes sense, especially when much of it seems based in a romantic myth about an ancient history. We can't hope to bring justice to the Jewish people by creating a fortress in the desert, where even if everything works out as promised, it will still be an isolated oasis. The solution to the Jewish question has to be a global solution, which can only be found in a righteous and just world. If we displace one group of people to build a homeland, how does this contribute to such a world?

"Also, on the historical question," Louis continued with growing fervor, "I fear that we are privileging a long-lost history, captured in biblical poetry, over our lived reality of the last two thousand years. Jewish culture and essence don't live in Palestine; they live in the diaspora. Here, in Paris. Back in New York. In England and Africa. The diaspora is our homeland—Jerusalem is just a dream—but the Zionists want to treat thousands of years as if they were but a temporary accommodation, a tent in the desert. We're People of the Book!" Louis declared, "and if that means anything. . . ."

"I'm sorry," Juliette interrupted. "You seem very passionate about this, and I can sense your certainty. But you said you were struggling, and I don't hear it. What is it that you are having trouble with?"

Louis realized he'd grown stiff again, and he took a deep breath, willing his muscles to relax. "Yes, yes, apologies," he said, spreading his hands. "It's all I've been thinking about, so it's sometimes difficult to not continue down the usual path. But maybe it's good to attack one's enemies before criticizing one's friends. And you know, there's always more clarity in attacking one's enemies."

Juliette felt slightly bad for interrupting Louis, but she was already regretting making the offer to help him with his work. She didn't care much about Zionism or anti-Zionism. Let the Jews leave or stay; she was tired of them getting all the attention during the war, and now in the Displaced Persons camps and their family reunifications. Everyone had suffered and lost family during the war. She'd searched and searched for her missing brother, to no avail. Over the years in Vichy, it had always been about the Jews, and now after the war, it was again all about them. Juliette liked Louis. There was something about him that intrigued her. He was kind and gentle, and somehow still had hope in his eyes. But sometimes, when he went on about the Yiddish paper and the petty infighting, she felt like she couldn't breathe. Though she was well aware she'd opened the door to the conversation, she now just wanted to move on.

"Before you continue, do you mind if we walk a bit?" she said. "I had been sitting here for a while before you came, and I am feeling a bit pressed upon."

* * *

Louis sensed Juliette's discomfort. After years of organizing, he had become finely attuned to awkwardness, and now that he had less occasion to use it to his advantage, he tried to avoid it like everyone else. "Yes, let's walk," he said, pulling two cigarettes from his pocket and handing one to Juliette.

With nowhere in particular to go, they both started in the direction of the river, and looking toward the ruins of a once-grand structure, Louis asked, "Do you know it?"

"No, I do not think so," Juliette responded.

"Excellent. Then, the game. What do you think: palace, museum, or administrative building?" Louis asked. On their walks, they'd often made a game of trying to guess the former lives of certain impressive ruins.

"That is a difficult one," Juliette said, smiling. "It was not a museum. Too small for a grand museum and too grand for me to not have known it. I'm going to guess administrative building."

"Not a palace?"

"No. I do not think so. Those window arches were not ornate enough. Plus, there are no balconies. This was the daytime dwelling of civil servants."

"You sound quite certain."

"I have spent a lot of time in administrative buildings, between my research here in Paris and my work in . . ."

"Vichy," Louis said, recalling she'd mentioned she worked for the government there.

"Oui. Vichy." Though Juliette tried to avoid the subject for obvious reasons, it always had a way of slipping out, because the years in Vichy had been among the happiest of her life.

"Do you mind if I ask you what you did in Vichy?" Louis inquired, breaking his rule of not asking how people spent their war years.

"Very little," Juliette said quickly. "I went for a government job when I lost my research funding. But I was a low-level bureaucrat, filing and moving papers around."

"But what was the subject of your work?" Louis pressed. "Your research was in linguistics and regional markers, so I'm curious as to what they had you doing."

"Truthfully, I could not tell you," Juliette replied, waving her hand dismissively. "I did what my supervisors asked of me, but I did not really pay attention. It was all small pieces of projects for which I never knew the whole. Despite what title I had, I was basically an office secretary."

"Did you have any family in Vichy?"

"No, no. My family is from Paris. We have lived in this city for hundreds of years, since before the Revolution."

"In America, your family would be quite wealthy. The old families own most of the country."

"And when did your family emigrate from Hungary to America?" Juliette inquired, relieved to change the subject.

"My parents came over in the early part of the century." Louis paused. "How did you know that we came from Hungary?"

"Your name. Kleinmann. It is one of the four Hungarian names given to Jews."

"Four names?"

"Yes, all Jews in Hungary were called one of four names, depending on a physical characteristic: Schwartz, Weiss, Gross, and Klein. Black, white, big, and small. You must have come from a small man. But it looks like you've outgrown it, so mazel tov, as your people say."

Louis laughed as they arrived at the bank of the Seine between two bridges. They stood for a moment, and he gestured at the island rising from the middle of the Seine. "You know, in Manhattan in New York, we also have an island in the river, but we built a prison on it."

"Really?" Juliette responded, arching her brows.

"I've seen it from the inside and the outside," Louis said, surprised to find himself discussing his time at Rikers Island. "I think you made the better choice with a cathedral, even if it is a bit of a prison in its own right."

"Why were you in prison?" Juliette's tone conveyed, not condemnation, but curiosity.

He chuckled. "The usual, I suppose."

"Is that where you got the limp?" Juliette asked, having wanted to broach the subject for a while. One reason she liked Louis was because she couldn't quite figure him out. He seemed a smart, able, charismatic person— so why would he leave booming America for war-torn Europe? She'd wondered if it was connected to the limp.

Louis touched his leg like it was a foreign body that he was both appeasing and paying tribute to. "No, but I suppose it's not unrelated."

"In what way?" Juliette pushed, refusing to allow Louis to get away with waxing on about his ideas, then revealing nothing of himself.

"Both were the result of an overexcited policeman." Louis took a deep drag of his cigarette. "It really amazes me how quickly a cop will take away one's liberty or legs without any forethought."

"How was it? Prison? Is it as bad as people say?" Juliette asked, revealing one of her deepest fears.

"I misspoke. It was jail, not prison, and only for a few weeks. It was fine. The fellows were all right, not the cutthroats that everyone imagines. And I was surprised to find more solidarity among prisoners than at any labor union I've ever been a part of." Louis smiled. "Maybe the world would be a better place if all management wore uniforms and beat you with a stick. Class consciousness would certainly increase."

"Speaking of authorities," Juliette began, jumping on the chance to discuss what was weighing on her. "I have been intending to ask a favor. I have had trouble locating my brother, who disappeared. A few years back, I enlisted the help of some of my colleagues in the government, but things became hectic before they had a chance to report back. And now I do not really have any government contacts. I was hoping maybe you could help."

"I'd love to help, Juliette, but I'm not sure how I could." Louis knew nothing good would come of looking into war records, and hesitated doing so. "I don't have any government contacts, either, except for the woman at the immigration office that stamps my paperwork every few months. And I don't see her being of much use."

"I know you and your colleagues at the newspaper work with people at the Displaced Persons camps," Juliette responded in a pleading tone. "Maybe you could ask around? See if he is there or if anyone heard anything from him?"

"I can try. What's his name?" Louis reached into his pocket to get a pencil, already regretting that he'd relented.

"Charles." Juliette produced a piece of paper where she had prewritten his full name and identification number and handed it to Louis. "His details are all here."

YAAKOV

On the first day of the month of Iyar, in the year 5708, Yaakov Pasternak ate two death cap mushrooms that he had plucked from the thickets of Central Park. When Yaakov was a young child in Stawsk, his mother would take him foraging for herbs and mushrooms, and she always pointed out the death caps, warning that consuming even one bite could kill you. She would further caution him to not even touch the mushroom, because the poisons could be absorbed through the skin. As a result, whenever Yaakov would walk through the park to get to work, he took notice of a small patch of death caps under a stand of oaks, and kept a respectful distance.

Seven days earlier, he had received news of his mother's death six weeks prior. Five days earlier he'd begun to weep, which he did uncontrollably for two days. Four days earlier, he'd grown silent. Three days earlier, he'd approached the mushrooms. Two days earlier he'd plucked them, his hand inside a brown paper bag, which he then used to transport the mushrooms. He'd torn the bag open when he got to his room in the tenement apartment he shared with his sister, exposing the death caps to the air and light. For two days he lived with the mushrooms, staring at them, watching them droop and shrink, changing from a pale olive green to a dark white. When Yaakov had pulled the mushrooms from the ground, he'd been surprised by the smell they released, honey with hints of thyme. For two days, that faint saccharine smell had slowly but noticeably grown more pungent, a rank and decaying sweetness, like fruit left in the sun. The flies that buzzed around his room in early May hovered about the mushrooms, creating an everchanging cosmos to the death caps' world, but never landing. One day earlier, he had resolved to eat them, because doing anything else felt impossible.

The death caps tasted nutty and woody and brought to mind acorns and dense woods. For a surprising moment, Yaakov enjoyed the mushrooms, then felt a deep sense of guilt. After swallowing them, he sat on the edge of his bed and waited. Yaakov had never been poisoned before, but he imagined that something would happen quickly. In the stories of snake bites and arsenic that he remembered from school, people reacted urgently because the poison spread with the speed of blood pumping through the body. He remembered his teacher remarking that blood pumps at the same speed as a brisk walker: four miles per hour, one mile in fifteen minutes, six feet per second. But for several hours nothing happened, no aches or cramps, no seizures or strokes.

Yaakov got up and walked a few feet to his desk. He pulled a notebook from the single drawer and began writing.

Dearest Imma . . .

Yaakov's sister found him lying on his bed later that night as she arrived home from work at the shirtwaist factory. She passed by his room, saw the light on, and was drawn in by the terrible stench. She called his name as she approached the bed, but he did not respond. As she came closer, she noticed his trousers were wet. She grabbed his arm below the shoulder to wake him, but he was cold and slightly stiff. She shook hard, moving his whole body from side to side, and feces pressed out over his waistband.

Yaakov's sister ran outside to a pay phone and dialed 0, pleading with the operator for emergency help. After being told that an ambulance was on its way, she stood on the street, breathing rapidly, unsure what to do next. She picked up the receiver again, dialed 0, and asked to be connected to Rav Moishe Minsky of Brooklyn.

Rav Minsky arrived before the ambulance, and he followed Yaakov's sister up the five flights of steps to the tiny apartment. He approached Yaakov's body on the bed, splayed in an unnatural position, and upon touching it knew immediately the young man was gone. Rav Minsky kept his hand on the body and said a prayer, slowly and loudly. He turned to Yaakov's sister and said, "I am sorry. May his memory be a blessing."

"Rabbi," Yaakov's sister replied, holding something tight in her hands. "He wrote this tonight. It's a letter to our mother." She pushed the paper into the rabbi's hands.

Rav Minsky read the letter slowly and carefully, understanding its implications. "Has anyone else seen this?"

Yaakov's sister shook her head.

"I am going to take this with me. Never tell anyone about this, even your family. Do you understand?"

She nodded.

"I will make sure things are handled properly." Rav Minsky stuffed the note into his coat. "But you must never mention this. For your brother. For the community."

"I understand," she said solemnly, staring out the dark window.

The next afternoon, several dozen people stood awkwardly at the indigent Jewish cemetery in Staten Island, the Chebra Agudas Achim Chesed Shel Emeth. Yaakov had been a young man in good health, and in the eighteen hours between his death and his burial, rumors wound through the community concerning the circumstances of his demise. As the mourners stood around the rectangular hole in the ground, waiting for Rav Minsky to start the service, the people gathered there whispered. Some speculated he might have been ingesting animal tranquilizers, others that he'd suffered from a mental disorder, and still others said that he had killed himself. All sad stories, they agreed. Though only the third, if true, would have kept him from being buried in a Jewish cemetery. Yet here they were, placing young Yaakov among other Jews in a community of the dead, so the talk of suicide was just talk.

Rav Minsky began with the particular variation of the Mourner's Kaddish that is only said at the grave. After the common initial phrase, Rav Minsky declared in Aramaic that one day Hashem would revive the dead and raise them to eternal life, that he would rebuild the city of Jerusalem and in it reestablish His temple. In response, several crying relatives repeated in verse, and the rest said *Amen*. Rav Minsky then walked up to Yaakov's two brothers and his sister, pulled out a small knife, and sliced their shirts above their hearts. These would be their mourning garments for seven days of shiva.

The body, which had been wrapped in a clean white linen and placed in a simple pine box, was lowered into the ground. Rav Minsky said a series of short prayers, and the mourners said *Amen*. Picking up a shovel, Rav Minsky lifted a scoop of dirt and dropped it on the casket, dust rising up in return. He handed the shovel to Yaakov's brother, who followed the rabbi's lead in depositing a scoop of dirt and then passing the shovel to his brother. Then sister. The process continued with the mourners. When handed the shovel, each stepped forward, added to the dirt in the grave, chose the next recipient of the shovel, and then went to stand in the second mass of mourners. After everyone had moved from the first grouping, through their silent duty, to the second grouping, the hole was more than half filled. They continued gossiping about Yaakov and his family as several yeshiva students, who had helped transport the body, went to work filling the rest of the hole. Rav Minsky turned to the mass of mourners, now standing to the right and downhill of the hole, and spoke: "Today begins the first day of shiva for Yaakov's family. This is the second tragedy faced by the family in a short time, the first being the loss of Yaakov's mother, who after suffering the tragedies of the Shoa, died in a Displaced Persons camp while waiting to be reunited with her family. Anyone close to Yaakov would know that his mother's death affected him deeply. Indeed, it affected his whole family deeply. But perhaps Yaakov more so because he was the youngest, and his mother stayed in Poland so that he could be saved. I have heard whispers of a shanda surrounding Yaakov's death. It is lashon harah—the evil tongue— and it should stop immediately. Whatever Yaakov did, he did. But he was not in his right mind in his final days—that much is certain—and therefore the Talmud counsels that he cannot be judged for his actions. This family has suffered more than its share of sorrow; the community should not add to it with lashon harah."

Lillian watched her father before the crowd and was proud of his forceful rebuke. Looking around to gauge how his words were being received, she noticed someone she hadn't seen in a while.

Lillian walked over to Rivka, whose efforts to force a Get had been refused, even three years after her husband abandoned her for Zion. Knowing what it felt like to be let down by Rav Minsky, Lillian had pitied the "chained" woman. But now, seeing Rivka standing beside a man who was not her husband, she found her curiosity piqued.

"Rivka, may Hashem comfort you among the other mourners of Zion and Jerusalem," she said.

"You as well, Lillian," Rivka responded politely.

"How have you been?" Lillian asked with a sidelong glance at Rivka's companion. "It has been a long time since we saw each other last."

"I've been well. Bli neder."

"And your husband?" Lillian asked in a hushed tone. "Have you spoken with him, or reconciled?"

Rivka's eyes widened. "Lillian. I am divorced. You didn't know? It was your father's beit din that annulled the marriage."

Lillian frowned. "No. That can't be," she said. "I remember typing up the decision for my father when he denied the Get." For a moment she wondered if her father had decided, at the last minute, not to issue the decision. But if so, why wouldn't he tell her?

"Yes, he denied it at first, but then someone noticed something about the wedding that allowed for an annulment," Rivka confided. "A sort of legal loophole."

Lillian stood shocked, completely forgetting about the man standing there, silently watching the filling of the grave. "What! What was the thing, the fact, that was noticed?" she said. "If you don't mind my asking."

"No, of course not." Rivka chuckled quietly. "I thought you already knew. It was a wonderful miracle that it happened. That day, when your father delivered his decision, I began crying. I brought my hands up to my face to cover my tears, and my wedding ring rubbed up against my nose. Upon feeling it touch my face, something came over me. I pulled the ring off, slammed it on the table, and told the rabbis that if I was going to be an agunah, I wasn't going to wear the silver chains my husband gave me around my hands for everyone to see." Rivka stopped speaking and let the words hang in the air.

"And?" Lillian said impatiently.

"The ring was silver. Do you understand?"

"I'm not sure I do."

Rivka grinned. "I didn't either. But your father recognized it right away. Jewish law demands that a bride be given gold, even as thin as gold foil, but gold. My husband, in his thrift, gave me a silver ring. And that turned out to be enough to annul the entire marriage."

"Wait. So after all the inquiries into abandonment, bad breath, the fundamental duties of a husband, and the declarations of how sacred marriage is, you're saying it was just shtuyot. All that mattered was that he gave you a silver ring?"

"He could have attached an almost worthless piece of gold speck, and that would have been enough. But the law is clear. The ketubah says he was to give me a golden thing of value."

Rivka was smiling widely, and Lillian was both happy for her and furious at her father. When she'd typed up the decision, he'd explained to her that the rules mattered, because "our morality is borne of the heavenly rules." Looking over her work, he'd commended her on its lack of errors, saying that it showed great care, and he hoped she had learned from it. She wondered why, after all that, her father had purposely withheld the end of the story—how the whole matter hinged on the meaningless distinction between two precious metals.

Rivka looked around at the mourners and the now-filled hole. "Yaakov. It is such a shame."

Lillian didn't respond, still fixated on the ring.

After an extended silence, the man standing beside Rivka spoke. "You know, I knew Rochel back in Stawsk."

Startled at hearing him speak, Lillian asked, "Who is Rochel?"

"Yaakov's mother," he said somberly. "I did not know her well, by any means, but I had spoken to her on a few occasions."

"It's so sad," Rivka said. "She got the family out of Poland, and she somehow survived the war and the Shoa, only to die while waiting in a DP camp. I saw Yaakov after he heard. When she died, so did he." Something caught Rivka's eye. "Excuse me, I should go over and express my condolences to Yaakov's brothers and sister."

Rivka strode away, but her friend remained with Lillian.

"I don't believe I have introduced myself," he said. "My name is George. George Mazar. I just came over a few weeks ago, and I'm staying with Rivka and her family until I get settled. They are doing a mitzvah in opening their home to me."

"I am Lillian," Lillian said. Then added, "Minsky."

"The rabbi, is he your father?"

"He is. Did you say you just came from Stawsk a few weeks ago?"

"No. No. I am from Stawsk, but I left years ago. I have been living in France. In the countryside."

"Through the war?" Lillian asked, knowing she shouldn't. "Or . . . ?"

"Yes." George nodded quickly. "I worked as a laborer on a farm that bred rabbits."

Lillian couldn't say why, but she felt comfortable around George. "How was that?"

"The farm? It was all right. It smelled most of the time." George smiled. "They of course didn't know I was Jewish, which was tough. But I will tell you a secret." He leaned in and whispered, "There was another fellow on the farm, similarly Jewish. I knew right away and called him Yankel in my mind. And some days, when the wind was strong, I would get on the top of a pile of hay on a cart, and he would get on top of a pile of hay on another cart across the field, and we would yell Yiddish at each other."

Lillian laughed loudly, then quickly caught herself. Covering her mouth, she asked through her hand: "What did you yell to each other?"

"What does anybody yell about in Yiddish? News, politics, weather, jokes. It just let me feel at home for a few moments. Sometimes you just need something that reminds you of who you are."

"I know what you mean," Lillian said. "My days at work, at the store, I speak English. And I am good at English now. I dream in it, even. But it exhausts me. Some days I say funny English words out loud just to hear the silly sound. When I get home, I hear Yiddish, and there is something about it that makes me feel more like myself. Not that I want to be in Poland or even visit Poland. Trust me."

"Which words?" George asked.

"What?" Lillian replied, confused.

"Which words do you find funny?" he said.

"Oh, yes," Lillian said, her fingers fluttering nervously. "Well, *blouse, trickle, satchel*." She found herself chuckling, and George also chuckled in response.

"Has anyone shown you around the city at all?" Lillian asked, feeling oddly bold, something she associated only with her union activities.

"No. I have wandered a bit, but mostly through the neighborhood."

"Would you like me to show you around? As a mitzvah. I am sure it is quite a change from Stawsk. Or the rabbit farm with Yankel."

George dipped his head respectfully. "Are you sure it is not a problem? With your work? And your father?"

Lillian felt her face harden. "It will be fine. I'll show you the city. I'll call Rivka to arrange a time."

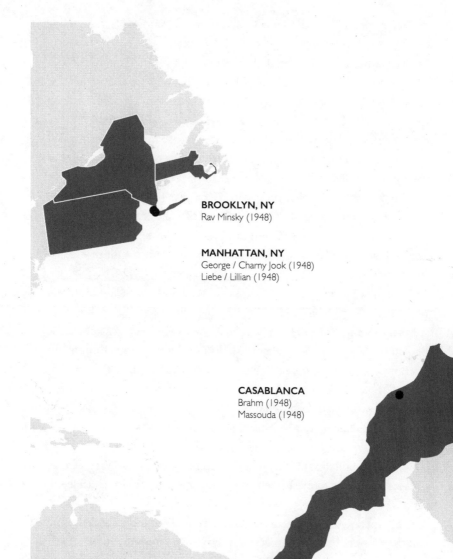

BROOKLYN, NY
Rav Minsky (1948)

MANHATTAN, NY
George / Charny Jook (1948)
Liebe / Lillian (1948)

CASABLANCA
Brahm (1948)
Massouda (1948)

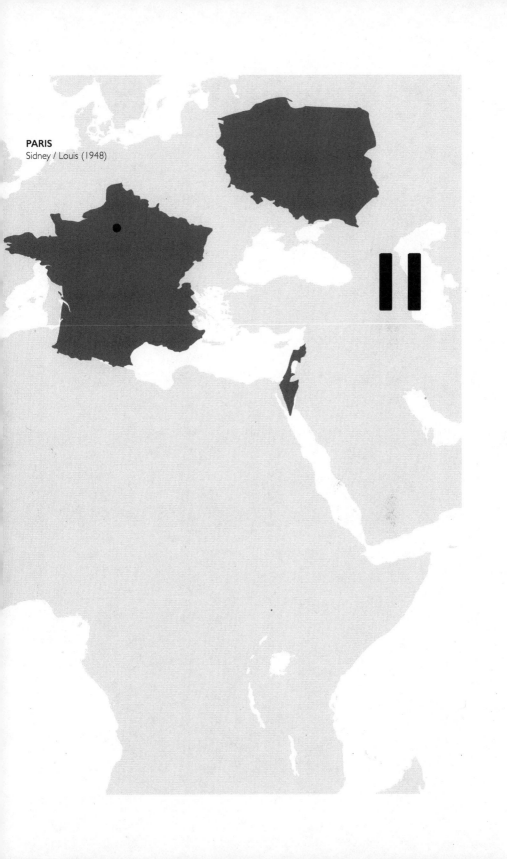

PARIS
Sidney / Louis (1948)

ISRAEL

At 4 p.m. on May 14, 1948, the radio station Kol Yisrael—the Voice of Israel—crackled to life. As the transmission began, David Ben-Gurion choked on his air, letting out a gasp and then a cough. People adjusted their radios, believing it to be static, turning the dials to the right and left, searching for the Voice of Israel. Then Ben-Gurion spoke in Hebrew, explaining in a monotone: "I shall now read to you the founding document of the State of Israel that was approved by the People's Council."

The British Mandate had ended earlier that day, and her majesty's ships had unmoored from the ports of Yaffo and Haifa, beginning the long-awaited separation of the British from the Levant. Rumor had suggested that the month of May—following what was purportedly a year-long civil war that, in actuality, had been fought in fits and spurts for decades—would bring with it a declaration of independence, but the name of the new land remained elusive. Many referred to the soon-to-be state as Palestine, assuming that its longstanding name would be carried over. Others speculated it would be Zion, from the Bible and collective imagination. To hear Ben-Gurion explain it, it was a tautology; the state would be called what the land was called, and who could argue with the logic? Speaking for thirty-two minutes, Ben-Gurion began at the beginning, declaring that the land-become-State was "the birthplace of the Jewish people," and it was "here their spiritual, religious and political identity was shaped. Here they first attained to statehood, created cultural values of national and universal significance and gave to the world the eternal Book of Books."

Ben-Gurion went on to recount the forcible exile and dispersion of the Jews and summarized the vast breadth of Jewish history as the attempts by every generation to reestablish themselves in their ancient homeland. He relayed how, in 1897, modern Zionism was born, and the European nations reaffirmed the rights of the Jewish people in Palestine before murdering them in the Holocaust. He relayed how, on November 29, 1947, the United Nations recognized that the right of the Jewish People to establish a State was irrevocable. After laying this history and evidence before the world, Ben-Gurion, breaking the boundaries of tenses, brought his speech to a close: "Therefore we gathered, we members of the People's Council, Representatives of the Hebrew Community and Zionist Movement, on the day the British Mandate over the land ends. By the virtue of our natural and historical right and based upon the UN Resolution, we hereby declare the establishment of a Jewish State in the land of Israel, which would be called The State of Israel."

Stating dryly, "The State of Israel has arisen," Ben-Gurion then paused at length and concluded: "This meeting is over."

The radio erupted in crackled claps, and people poured into the streets. Photos and quick dispatches were sent to London and New York, Paris and Berlin. The world had grown used to seeing images of the poor Jew, barely more than a skeleton, being liberated from camps; or huddled in masses of refugees, cold and sullen. But here was a new image—the dancing, healthy, strong Jew, in front of Hebrew signs of a territory newly claimed. The news whipped across the globe.

*

On May 14, 1948, in Paris, Louis sat beside a radio in the fifth-floor studio apartment he shared with Juliette, struggling to transcribe Ben-Gurion's speech for his editorial in the paper. He was translating Hebrew to English to French because he couldn't translate directly from Hebrew to French. As he looked at the intermediate text, he saw that he had written that *Israel was almosting it*. He laughed at the absurdity before making the correction.

He had spent the year arguing vehemently against the establishment of a state, but now, as he heard its name—"*Yee-sra-el*"—he choked on conflicting feelings. It sounded so biblical—Israel—a land for the wandering Hebrews.

Louis shouted for Juliette so she could come listen to the news, then recalled she'd gone out. Earlier in the day, she'd surprised him by suggesting that they marry—a sort of civil union to make the administration of their affairs easier. They already lived together, sharing a kitchen and a table, a bedroom and even a bed, as well as (with two other apartments) a bathroom. Combining their attributes would make things easier: American with ties to Jewish communities and labor wed to a Frenchwoman adept at navigating postwar bureaucracy. She proposed it as a paper marriage that would, in effect, change little about how they lived. And yet Louis hesitated to reply, swallowing his answer. He asked if he could think about it, today being a big day, his mind occupied with other matters. Juliette had responded, with sarcasm, that *of course he should take his time, ponder it in between thinking about Palestine*, and that she was going for a walk.

Staring out the window, Louis recalled the debates he'd had over Zionism. He'd warned that it was a mistake, arguing over and over that establishing a state would disrupt the lives of Jewish communities in Arab countries and increase violence. Louis now took in the Paris streets below, the French buildings with their proud plastered facades, and considered Israel. Instead of devoting that day's column to pointing out the error of what had occurred, he decided instead to celebrate it. He remembered what he used to say at union meetings—how you debate vigorously until the first shot is fired, but once you smell the powder, you fall in line. Solidarity requires a single voice.

Louis began pondering how he could help beyond his position at the paper, and he remembered that several months earlier, he'd heard about the children making the long journey to Palestine from Europe and North Africa, many of them alone either because they were orphaned or because that was the only way for a family to afford the trip. He'd also heard that to overcome bureaucratic difficulty—as Jews were often forbidden to leave their countries of origin—some were utilizing elaborate schemes involving temporary adoptions and adoptive parents along the way. When Juliette returned, he decided, he would tell her that a paper marriage was a splendid idea . . . and ask if perhaps they should also adopt paper children to help the cause.

*

On May 14, 1948, in Brooklyn, Rav Minsky was late for morning prayers. In his mind, he was almost at the synagogue, reciting passages in his head that he had long ago committed to memory, but in reality he was only a few blocks from his apartment. As he walked briskly, he pressed his arm against the front of his coat in his usual nervous manner but didn't feel the familiar hardness. He stopped murmuring the prayers and patted his entire coat, but still he felt nothing. Standing for a moment in the street, not praying and not moving, he realized he'd left at home the small bag containing his tefillin. While the scrolls were not completely necessary for the prayer, he couldn't imagine the congregation looking upon him without them, and he turned to retrace his steps.

As Rav Minsky inserted the keys to his front door, he heard the phone ringing. He considered not answering but thought about Yaakov's frantic sister and realized he had to pick up.

"Hello?" Rav Minsky tried not to sound rushed. A thin buzz met his ear, indicating there was someone on the line, but no voice was carried. "Hello! Hello!" Rav Minsky repeated, now with some impatience. "Is someone there?"

"May I please speak with Rabbi Moishe Minsky?" a man with an eastern European accent inquired.

"This is he."

"Hello, Rav. I have tried several times to reach you by various channels, and I am glad to connect. Perhaps it is Hashem's will that I finally make contact on this most happy of days, when Yisrael has announced herself as a state."

"Excuse me?" Rav Minsky had not heard anything of the sort, and he could not process it. His mind was deep in prayer.

"My name is Shlomo Levin, and I am calling from the Jewish Agency in Yerushalayim. I have something quite exciting to discuss with you. . . ."

A call from Jerusalem? Israel a state? It was too much to absorb. Rav Minsky glanced at the clock on the wall. "I am sorry, but I am just now on my way to shul. Can we talk later?"

"Yes, of course, but this is a matter of some urgency. While I have you on the telephone, please allow me to briefly explain the matter so that you can consider it."

Rav Minsky ran his fingers along his battered felt tefillin bag, which he'd used continuously since his bar mitzvah in Stawsk. His mind began sorting through the implications of who Shlomo Levin was and what the man had just imparted. Though Rav Minsky was running late, he wasn't leading the service that day, and he knew they would have a minyan without him. And Yisrael. Yisrael! It was a day of immense import. "Please proceed," he said. "I cannot speak long, but I would like to make sure I understand."

"Todah," Shlomo Levin replied in an awkward attempt at Hebrew. "And I appreciate your desire for quickness. Time is quite sensitive for us as well. As you know, we now officially have a Jewish state—baruch Hashem—and now our task is to help establish the soul of the nation."

"And . . ." Rav Minsky began, wondering how Shlomo Levin had come to call him.

"We have been working on bringing esteemed rabbis to Palestine— excuse me, Yisrael— and you have been identified by several prominent scholars as a great rabbi in a long tradition of great rabbis who could establish a yeshiva and serve in a beit din. I would like to discuss the possibility of you and your family making Aliyah to the holy land." Shlomo Levin paused and took a breath, then continued, "Do you know Yavneh?"

Rav Minsky had been preparing to interrupt and cut the conversation short until he heard that word.

Those two syllables—Yavneh—meant everything to Rav Minsky, just as they had to every rabbi in his family. Some Jews had Jerusalem, but for him, Yavneh was the true dual city. Though he knew it physically existed, it was more an idea and ideal than a locale, a place of ethereal divergence—like Mount Sinai or Sodom and Gomorrah—where a choice was made that was a turning point for the world. The sound of the word on Shlomo Levin's tongue struck Rav Minsky in a way that he had not anticipated, especially since the man who'd spoken it was in proximity to the city.

Do you know Yavneh? Rav Minsky had no idea how to answer the question. To not know it would be for his right hand to lose its cunning and for his tongue to cleave to the roof of his mouth. But what could it mean to *know* Yavneh?

When Rome had attacked Jerusalem, the great rabbi Yochanan Ben Zakkai faked his own death and was smuggled beyond the city walls in a coffin, only to rise up on the other side with a solution. Without Jerusalem and without a Temple, how could God be properly worshipped as commanded in the Torah? But Ben Zakkai had found a way for Judaism to survive—through Yavneh, through the Mishnah, through a dynasty of rabbis that Rav Minsky felt a part of. Yavneh was Judaism's resurrection.

The line cracked with static, bouncing between Brooklyn and Jerusalem and back again. Finally, Shlomo Levin broke in with his excitable rasp: "Rav Minsky? Did you hear my question?"

"Yes. Yes, of course."

"Good. We have recently acquired some land in Yavneh under some extraordinary circumstances, a citrus grove of almost a hundred hectares, with a house. Nearby is a location and building for the yeshiva and beit din. If you would be willing to make Aliyah and reestablish Yavneh, we can offer you the citrus grove and house."

Rav Minsky heard these words as well, and they didn't resonate as *Yavneh* did. Indeed, each raised a multitude of questions. *Acquired? Reestablish? Offer?* Of course his mind had all the tools to investigate the meaning of what was being said, his days filled, as they were, with examining the obscure and disentangling ambiguities. But he was accustomed to ancient tongues engaging in a dialogue that stretched across generations, transcended time. Here he felt an urgency, the need to seize a fleeting moment that might not ever return. He felt like Rav Yochanan Ben Zakkai, who when offered anything in the world by Emperor Vespasian, had saved Judaism by responding without hesitation, "Give me Yavneh and its sages."

*

On May 14, 1948, in Manhattan, Lillian and George were strolling through the streets. They had stopped in Brooklyn for bialys and blintzes before crossing the bridge, and now Lillian was showing George her world. She pointed out the five-and-dimes where the sit-down strikes had happened; Hearn's and Bloomingdale's, which were led by communist unions; and her Gimbels, where she was a union steward and they'd faced down both management and their International union. She told him about her comrade, Sidney, how he'd been arrested and then turned the arrest into a win. She told him about the communist purges in the unions and how Sidney decided to move to Paris to edit a Yiddish newspaper.

Lillian had heard George speak French casually on a few occasions and asked if he'd spent much time in Paris.

"A bit, but barely any," George replied.

When she asked how he spoke French, George responded that he was just good at picking up languages, then repeated the answer in Arabic and German to prove his point.

Crossing into the Lower East Side, George and Lillian began hearing a commotion. Men started spilling into the streets, howling and dancing, snapping their fingers and waving their arms, while women took to the windows, leaning on elbows and tugging at clotheslines sagging with fabric, calling out through the window network.

"What's going on? What are they saying?" Lillian asked, as if George's understanding of languages made it easier for him to discern distant indecipherable screams.

They both squinted to hear better, but could only sense the nature of the sounds. Happy. Maybe joyous. George suggested that they head toward the hubub to find out more, maybe join in, but Lillian resisted, saying it looked like shtus—nonsense. Grabbing George's inner elbow, she pulled him in the opposite direction.

As they walked toward Central Park, George talked about his work tutoring children in a variety of subjects. Lillian listened intently to what others might consider boring stories. She loved how he talked affectionately about each of the children. Even the ones who were clearly little schmucks he approached with equanimity and understanding, never with coldness or judgment. She watched his clean-shaven face as he spoke of his students— almost as if they were his own children—and found herself wanting to know more about him, what experiences had shaped his attitudes.

"Tell me about your time in Paris," Lillian said, surprising herself with the question. From his earlier response, it was obviously a subject he had no interest in talking about. Perhaps that's why she was asking. His answer had been almost too dismissive.

"As I said, I was there only briefly. And with the destruction it suffered since, I probably would not even recognize it."

"How long were you there?" she persisted.

"Not long. I was a student, so my head was in the books. I could have been in Marseille and I would not have noticed."

"I hope Sidney is doing well," Lillian said, somewhat wistfully.

"If he has a job, I'm sure he is fine." George paused. "Even if he does not, I am sure he is fine. New York works for those who work. But Paris is different. People sit all day and talk."

"I hope so," Lillian responded.

The noise from the throng in the street continued, as though it were following them. Lillian kept an ear tuned to the commotion and tried to direct them away, pretending each turn had been preplanned. But the noise made her nervous, and she felt nothing good could come from the crowds.

*

On May 14, 1948, in Casablanca, Brahm moved through the neighborhood and saw new friends everywhere. He walked slowly, with a cigarette hanging from his lips, his right hand in his pocket, and his left hand clasping and reclasping the right hands of people he knew. With some, he would lean in, roll his cigarette from one corner of his mouth to the other using only his tongue, kiss them on each cheek, and withdraw leaving a cloud of smoke in their faces.

Brahm's plan, hatched on the docks, had somehow worked. Starting with his few contacts, he'd found funding for his idea. Word spread quickly from a low-level smuggler he knew to former members of the French underground in Morocco to the London schmatta makers to the Jewish militias in Palestine to the group of eighteen Jewish millionaires who formed the Sonneborn Institute to a dummy corporation formed to sneak arms to Jewish fighters. Within six weeks of that night on the docks, Harry Rothstein, Vice President of the New England Plastic Novelty Company, made contact with Brahm and explained the company could assist with warehousing in Czechoslovakia and Palestine, could smooth over various customs issues, and had authority to spend up to two hundred and fifty thousand dollars for successful delivery of needed arms. Customs and borders were serious concerns for Brahm, but when he heard the amount of money in the mix, he could focus on little else.

The money appealed to Rafael as well. For a half-million-dollar payout, he'd agreed to join as a partner and get Moussa on board. Moussa resisted at first due to his general dislike of Brahm, but when Rafael explained that with an influx of seven hundred and fifty thousand dollars, their families could be set forever, Moussa agreed. Back at his metal shop, Moussa got his partners and neighbors to agree to stay silent—knowing there was no such thing as a big secret—by promising them a cut of the one million dollars that would come from America.

Brahm had received only a small amount of the money from America, but everyone knew he would soon have much more. For the first time in his life, Brahm could pay for the luxuries he wanted, and he found it funny that because he now had money, no one charged him. He'd made Sharona laugh by saying that he had figured out how to get rich; the key was to start out rich.

Brahm passed by the tin knocker stalls and saw a poor woman sitting in a tiny corner of shade, nursing a baby. He crouched beside her, grabbed her hand and pried it open, and deposited a fistful of change. She did not raise her head, but said "Shukran" softly. "May God be with you," Brahm replied, continuing on to his favorite café to drink strong coffee and tell the boys his latest stories.

Several blocks away, Massouda sat in a café, eating a cup of yogurt and straining to hear the radio. Crackling over the waves was a short French dispatch being repeated over and over on six-minute loops. This was at least the fifth time she had heard it, and each time it excited her like the first. After two thousand years of existence in the collective imagination, the state of Israel had been reestablished on Earth. It was suddenly real, the radio announced—playing short snippets of Ben-Gurion—and it was there. Just over there.

As she struggled to listen to the dispatch for a seventh time, a group of young men at a table near her hissed and jeered the voice of Ben-Gurion. Their comments didn't add or detract from her understanding of the event, because she didn't speak Hebrew, but still it annoyed her. A sharp noise interrupting a dream. She spun and fixed a disapproving look on the men until they quieted. She turned back to the half-eaten cup of yogurt, closed her eyes, and waited for the news to begin again.

ISRAEL

In the early morning of May 15, 1948, the Arab League sent a cablegram to the United Nations Secretary General announcing their intervention in the establishment of the State of Israel. The document set forth a history of the land and the people that was quite different from Ben-Gurion's, beginning with the facts that Palestine had been part of the Ottoman Empire and that the majority of its population had always been Arabs. Through the early twentieth century, the Arabs had asked for freedom and independence, but promises by European powers were made and broken. The League described Palestine as "an Arab country, situated in the heart of the Arab countries and attached to the Arab world by various ties—spiritual, historical, and strategic."

Months earlier, when the United Nations General Assembly had recommended a partition into two states—with Jerusalem held under the World's trusteeship—Arabs had loudly objected, voicing the injustice of this solution, explaining that it could not be achieved peacefully.

In its May 15 cablegram, the Arab League had protested that with the end of the British Mandate, the rule of Palestine should revert to its Arabic inhabitants. The Zionists had shown their aggressive intentions and committed multiple massacres, and the rule of law needed to be restored. They declared it was therefore incumbent upon the Arab states to intervene, stating their aim as "nothing more than to put an end to the prevailing conditions in Palestine." They emphasized that they were not aggressors and invited the intervention of world powers if it was deemed necessary.

As the cablegram made its way to New York, the armies of Egypt, Syria, Iraq, and Transjordan began moving on the small new country. The civil war between the Jews and Palestinians—marked by small-band raids and riots—had ended *several months earlier, and now something new had begun. No longer were people, and peoples, fighting between and in neighborhoods, but states were in combat across contested borders. Maps of the region were taking shape, with colored lines across sand and hills, layering a new world atop the old.*

The fact of war took no one by surprise, but the damage and the victors were yet to be decided. The Arabs' plan was articulated in various voices in public and private. Egyptian generals advised the king that, with the army marching on Tel Aviv within two weeks, it would be less a war than a parade, a military picnic. The Lebanese and Jordanians spoke of freeing their brothers in Palestine, who had been fighting the civil war for decades, and returning the land to its rightful owners. Newspapers noted this year was the nine hundredth anniversary of the 1148 Siege of Damascus, when Muslims defeated the Crusaders and drove them back to Europe. In Syria, there were public declarations that the Jews would be routed, pushed into the sea.

Those in the newly born State of Israel heard these statements and believed a new Holocaust was upon them. But they had few light weapons and fewer heavy weapons, so to compensate for the imbalance in arms, they unleashed a viciousness few expected, and they spread word of what they had done. When Egyptian soldiers captured two Palmach scouts near Jibalya, they found the men's thermoses filled with water contaminated with diphtheria and typhoid. The scouts reportedly had poured some of the deadly mixture in one well and had plans to poison the Gaza Strip's underground water supply. Upon committing atrocities at Deir Yassin, Lydda, and Tiberias, Israel telegraphed the news of the hundreds murdered and maimed, sometimes detailing how their fighters made the old women and children scream before exterminating them. Nearby villages emptied in terror of Jewish marauders, and the name Deir Yassin was whispered and repeated by those abandoning their homes.

In Benny Morris's 1948, one Israeli commander present at Deir Yassin describes the "conquest of the village," stating it was "carried out with great cruelty. Whole families—women, old people, children—were killed, and there were piles of dead. Some of the prisoners moved to places of incarceration, including women and children, were murdered viciously by their captors." Years later, an Israeli historian found the carnage documented in military records, which are quoted in Morris's Righteous Victims: *"Whole families were riddled with bullets and grenade fragments and buried when houses were blown up on top of them; men, women, and children were mowed down as they emerged from houses; individuals were taken aside and shot. At the end of the battle, groups of old men,* women, and children were trucked through West Jerusalem's streets in a kind of 'victory parade' and then dumped in (Arab) East Jerusalem."

In the north, Israel had the Davidka, a loud mortar that its soldiers employed continually night after night, the thunderous sounds in the echoing valleys. Though the bombs themselves were weak and inaccurate, the Israelis spread rumors that they were atomic. Memories were still fresh of the horrors Jewish scientists had unleashed on Nagasaki and Hiroshima. Who could say with certainty that the same could not happen in Yaffo and Haifa?

To the watching world, a major conflict was unfolding in the heart of the Middle East, but on the ground the battles were relatively small: several hundred people fighting several hundred people on dusty mounds and behind rock structures using out-of-date European weapons transported in by sea and ancient smuggler routes.

When the first truce went into effect on June 11, each side had lost hundreds in combat. Israel had suffered the greatest losses, but the fact that it hadn't been defeated outright was perceived by many as a victory, and during the course of the month-long truce, Israel realized it could prevail. The weapons embargo imposed during the cessation of hostilities meant Arab countries, which engaged largely in legal trade, couldn't stockpile arms, but Israel acquired its weapons illegally, smuggling them in, and throughout the truce they expanded their munitions.

When the United Nations mediator proposed a partition plan similar to the previous one that Arabs had found objectionable, both sides rejected it, and on July 8 the Arab countries attacked full force. In the ten days that followed, little land changed hands, and despite there being no victor when the second truce went into effect on July 19, Israel was seen by many to have succeeded merely by not succumbing to defeat.

In late September, the United Nations mediator introduced a new plan, this time with a call to internationalize the city of Jerusalem, thereby removing it as a subject and site of conflict. Before his proposal could be officially published, however, the mediator was assassinated by terrorists of the paramilitary Jewish organization LEHI (Lohamei Herut Israel, or Fighters for the Freedom of Israel). When hostilities recommenced, Israel focused nearly all its energies on the last Arab army still fighting, Egypt's, with occasional skirmishes with the Syrians in the north.

In January 1949, on the brink of defeat, Egypt announced that it was prepared to enter armistice negotiations. Israel agreed to a ceasefire, but before it went into effect, Israeli commandos laid a massive mine that blew up an Egypt-bound train carrying hundreds of injured soldiers. In March, Israel reminded the world once again that it saw itself as a fierce and vengeful force, conquering the vast Negev desert, which included the infamous hilltop of Masada, where Jewish militants had, two thousand years earlier, built an impregnable fortress. It was there they'd taken their final stand against Rome in 73 CE, before committing mass suicide to avoid capture. The event, and Masada itself, would become central to the Israeli self-defined identity as an uncompromising people who would die fighting.

Following the Egyptian–Israeli Armistice, borders were shifted and land transformed. The Palestinians, forcibly expelled and dispossessed, clustered largely in the Jordanian West Bank, the Egyptian Gaza Strip, and refugee camps in Syria and Lebanon.

On July 18, 1949, David Ben-Gurion gathered a group of nine scholars of cartography, geography, archeology, and history in his office in Tel Aviv, reconvening the Names Committee that had been created by the Jewish National Fund in the 1920s. The goal was to create the official map of Israel so there could be no question of what the recently conquered land was and always would be.

The making of maps has never been a neutral or academic endeavor. As preeminent cartographers J. B. Harley and David Woodward wrote in History of Cartography: "Mapmaking was one of the specialized intellectual weapons by which power could be gained, administered, given legitimacy and codified." Israeli scholar Meron Benvenisti echoes this sentiment in his book on the renaming of Israel, Sacred Landscape, explaining, "Cartographic knowledge is power: that is why this profession has such close links with the military and war."

Benvenisti's research shows that the mission of Israel's Names Committee was not to honor ancient archeological places and bring them forward into the contemporary landscape. It was erasure. As Ben-Gurion wrote to the members of the committee: "We are obliged to remove the Arabic names for reasons of state. Just as we do not recognize the Arabs' political proprietorship of the land, so also do we not recognize their spiritual proprietorship and their names."

Place names constitute stories, and not just of cities and villages, but of the land itself— geographical features, hills and valleys, springs and oases—perhaps telling of features that once existed but are no longer visible. Some names even refer to events instrumental in forming the place and the identity of its inhabitants. To acknowledge these organic place names is to acknowledge a living people connected to the land and a cultural heritage. In 1949, the story Israel sought to tell would skip over Palestinian habitation from ancient times to the present.

Though for some places in Israel the renaming was an act of recovering biblical heritage, for most, it was an act of fabrication. Hebraic names were simply created, ones that had a biblical ring to the modern ear. (Thus Bir Abu 'Auda and Rahma became Be'er Ada and Yerucham.) And in some instances, names of unknown places mentioned in the Bible—such as Yotvata, Evrona, and Mount Hor—were bestowed upon new Israeli sites like prizes. This practice occasionally caused controversy, such as when a religious kibbutz was granted the requested name of Yavneh, though it had no connection to the ancient rabbinical site. Yet when the Arab village of Yibna, which actually sat atop Yavneh, was captured, it was quickly stripped of its name so the place could be more accurately assigned.

Strangely, in 1956, when the first of the official Israeli maps were issued, many former Palestinian locations were included—with an ominous word next to each vanished place: harus, meaning destroyed. These were quickly replaced with a map without those markers of what had been, but for a brief moment the Israeli maps told a greater story than a land without a people for a people without a land. They told of the destruction and erasure of a people and places and of a cultural heritage. They showed the tombstones writ with Palestinian names, these markers proof that the places had been there for long enough to have stories and people and homes.

In Sacred Landscape, Benvenisti recounts an Arab legend from Israeli scout and ranger Alon Galili, relayed to him by elders, about the origin of the name of Bilad al-Ruha: A father near death decided to divide his property among his sons. He took them on a tour of the land so they would not confuse one place with another and each would know what was rightfully his and not fight with his brothers. Beside the first spring they visited, they saw an old drunk man, so the father said to his sons that this place should be remembered as Ein al-Sakran (Spring of the Drunkard). Upon ascending a hill, they saw a ridge from which flowed eight wadis, so the father said this place should be remembered as Ras al-Matmuniya (the Octagonal Head). As they proceeded, they were greeted by the mukhtar or village chief, who had just risen from a nap and as a result was bareheaded, with his hair blowing in the wind. So the father proposed that this village should be called Abu Shusha (Father of the Forelock). From there, they descended to the valley, where they saw camels loaded with sacks of salt, and the father declared that this valley should be remembered as Wadi Milh (Salt Wadi). They then met some young pretty woman in a village that they deemed Umm al-Zinat (Mother of the Pretty Women). Continuing on, they climbed the highest hill, which had a breathtaking view, and the father declared the spot Umm al-Shuf (Mother of the Sights). Walking a bit farther, they encountered a group of villagers who annoyed them and decided the place should be remembered as Kafr 'Ara (the Damn Village). Finally, as they started back toward home, the girls of a village came out and beat drums and danced for them, and they named the place Umm al-Dufuf (Mother of the Drumming Women). Throughout their trek, they'd experienced pleasant sea breezes, and upon arriving home, the father said the area should all be called Bilad al-Ruha (Land of the Winds).

This walk is likely apocryphal, and it's far more likely that these names—which persisted for generations—grew organically based on the topography, geography, and inhabitants. But they represent a way of understanding the world, a way of life, passed down from elder to child, and how a people saw the landscape and themselves.

In "The Place Itself, or I Hope You Can't Digest It," a poem about his village, which was destroyed in 1948, Taha Muhammad Ali wrote:

And so I come to the place itself,
but the place is not
its dust and stones and open spaces . . .

Bilad al-Ruha no longer exists. It is now Ramot Menashe, meaning the Heights of Menashe, on the official map.

*

In Israel, the 5th of Iyar on the Jewish calendar became Yom Ha'atzmaut, or Independence Day. On that day, fireworks and parades fill Israeli cities and towns, and families take to the land to grill meats and celebrate the rebirth of modern Israel, laid on the foundation of an ancient civilization. Because it is celebrated on the lunar calendar, Yom Ha'atzmaut can fall on any Monday, Wednesday, Friday, or Saturday of the month.

For Palestinians, May 15th of the Gregorian calendar is Al Nakba (The Catastrophe). On this day, Palestinians remember the forced expulsion, the loss of their homes and homeland.

Because one occasion is measured by the moon and one by the sun, in some years, the days coincide: one culture celebrating, the other mourning.

LAWRENCE, MA
Liebe / Lillian (1969)
Misha (1969)

PITTSBURGH, PA
George / Charney Jook (1963)
Misha (1963)

CASABLANCA
Brahm (1955)
Channa (1955)
Massouda (1955)
Miriam (1955)
Rafael (1955)
Sharona (1955)

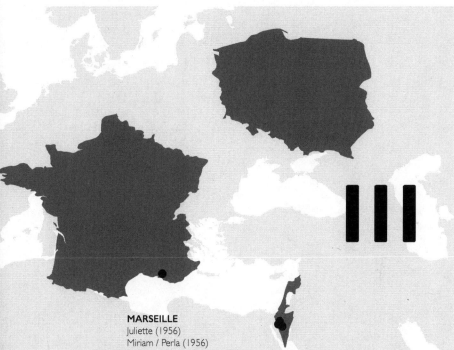

MARSEILLE
Juliette (1956)
Miriam / Perla (1956)
Sidney / Louis (1956)

HAR HAZIKARON
Juliette (1961)

JERUSALEM
Brahm (1965)
Massouda (1965)
Miriam / Perla (1965)
Sharona (1965)

BEIT GUVRIN
Misha / Oojie (1972, 1973)
Miriam / Perla (1973)

CASABLANCA

1955

Roses grew in the valleys of the Atlas Mountains with such sweet abundance that it was indescribable. That's what Massouda's family said to her and what she shared with her children. They then would proceed to describe it: the bushes grew in bands of color, with red and pink and white bleeding at the edges. When you were among one varietal, it was all you could see or smell, but if you went up the hillside and looked down, clear lines of the rosebushes were visible, grouped by hue, the rows extending beyond what could be seen through the length of the valley.

The roses were first planted in the Atlas by an Amazigh cousin, who'd carried them from Syria hundreds of years before. With a handful of flowers, she had changed the landscape of the Moroccan mountains forever. Now the mountains smelled of honey, nectar, and citrus. Roses were special and changed everything they touched. In the early mornings, they touched bees, whose echoes filled the chasms between peaks, and between the seasons they hugged the white rocks, which changed colors from centuries of contact. In the mornings, Massouda would add a splash of rosewater—water that roses touched—into a filled basin to clean the children. Throughout the day, each would be reminded through casual contact and sniffs that roses had touched them too.

On this day, Miriam, the youngest of Massouda and Rafael's children, hid in a solitary rosebush, alone in a wild hedge of other bushes and trees. Out with Massouda one day, she had noticed the smell of roses and noted the bush's location. She'd gone back and visited the roses several times, observing the petals and blooms but never touching them for fear she would disturb them. She even took to calling the bush *Maman*, as the other children called their mothers, though she called hers *Imma*.

Imma had sent the children out to play in the streets—Miriam knew this was so she could fight with Baba—and she'd put Channa in charge of them. Outside, they played a grand game of hide and seek, with the walls of the city as the borders. Channa and Hassan—a neighbor boy—were *it* because they were the oldest, and the rest of the children were dispersed and hidden, trying to elude them.

Massouda didn't mind fighting in front of the children, but she didn't feel like throwing a shoe when they began to imitate their parents. Even then, the children only retreated and watched from an obvious corner of the room. So she sent them out, and before Rafael could leave the house, she asked where he was going, a question that always annoyed him.

Rather than responding that he was going to work, which was true in part, Rafael asked why she was asking.

"Shouldn't a wife know where her husband spends his days . . . and nights?" she added, knowing what it implied.

"A wife should trust her husband," he said sharply. "You know that everything I do, I do for this family."

"And what do you do? What do we need so much?"

"Now you are complaining that we have too much?"

"You invite the jinn flashing money around."

"Pshht," Rafael hissed, weary of the constant talk of demons and ghosts.

"You made me a promise when we married that we would move to Palestine. And now, years later, we have seven children and all this stuff, but still we're here." Massouda pointed around at nothing in particular. "Did you know that Abraham is now in Israel? He is younger than me, and he did it with nothing but a rock."

"I am trying to make it possible. We can't just go. We need money, for us, for the children. So we don't end up like my uncle in Tsfat, may his memory be a blessing."

Massouda had heard so little so often about that uncle. As always when he came up, she fought her curiosity. She knew better than to ask out loud and even tried to dispel the thoughts from her mind.

"Well, then, explain to me what you're doing," Massouda asked, hoping to get a straight answer. "So I can understand why it has taken so many years."

Rafael had been tempted to explain his side work to Massouda on a number of occasions, but he was afraid if he did, she wouldn't let him gamble and spend. It was one thing to consider telling her when things were going well, but currently things were not going well. Rafael and Brahm had taken everything they'd saved and cut out Moussa and the rest of the group to invest in a separate venture, smuggling a load of arms to a radical Jewish militia. But the ship had been attacked and captured, the arms seized, and their entire investment lost in the Mediterranean. Now was not the time to talk about it. First, he had to gain back ground. To that end, he'd borrowed some money from Moussa, planning to change his luck at a card game.

"I don't have time for this. I have to go," Rafael said, exasperated. He left the house, half expecting to dodge his wife's thrown shoe.

As he walked through the narrow alleys of the city, Rafael stopped at every public fountain to sip from the communal cup. It was his custom even when he wasn't thirsty. The one closest to his house was tiled mostly in green, like a mosque, with gold mosaic eight-pointed stars throughout. Picking up the tarnished tin cup that sat upside down on the brown tile base, Rafael first wet his face and ears like a Muslim. He had picked up the habit from his employees, watching them do it each day, several times a day, splashing water on their faces with such care, rubbing it behind their ears, breathing in the cold and wet to calm and relax them.

As he carried out the practice, Rafael thought of Abraham, who used to work for him, sweeping up and preparing the tools. He was a boy, Massouda's little friend, whom Rafael had hired at her urging. Abraham too always spoke of going to Palestine. Every day in the workshop he would talk about some fact or other he'd heard about life there. Then one day he'd come in so excited. He'd been at the orphanage, where his father would drop him off to go drink and gamble for days at a time. While Abraham was there, the American president's wife, Mrs. Eleanor, came for a tour. She'd had tea with some of the boys, including Abraham. Something he said touched her, and she'd spoken to the administration and then told Abraham that if he liked, and if his father agreed, she would adopt him and take him back to America. Abraham had come into the shop screaming and howling about how he was going to be American and be the president's son. And that if the president didn't have any other sons, that meant that he—Abraham—would become the next president of America when the mister died. Rafael cautioned Abraham to go home and talk to his father. Rafael played cards with the father and knew the man beat Abraham often, but also that the boy was his only son, and he would not give Abraham away for nothing.

A few days later, Abraham had returned, sullen and angry, with bruises on his cheeks and neck. His father had said no. When Abraham pleaded, his father had yelled at him. When he'd argued, his father hit him with an unfinished leather strap. It had left marks all over his body, and his face had lost its cuteness, his eyes no longer large.

Weeks later, Abraham had gone to the orphanage with a rock and broken all the windows. He was taken from his father and sent to jail—but his new status as a Jewish orphan made him eligible to be sent to Palestine. Rafael would occasionally visit him in jail, bringing him sweets, and Abraham would talk excitedly about the list he was on. Rafael couldn't believe it when Abraham had actually been chosen and sent to the land he'd spoken of so often. Though he'd been happy for Abraham, Rafael had wished Massouda hadn't heard the news. Nothing good came from her knowing such things.

Miriam crouched in the rosebush, trying to stay still so no one would see her, and because every time she moved, she felt a thousand points of pain. In all the stories of the rosebushes in the valleys of the mountains, no one ever mentioned the hidden army of small, sharp, awful thorns!

When her father approached the fountain, Miriam watched him from the belly of the bush as he washed his face and ears. He looked sad. She called out to him, screaming, "Baba! Baba! Baa-Baa!" from the rosebush, thinking it would cheer him to see what a good hiding place she'd found. She also hoped he would help her out of the bush without her cutting herself. Men on the street kept turning and looking in her direction at her cries, but none saw her. Miriam's hiding place was excellent.

Her father didn't hear her, however. After watching him stand still, silent, and slightly hunched over the fountain for a long period, Miriam saw him suddenly stand straight and walk away. She continued to crouch awkwardly, in pain from the pressing thorns, but remained proud of her hiding place.

In the hot midday sun, Brahm was sweating as he turned down half-shaded alleys, stalking past temporarily abandoned stalls in search of Rafael. He'd forgotten his hat somewhere, and perspiration dripped into the canals that led to his eyes. He moved quickly through the streets, creating a breeze on his face, his lips pursed around a cigarette.

Brahm had first gone to Rafael's workshop, but it was locked and empty. Though he'd rattled the metal gate three times, yelling Rafael's name louder each time, there was no response. At Rafael's house, he'd found only a few of the children. The wet nurse said she didn't know where Rafael was but asked Brahm if he could stop by the market to pick up some butter and eggs for the snakes. Brahm had taken the coins, but he had no intention of returning. He thought it absurd that women wasted good money feeding house snakes and shuddered at the thought of small snakes suckling on the breasts of wet nurses, to keep their milk from drying up.

Brahm stopped by a couple of cafés, but no one had seen Rafael in days. Or at least that's what they said. After speeding through one street a second time, Brahm stopped at the green fountain to think, asking himself *Where would I go if I'd just ripped off my partner and had extra cash to spend?* Rinsing his fingertips, pushing water into the cracked skin, he recalled all those times Rafael had cheated him at cards, and how he'd let it slide because Rafael had a nice wife and a family. He thought about how, despite everything Rafael had done, Brahm had given the man another chance and a prime opportunity to make money. Then he thought of Sharona. Yes, Sharona was where to go.

Miriam watched him, the man, rub water into his hands and through the stubble on his face. She had seen him around before and wanted to call out for help, but she didn't know his name. She yelled "Baba," assuming he was a father and that all fathers responded to the call, but he didn't turn. Instead, he turned to a nearby man, said something, and quickly walked away.

Channa searched with Hassan through each of the narrow alleys and larger cross streets. They'd found most of the other kids and dutifully tagged them, but they had not yet found Miriam.

Hassan began taunting Miriam loudly to get her to stir. "The men with the knives are coming," he yelled with his hands cupped over his mouth. "You better come out quickly or they might mistake you for an Eid sheep."

Channa pictured the wagons—packed tight with bleating sheep—that would soon be pulled down these streets. The animals would be brought in by the hundreds, the tight streets made narrower by makeshift pens. For a week, the children lived in a zoo, petting and feeding and playing with the sheep. Other creatures, smelling the sheep, would emerge and take to the light. Cats hanging from rafters, dormice dancing in the streets, big fat creatures that no one recognized suddenly digging holes in bushes. A whole menagerie out of nowhere.

And then came the slaughter. The men with the long, sharp knives would walk along two by two, say a short Arabic prayer, and then slit the throat of every sheep they saw. Young boys were tasked with carrying the whetstones, while older boys were ushered into manhood with a knife and a swift stroke. Sometimes the boys wouldn't do it right, and the wounded sheep filled the streets with their screams before the men descended to finish the kills. Blood ran down the streets too fast for even the cats to lap up. From balconies, blood rained, then drizzled for hours until it hardened and stained the walls. In an instant, the petting zoo transformed into an abattoir, and Channa dreaded that moment for the rest of the year.

"Come on, come on, Miriam. We know you're here. Baa baa baa," Hassan yelled down an alley filled with bushes, including a sole rosebush, as both he and Channa stopped to listen for a reaction.

"Yeah." Channa joined in. "You don't want to end up like Nissim. Remember Nissim?" she called into the silence. "Remember Simi and Nissim at the beach?"

"That's good," Hassan said quietly, then yelled, "If the men with knives don't get you, the sea will. Come on out."

"Was it the sea or was it the jinn?" Channa projected her voice down the alley. "Is he here now, hiding?"

Nothing stirred, so they turned at the fountain toward the next alley.

Sharona was cooking when Brahm arrived. He looked like he hadn't slept and was acting more nervous than usual. Almost immediately, he started screaming about "that cheat, that thief, he thinks he can trick me!" Sharona tried to slow him down, attempting to distract him as one does an angry child, but he was looking through her, peering into a fog only he could see, so she tried to understand. "Who? Who? Who are you talking about?" She couldn't get Brahm to focus, and kept repeating "Who?" hoping one of the syllables would break through.

Finally, he heard. "Who? Who? Rafi! That snake. He thinks he's better than me. Thinks he can cheat me! Where is he? He has to be somewhere!"

"Have you tried the card game?" Sharona asked. She offered Brahm a bowl of spicy fish stew, hoping that in the time it took for him to eat it, he'd catch his breath. Brahm pushed the soup away, however, and hurled his body out of Sharona's house, colliding loudly with the door.

Early the next morning, a crowd gathered at the tin gates of the Jewish cemetery, which was tucked in a corner of the old city. Beside the barbers' and the butchers' quarter, the graveyard was invisible to most, despite the field of Jewish dead residing in the beating heart of the marketplace. A high wall of buildings surrounded the cemetery, the only entrance and exit a tall pale-green sheetmetal gate guarded by an elderly Muslim woman and her daughter, who required a toll of several specific coins to enter when no funeral was taking place.

Before anyone could breach the walls of the grounds, the body had to be carried in, and afterward the mourners would follow, a mass of the living trailing the dead. Immediately behind the body this morning were Rafael's aunts and his wife, the women of his life, who were in unison emitting loud ululations. Their tongues dashed up and down, beating individually yet combining to create a sound that bounced off the backs of the buildings and caused the gate itself to tremble. Behind them were the children, then Rafael's friends and neighbors. In a short time, the hole had been dug, dirt and rocks mounded beside it like a monument, with several shovels for mourners to use to cover the body with their respect.

The funeral was wordless but not silent. Wearing long dark garments shorn above the heart, the bereaved screamed a mixture of anger and prayer. Tears and spit fell on the dusty ground, sitting on its surface for a moment before being drunk down. Down, down, down. The wretched procession marched along the pathway, avoiding the squat trees and broad wormwood plants, to the appointed hole. Once the body was lowered and the covering began, the cries became muffled, no longer directed toward the sky and sun, but into stained handkerchiefs. The mass that had entered as one started to splinter as individuals turned and walked away in their own time. Nothing left to say, so nothing was said: the ending marked simply by departure.

Tea after the funeral was at Rafael's aunt Miriam's house. Almost everyone attended, filling her salon and courtyard, smoking and drinking tea, laughing and crying. Stories and gossip were exchanged, each person thirsty for information of the night prior, but no one willing to ask or tell, lest such words invite the evil eye. Instead, anecdotes with both humorous accusatory undertones were traded and hoarded for another time. Truth was exchanged not in words but in glances and groans, confirming or denying suspicion.

Massouda was at home, hoping her brief absence would be attributed to a widow's grief. Underneath piles of fancy linens that were rarely bothered, she extracted a small wooden box with ivory inlay, constructed the previous century to hold a backgammon set. Inside were no pieces or dice, but instead a small purse filled with gold coins and 1924 quarter pieces, a small chamsa with one of God's names scratched into it, identification papers for her and each of her children, as well as a list of names with numbers and addresses beside them. She knew exactly what was in the box, having opened it often, but still she inspected everything closely, knowing she had to act fast. She took out the chamsa, tucked it beneath her dress, and slid the box back under the linens. It was time to be with family. The box and the plan were safe.

MARSEILLE
1956

"Come on. Let's go!" Louis said, drinking the remainder of his coffee and slapping the small cup down on the metal table. "I see the ship."

Juliette turned slightly to look behind her at the old port where Europe abruptly ended and the seas to Africa and Asia opened up. "It is still at sea. Not even close to port yet. Why should we go down to stand with all the Africans? It will be a few hours until she is off the ship and processed."

"I know. I know. But she's on there, somewhere on the ship. That ship! And in a few hours, we will be meeting her and taking her home. It's exciting, no?"

Juliette sat for a moment with the rhetorical question, trying to re-create the steps in her head from how an administrative search for her brother had led them to the grimy port of Marseille. "We have not discussed what we'll call her," she said with a sigh. "What her new name will be."

"Her name is Miriam. Why can't it just stay Miriam?" Louis asked.

"Well, if we were really adopting her," Juliette began, putting an emphasis on *adopting*, "and if we were really a Christian couple, then we would change her name. This should look right. How old is she again?"

"That makes sense," responded Louis, who'd learned long ago to defer to Juliette on bureaucratic truths. "I think she's four or five. I haven't received a clear answer. I'm not sure anyone knows for certain. Not even the family."

"D'accord. Four- or five-year-old girl. Amazigh heritage. Cave-dwellers. Casablanca. Ruddy, but probably pretty in a way. What was the name of that Moroccan footballer in Marseille that everyone is crazy over?"

"Larbi? Larbi Benbarek?"

"Oui, mais. What was his sobriquet?"

"La Perle Noir?"

"Oui. That's it. We should call her Perla. It is Latin, European. But also pays homage to her homeland. And it is a pretty name for a young girl."

"It's very nice," Louis agreed, "but how about Lillian? That's also a nice name for a little girl."

"After your American friend?"

"No. Well, yes. But no. I just like the name. It's pretty, right?"

"You've mentioned her before. Should I be worried?"

"Hah," Louis honked. "Don't worry. If I had a fake mistress, I would do it in the French manner and be open with my fake wife."

"Relax, Louis. I am just playing with you. You can have all the mistresses and manstresses you'd like. Just as long as you always come home to me."

Louis smiled. He thought of their new home in Marseille. It was so different from anywhere he had previously lived. L'Unité d'Habitation, La Cité Radieuse. A concrete block like nothing he'd ever seen. An inhospitable material turned into a unit for mass habitation. An experiment on the hill. La Maison du Fada. Juliette had secured it, and at first he hated it. The structure was cold; it felt cold. Not stone and not brick, it was undifferentiated cement poured into a mold. A massive beached ocean liner drydocked and stranded on the hill. But it quickly grew on him. He hated to admit that Le Corbusier could be right, because Louis disliked his brand of managed-housing socialism. But living in this building somehow felt natural, despite its artifice. In Paris and in New York, it had felt like he was living in the past. But the community created by Le Corbusier felt like the most present place he had ever been.

"It is going to be so strange suddenly having a little girl in our lives," Juliette remarked.

"A daughter. Our daughter," Louis corrected her.

"Remember, Louis, we're not keeping her. We're just a step on her journey."

"Yes. No. Of course. I know. But it's exciting, no?" Louis repeated.

Juliette sipped her coffee and felt slightly nauseated. Louis was a sensitive man, and she knew he had a desire for children. Though this was largely biologically impossible for him, he wanted to be a father, and she feared that despite his assertions they were adopting for the cause, he was going to be heartbroken when Perla left in a few months.

"What should we do with Perla tomorrow?" Juliette asked. "I have very little experience with children."

"I don't know. Maybe take her for a walk around the neighborhood, let her get used to her new home."

"Sure," Juliette agreed, though she felt uneasy at how Louis was framing it. "But after she is settled. She speaks French, right? We need to find things for her to do. I think you have to keep children busy."

"Oh, I read in the paper that there is a music festival next week. It's free. We can take Miriam. Perla. Kids love music, right?"

"You know next week is Charles's birthday," Juliette said. "He would have been thirty-eight."

"I'm so sorry, my love."

Louis only called Juliette affectionate names when he felt guilty. She tried to picture Charles but could only recall Louis's face the day he came home with the news. Through his contacts at the paper, he'd reached out to the former underground. Charles had showed up in their records on several occasions, but suddenly there was no more mention of him. She'd asked Louis to find out what had become of Charles, if he was still alive. Now she wondered if it would've been better to remain ignorant, hopeful. Knowing what she knew, she could no longer conjure up the awkward, funny, clingy teenager who'd always tried to be a part of her group of friends. Instead, she saw the copy of the report that Louis—being unable to parse the French cursive—had brought home for her to read. She thought of the stylized script that a seemingly calm hand had used to write Charles's story.

As the ocean liner made its way toward the Port of Marseille, Miriam peered from the port-side deck at the city revealing itself. She'd spent the first part of the journey looking down at the water for any signs of a body. Every salty wave cast an oily shadow that could be someone, dead or alive. Dolphins and large fish that broke into the air appeared as a swimmer for a moment. She dreamt of him having grown fins, making friends with the sea creatures, swimming and dancing just beneath the surface. A few times, she yelled out Nissim's name, knowing he was in the water somewhere, but no one ever called back.

They'd been on the ship for four days, first hugging the coast of Morocco, passing the minarets and cliffs, until Gibraltar. Once they squeezed through the straits, everything flipped, and Africa became lost at sea. The

Spanish coast seemed so green compared to Morocco's, but nothing prepared her for Marseille. The city rose from the water to a mountain with a castle on top. "The Good Mother lives there," she'd heard someone say, pointing at the peak. The good one, not the bad one. The good mother has good children. Miriam's mother had sent her to Marseille so they could all be together again in Israel. Simi had already left to marry a man there, and Amram and Mousa were working on different ships like hers. And the ships were working their way across the ocean. Everyone and everything working, because it was important. Baba was not working that day in Casa. He was walking and washing his face and playing. Imma was still in Casa with the middle kids because, she said, Israel would not let her bring more than three. Three was the most because four was a nice number. So the oldest and youngest had to get in on their own. Everyone would go by ship, and everyone would stop in France, just at different times. That was how it had to be.

Miriam was told that a nice man and woman would meet her in Marseille. She was to call them Baba and Mama, but they were not her baba and mama. Baba had died that night she hid in the rosebush and was buried the next morning near the sheeba bush, where everyone screamed and cried. Imma screamed the loudest, and she was still in Casa with the middle children, but they would all meet in Israel and then she would call Imma mama again. Baba wasn't coming. Nissim wasn't coming either.

But first, four days on the boat. The bag was packed for her, and everything was dry. Dried fruit and cheese and bread. Because you take dry things on the wet water. On the boat, Miriam was to ask for water. But not the water from the ocean because that water made you more thirsty. It was not clean water like in the fountains outside the house, which you could drink. And when the people that she would call Mama and Baba picked her up, she was supposed to be nice to them. And she was to speak only in French. No Moroccan because Moroccan was for Morocco and Morocco was in Africa. But the nice people were in Marseille, which was in Europe. And Israel was not in Africa or Europe. It was in the Torah. And once they were together in Israel, everything would be better than it was in Casa. Which was good because Miriam liked Casa.

"Did you know that Marseille was briefly stripped of its name?" said Louis, who'd researched the city's history rigorously before their arrival.

"Non!" Juliette responded. "I've never heard such a thing. How do you have a city with no name? It seems impossible."

"Oui. After initially supporting the Revolution, it led a counterrevolutionary rebellion."

"Yes, I knew of this history."

"When General Carteaux's army, and a young Napoleon Bonaparte, retook the city, they brought trial and punishment. First, they tried the people involved, the anti-Jacobins. But then they wanted to punish the city itself, to mark it with a permanent stain. So they passed the law of 6 January 1794—or whatever the Revolutionary calendar equivalent was, maybe Nivôse, snowy?—which designated Marseille as an outlaw city. As part of that, its name was officially stripped."

Juliette frowned. "I don't understand."

"Well, names are given, and so they can be taken, I suppose . . ."

"No. I understand *that*. What was it called after they took the name? There is a need to call it something, right? What did the people call it? How was it listed on maps? Marseille is a major city, with an important port." She paused, waving her hand around them. "What was the port called by sailors?"

"It was called ville sans nom. So, I suppose the port was called the port of ville sans nom."

"Oh," said Juliette, smiling her sly smile. "So it was not actually stripped of a name. It was renamed City Without a Name."

Louis chuckled, but dug in. "I do not see the distinction," he said.

"Everything needs a name, because it gives us a way of pointing to it, of talking about it. And names always tell a story of sorts." Juliette began to feel like she was in graduate school again. "Names mean things. Like *Berlin* means *swamp*, because it was presumably a swamp at one point. And *Dublin* means *black pool*, because it too was presumably a swamp. It maybe still is. *Rabat* in Morocco . . ." Juliette gestured over her shoulder out over the ocean, aware that Morocco was somewhere out there. " . . . means *a fortified palace*, because that is what it was and is. And even Marseille comes from the Arabic for *harbor*, because . . ." Again Juliette waved her open palm at the water. "So calling it la ville sans nom was a renaming. It changed the city's story, yes, from being about the water to being about its betrayal. But it still served as a name of sorts and a story."

"I suppose you're right," Louis conceded.

"Of course I'm right. Names are necessary."

"Well maybe that's why the name *Marseille* for Marseille came back so quickly. I don't think the law lasted long. And perhaps this necessity of names was why the attempt to strip it away failed?" Louis said, seeking a compromise. "So maybe it actually had no name—like I said—but that couldn't last because cities need names—like you said."

"No. That's not correct." Flustered, Juliette tried to drink from her empty cup. "You are describing a fight over names where the stronger one won. That happens all the time. Cities are palimpsests, with layers written on layers. You cannot easily impose an artificial name on a city through law or force. It can be done, but it takes constant vigilance to keep the new name in place. It is like gardening; you cannot simply plant a new plant and expect that the native growth will never return. If it was there once, it will always find a way to break through. This is a harbor city, not a city without a name. No matter what the little Corsican general says."

Though most of the passengers stood at the front or sides of the ship to watch as Marseille unfolded before them, Miriam stood in the rear, watching the little tugboat push the great vessel. How? she wondered. Something so small pushing something so big. Weird that the tiny boat was more powerful than the giant. Smoke forced up, like out of a man's pipe. Poof, puff, poof. Miriam tried to mimic the sounds it made. Puff, poof, puff. Magic. So small but loud. Why wasn't it larger? Why was their big boat not able to push itself? Was the boat tired? Such a long trip it had taken. Miriam remembered being carried back home after the beach. Did the water make you tired? Yes. Yes, the water was cold, and cold made you tired. But so did hot. Water in the ocean was never hot. Only soup and baths were hot. And the hamam was hot too. But the ocean also pushed and pulled, and that also made you tired. Yes, Miriam determined: the big boat was tired.

"Le remorqueur," a voice suddenly announced.

Looking over her shoulder, Miriam saw a finger outstretched over the ocean, the finger attached to a hand, and the hand attached to an old man.

In a black sailor's coat, the old man spoke again. "C'est un remorqueur." He was pointing toward the tugboat. "Ça s'appelle un remorqueur."

Miriam nodded but wondered how he knew the small boat's name. Looking closely, she saw pictures of anchors on his coat buttons. Miriam knew it was part of a ship—she had seen the shape before—but did not know what it did, nor the name in French. She pointed at a button near his pocket.

"Et ça?" she asked.

The man looked down. "Ahh, oui." He reached into his pocket and pulled out a handful of walnuts. Seven of them, still in their shells. "Voici quelques noix." He smiled and kept his gaze above her, looking out at the tugboat, and beyond, at the calm sea.

She grabbed the nuts with both hands, thinking of the story *Smeda Rmeda*. Putting them quickly in her own pocket, she wondered which of the nuts would contain the Samsam-Kamkam demon that would save her.

The boat had docked and sat, not moving, but not yet releasing its passengers. Louis could see movement, passengers gathering in the front, sailors gathering at the pier, ropes being tossed back and forth. Looking at the number of people, Louis hoped that Miriam knew to wait at the sanitation or hygiene office at the port.

"After showing her the flat," Louis began, "I'd like to take Mir . . . Perla to the passages."

"The passages?" Juliette asked.

"Yes, well, I'm not sure what it's actually called. But I call it the passages, at least in my mind. It's the stretch under the pillars of our building."

"Ahh, yes. You have mentioned the area before. I know you go there sometimes. What is it you do there?"

Louis shrugged. "Nothing. I walk; I sit; I watch the shadows creep in parallel along the ground. I don't know if she'll like it, but it's quiet there. And I remember when I arrived, I needed a quiet place to be alone. Where I could relax. Plus, I think I've heard children playing nearby, so perhaps she can also meet someone her age. She can choose one or do both."

"I think that is a wonderful idea," Juliette responded. "And I wanted to ask if you minded, after we get to the flat, if I left you two and went to the cemetery."

"Which cemetery? Why?"

"I do not know. Probably Saint-Pierre. To be with Charles."

"But . . ." Louis thought for a moment. "He isn't buried here."

"Yes, I know. But it is all the same when you are in the house of the dead. Those there are not really *there*, so I suppose those elsewhere are there as well."

"I understand," Louis said somberly, though he was excited to have the day alone with Perla. "It's just a different kind of quiet place."

HAR HAZIKARON

1961

Juliette sat on the park bench at the edge of the forest. She'd arrived early but could not bring herself to put her questions in order. Instead, she sat trapped. Trapped in her mind, thinking about the book she'd been reading between the forest and the museum—named a hand and a name—on a hill with two names commemorating remembrance and revision.

Her purpose in Jerusalem was to report on the Eichmann Trial. She'd pushed hard for the assignment, arguing that her knowledge of the languages and cultures, as well as her lack of biases, made her the ideal person to interpret the proceedings.

Before leaving Marseille, she'd bought a book for the inevitable boredom of sitting in lobbies and hallways and quiet courtrooms.

When Louis had asked why, if she wanted to read for distraction, she'd chosen dense philosophy, Juliette replied she was hoping to make her time in Jerusalem reflective, to be a student once again. Louis had raised an eyebrow at her bringing a book in the original German to Israel, but she'd insisted it would keep her sharp, since much of the testimony would likely be in German.

"But don't you think reading Heidegger in Jerusalem might be controversial?" Louis persisted.

"Israel kidnapped a man from Argentina and will be holding a trial for the violations of laws that didn't exist," she snapped, "against people who had no association with the country. I don't think anyone will focus on me reading *Sein und Zeit*."

Louis raised his hands in surrender and changed the subject. "Will you be able to see Perla?"

Juliette frowned. "I don't know. I think my schedule will be quite packed. I hope to get the chance to talk with Hannah Arendt."

Though it had started as a protest and a provocation, *Being and Time* had gripped Juliette. Heidegger's analysis of aletheia—the essence of truth—to be an uncovering or unhiding rather than a correspondence, possessed her. She had found a frame and propulsion for her work on the idea that truth was the opposite of forgetting or obscuring.

Juliette pulled her notebook from her bag, intending to put her varied thoughts on the trial in some order. She usually found her way toward meaning through discussion, but with no one to talk to, she was struggling. So she decided to write a letter to Louis that she might never send.

Dear Louis,

I am sitting outside Yad Vashem, waiting for my meeting with an archivist. The name of the museum is apparently a quote from Isaiah, so I read the book a few nights ago. Turns out it's pretty easy to find a copy in Israel. But what a messianic mess. And though the sentiment seems nice—a monument and a name—the full context leaves me confused. As far as I can tell, Isaiah is relaying God's message that, to the eunuchs who keep the sabbath and follow the commandments, he will give a monument and a name better than sons and daughters. It is not a promise to the Jews. The promise is that they will be remembered in posterity, which is in general the right sentiment for such a museum. Remember the dead. Remember the righteous who took the hard path. But in that way Israel just takes symbols from the Old Testament and reappropriates them haphazardly; they've done so here, to comic effect. In naming the museum Yad Vashem, they have inadvertently called themselves eunuchs.

I have been thinking quite a bit about symbolism and memory during these days of trial. The proceeding itself is not taking place in a courtroom, but rather a theater. It is a large building with ample seating, so it makes some practical sense. But does no one understand that the worst way to push back against the critique that this is all a show trial is to hold the thing . . . in a theater?

Furthermore, rather than have Eichmann sitting at a table where all anyone would see is the back of his head, they have him in a glass cage, on display, like some sort of animal in the zoo. I suspect this was done to isolate him, to show he is dangerous, but the effect is not as they'd hoped, because what I see each day is an old, mild-mannered German who comports himself with quiet dignity, while his captors have put him on humiliating exhibit. Maybe this will change once he testifies, but for now, I can't help but feel sorry for the little old man in the glass cage.

More importantly, I cannot help but wonder what the intent of this trial is, and what the result will be. It is clearly not a trial in the traditional sense, where a determination of guilt or innocence is the desired outcome. No one doubts that he will be found guilty and that he will be executed. Israel did not kidnap him and call the world's attention to absolve him of his alleged crimes. But something bigger is happening here; I can feel it.

It first struck me when I was listening to one of the many, many witnesses recounting their experiences. I realized they were not witnesses in the classical sense. What is it that they saw, witnessed? Few of them had an encounter with Eichmann. Instead, they are recounting the genocide, their loss, the suffering. One after the other, they go up to the stand, clutching some object for strength, and describe in Hebrew—not their native tongue—what they endured. And we all watch in that theater, like the audience of a monthslong avant-garde production that feels as though it will never end. It's as if this trial is creating a new national trauma, a new memory that all Jews will now share, which upholds and justifies the state of Israel. Though many Israelis and Jews did not experience the war or suffer during it, this new narrative, told in Hebrew, includes them. And perhaps just as importantly, it excludes all others. What of the Arabs? What of Christians? They have no access to this trauma, and I wonder how they can ever engage civically or have full citizenship without it.

Something is going on here, much different than what I imagined when I took this assignment. I don't know why, but I assumed that the trial of Adolf Eichmann would be an occasion for healing and closure, but instead it feels like a record is being created, one that can be consulted and referenced, that will keep the sore open, fresh, raw. I thought the trial might provide personal peace to the individuals who suffered, but this feels overwhelmingly like a political project. The Attorney General of the country, in consultation with the Prime Minister and the military, using the resources of a state museum, is weaving a new narrative of the nation and where it stands in history. All in Hebrew. But why? The defendant is German; all the witnesses are German; the judges are German. Why use a language that is foreign to everyone involved if not to infuse it into this new country's soul?

And the strategy appears to be quite effective. It has been fifteen years since the end of the war—a lifetime ago!—and yet as I sit in the theater, I feel it happening in the moment. I can feel rage toward its perpetrators and pity for its victims coming up in my throat. And I can sense that every member of the audience of journalists in attendance, as well as the far-flung audiences who read our dispatches, feel likewise. Even as we are briefly distracted by the present, such as when Yuri Gagarin was launched into space or America launched the Bay of Pigs invasion, we return quickly to the past, to which we've become emotionally and spiritually attached.

In some ways, this uncovering seems important. But it also feels dishonest, like a re-covering with a new shroud. There is no intellectual rigor to the examination. We are six weeks into the trial, and I remain lost as to what Eichmann's crimes are. I feel sad for these Jews, but I also feel shame and exclusion from this sorrow. And I am a tourist here. What of those non-Jews who live here, who have lived here? If the nation is being redefined by this mass trauma to which they have no access, how can they identify with it? How can they ever feel Israeli? How can the Nation accept them? I've realized that . . .

As Juliette wrote, someone cleared her throat. Between Juliette and a tree stood a woman, clearly waiting to be noticed.

Juliette jumped up and put her notebook down. "Hello. My apologies," she began. "Are you the archivist here at Yad Vashem?"

A woman about Juliette's height, of middling years, replied, "Yes. I am the archivist."

"Very good." Juliette nodded, smiling politely. "As I mentioned in my letter, I am here covering the Eichmann trial for a small French journal, and I wanted to talk in order to . . ."

"Yes, yes, I have your letter here," the woman interrupted, holding up a piece of paper, bent by its many folds. "I have read it, but I don't understand why this is relevant to the trial."

"That is not important." Juliette stiffened at the woman's tone. "Were you able to find any information about him?"

The archivist examined the paper she was holding. "This man, whose information you are searching for, he is not Jewish, yes?"

"No. Why is that relevant?"

"Well, you have come here to Israel. To Har Herzl, to Yad Vashem, and you are searching for information on a gentile who disappeared during the war. I have spoken with several of my colleagues, and we are not quite certain . . ." The archivist paused. "You are aware that the museum is formally consulting with the prosecution, yes?"

"Forget the trial," Juliette said, exasperated. "I only mentioned it by way of introduction. I am reporting on it, but I am here today in a personal capacity."

The archivist looked again at the unfolded paper. "But this man . . . this Charles . . . is not Jewish, and he is not a victim of the Holocaust."

Juliette's breathing sped up, and she felt her face get hot, her ears tingling. "How do you know that? Were you able to find any information about him? About what *happened* to him?"

"I am sorry, madame, I do not think we can help you."

"I don't understand why. Isn't this what you do? Why Yad Vashem is here?"

"Is there anything else we can do for you?" The archivist said in a bureaucratic tone of finality.

"You have not done anything for me," Juliette replied accusingly.

The archivist refolded the letter and walked away.

"This place is backwards," Juliette said loudly to the archivist's back.

"Excuse me?" For the first time, the archivist sounded interested.

"This place . . ." Juliette tried to calm her breath. ". . . this Yad Vashem is backwards. I read Isaiah. And the quote from which the phrase is taken. The context is that God will welcome into the community the foreigner and eunuch who do good. And to that foreigner and outsider he will create *a monument and a name* better than children. But what you have created here—this trial, this focus on the Holocaust that concerns itself only with Jews—is not about welcoming a community, but excluding them."

"Who do you think you are?"

"I am nobody," said Juliette, deflated. "I am just looking for some information."

"No. You are worse than nobody." The archivist raised her finger. "You are an antisemite. I can see it. I can hear it. You drip with bigotry."

Juliette vehemently shook her head. "I came here looking for help, and you . . ."

The archivist interrupted. "I have work to do. Please leave."

Turning again, the woman put the folded paper in her pocket. She slowly walked toward the front door, opened it, and went inside, all without looking back. Juliette saw the path to either side and the forest behind her. She put a stiff arm on the bench for support as she decided which direction to turn.

PITTSBURGH

1963

"I'm sure we can reach a satisfactory resolution," the rabbi announced to the table, hands outstretched symbolically to both sides. "If we all give a little and try."

The rabbi, young and cleanshaven, with a strong Trenton accent, sat at the head of the table in a small room in Pittsburgh's giant domed B'nai Israel Synagogue. To the rabbi's right was George Mazar, and to his left several of the synagogue's congregants.

One of the congregants responded, "I sure hope so, because Jewish education is very important for our family. That's one of the reasons we've donated so much to this congregation. And I know I speak for a lot of the B'nai Israel families when I say that we just want Principal Mazar to work with us."

All eyes turned to George at his solitary side of the table, and George nodded in approval of the sentiment.

"Well, good, good," the young rabbi said. "We're getting somewhere. This is good!" He turned to the congregants' side of the table. "Richard, do you want to explain the issue as you've expressed it, so we're all on the same page?"

"Sure. Sure," Richard Rosenthal replied. "And like I've said, we care so much—so much—about Hebrew education, and have so much respect for Principal Mazar, so I'm certain we can figure this all out.

"We feel that—and when I say we, I mean not just my wife and I, but a lot of the other B'nai Israel parents—that Hebrew education is taking up too much time. The kids have other activities—sports, music lessons, dance; I mean, there is just so, so much—and it feels like Hebrew education is at the expense of everything else."

"That is an excellent point." The rabbi announced, as if at the bima. "Maybe let's hear now what Principal Mazar has to say about this before continuing."

George waited and then spoke quietly: "What is there to say? One day a week for Hebrew and Jewish studies is not even enough, but it is being said that it's too much. I was brought here from New York to be the principal of this school, and it takes time to teach these children. Many do not know Hebrew, and fewer still have a good foundation in biblical studies. We do what we can with the full day on Sunday, but we need more time. I do not think it is reasonable to expect that we can cut the day in half and yet teach them properly."

"Well, what if instead of sitting at desks learning Hebrew, the students did something *while* learning Hebrew?" Richard opined aloud. "Maybe they could play sports in Hebrew? Or maybe there could be a musical component to Bible study?"

"Okay, so these are interesting suggestions," the rabbi declared. "Instead of dividing the pie further, we are growing the pie." He swept his face from Richard to George. "What do you think, Principal Mazar?"

"About what?" George answered.

"About the suggestion that maybe we can incorporate studies with more activities, so that the students don't have to choose and miss out on other things they want to do."

"You want we should do kharate in Hebrew?" George asked, giving the word a Yiddish kick.

The rabbi's smile faltered. "I don't think that's what they're saying, Principal Mazar. I think . . ."

"Well . . ." Richard interrupted, "what would be wrong with that? I mean, sure, maybe karate would be silly. I think that besides punching and kicking, it's mostly shouting. But maybe some sport or exercise. Why not do it in Hebrew? What we're proposing isn't so radical. I mean, think about how they must teach these activities in Yisrael, in Yerushalayim." Richard extended the Hebrew syllables in both place names. "They must be doing it in Eevreet, right? I mean, they probably teach about the Maccabees or even the heroes at Masada, baruch Hashem, who gave everything. But not in a boring old classroom. They probably hike to those places, incorporating physical activity with learning. And shouldn't we here learn from Yisroel?" Richard's voice had risen in pitch and volume. "Who better to teach us than the vanguard of Jewishness?"

George withdrew a single cigarette from his shirt pocket and waved it in the air. "Would anyone mind?"

"Actually," Richard said, "my wife is sensitive to smoke."

"Of course." George rose and went to the narrow window, turning the small, squeaky hand crank at the bottom. It let out a groan, then the window pivoted to its side. Lighting the cigarette with a paper match, he watched it burn itself to ash between his fingers. His lips wrapped around the unfiltered butt, he breathed in and thought of Israel and of Richard's talk of karate there. When he'd imagined Israel, he always imagined its holy sites, the Kotel in Jerusalem, the Tomb of the Patriarchs in Chevron, Yavneh. Now he pictured Israeli boys kicking and grunting, telling dirty jokes in Hebrew across latrines.

Outside the window, schoolchildren were playing, including his and Lillian's three boys—Mishael, Solomon, and Benny. George exhaled, watching the group of boys through a scrim of smoke that tickled his eyes. He saw Mishael, who'd just had his bar mitzvah, carrying a large tree branch and gesturing with it, as though urging the others, before turning and walking toward a large tree. Though Solomon was a year older, he looked to be following Mishael, along with four other boys. Benny, their youngest, trailed off to the side, spinning in his own orbit while the six older boys moved— nervously, George thought—around the tree, between the synagogue and the school, with Misha holding a branch like a bat.

George's quiet, academic manner hid a deep suspicion of all things. Holding his cigarette in the French style with his back toward the conference table, he wondered what the group of boys was up to. Lillian was teaching a class in the building, and George hoped she was distracted enough not to look out the window. She'd wanted to move from New York, but she'd become so nervous since transitioning into Jewish education, so agitated and afraid, that he knew she'd worry if she saw whatever the boys were doing.

Misha lifted and lowered the thick end of the branch into his own palm, hard for emphasis. He could feel the sting of the knots and stubs as they landed in his flesh, but he hid the wince. The pain was startling at first, but then it helped him focus, and the sound of the impact emphasized his point.

"Those shits can't do what they did to Pinsky . . ." Misha pointed the branch at a pale, skinny boy. ". . . and just get away with it. If we let them push us now, then it will never stop. That's how history works. Pinsky, tell them what you told me. What they did to you."

Robert Pinsky was the tallest of the boys, bespectacled and fair, aside from his bright red acne. His voice straddled two octaves, generally low, but breaking high when he was excited.

"Those boys," Pinsky began in excitement. "Those little schvartzes! They took my wood. I was walking home with some pieces for my shop project. And those schvartzes . . ."

The word agitated Misha, made his thoughts reel.

". . . they surrounded me and took my wood. And then they beat me with it." Pinsky held up his white, white forearms, speckled with flashes of flaming red. "And my mother saw these bruises and splinters. She knows I was beaten. There was so much iodine."

"Do they still have the wood?" Benny asked from the periphery.

"That's not the point," Misha said.

"Yeah!" Solomon yelled at his youngest brother. "That's not the point!" He stalked over and pushed Benny to the ground.

Misha felt the situation slipping from his control. "It's not that they're black. They're part of the Stanton Street crew, and we're North Clair. We can't let them push us around!"

Though only thirteen, Misha had watched the March on Washington and had followed JFK's speech on civil rights, which he felt strongly about. He'd also read Leon Uris's *Exodus* and Elie Wiesel's *Night*, and though he felt strongly for the Jews who'd been through the war, he believed in the new Jew. Not the Jew of his parents' generation, who'd walked through the gates of Auschwitz and Treblinka when ordered. When Misha had asked his father what he did during the war, his father said, "Nothing," and returned to his book. It was a shameful answer. His father couldn't even look Misha in the eyes when Misha asked questions. Though he'd pressed his father about the war, eager for any scrap of adventure, any action during the conflict, his father merely said that it wasn't worth fighting. His father could speak every language imaginable, but he had no words for why he did nothing.

Misha believed in the Israeli Jew, who was strong and fought back against the Arabs. The new Jew was powerful but fair; with the strength and skill to smite his enemy, but after showing that he could, he made peace that everyone respected. Misha wanted to lead his friends to victory, but also to a peace-of-the-strong with the boys on Stanton Avenue. They all went to Peabody Academy together, and Misha thought there was no reason they all couldn't get along.

"Yeah, let's go down to Stanton!" Solomon announced.

"Let's get those fucking schvartzes!" Robert Pinsky added.

George withdrew from the window, turning back to the table. He gulped purposefully and audibly. "So, where were we?"

"We were discussing a compromise position," the rabbi announced, "where you would teach what you teach, but maybe with some sports or other activity incorporated."

"Maybe soccer," Richard added. "It's team-oriented, not too violent, inclusive, and international. So maybe Hebrew would fit in naturally."

"Yes, of course." George resigned himself to the inevitable, recalling the young men playing football in the parks of Paris during the war. Kicking that ball and yelling to each other like it meant something, all above ground. Below ground, in the sewers, lurked unimaginable things. He looked at Richard and saw his teeth smiling and his small arms and elbows resting on the table, his voice a squeak that seemed to echo in the room. George could imagine Richard standing on his hind legs and sucking those two front teeth, tongue darting, with little creepy fingers moving in the shadows. George thought of that night in the sewers and laughed.

"So, we are all settled then?" the young Rabbi coaxed. "That Principal Mazar will teach Hebrew and Bible studies, along with soccer. Or, as Principal Mazar certainly calls it, *football*."

"Sounds good to us . . ." Richard began.

"But . . ." George interrupted.

". . . really glad we could reach such a happy compromise . . ."

". . . but I do not know soccer. I am not a coach. I am a . . ."

"It's easy," Richard said with a breezy wave of his hand. "All the world plays it."

"Kids in third-world countries play it in alleys," the young rabbi added.

"Arabs can even figure it out, so how hard can it be?" Richard honked a laugh, and his wife followed with a soft chuckle. "So I'm sure you could learn it, chik chak."

* * *

Stanton Avenue enclosed one section of the neighborhood, cutting across Negley at a point not far from B'nai Israel. Neither Negley nor Stanton was a straight street, because streets in Pittsburgh snaked along ridges and through valleys, creating and cordoning off ethnic enclaves along the way. When someone announced what street they lived on, they announced their ethnicity and allegiance. If you were from Negley and its side streets, that meant something, and if you were from Stanton and its side streets, that meant something too.

"So when we get there, we're going to teach those schvartzes a lesson, right?" Pinsky said, smacking his fist into an open palm, missing the center ever so slightly.

"You bet we are!" Solomon replied, striding purposefully ahead of the others. "They can't come into our neighborhood and pick on one of us."

"Well . . . technically," said Benny, only partially engaged, "Pinksy was over on Janero. Isn't that part of their area?"

"Shut up!" Solomon put his face inches from Benny's, spitting as he shouted, "Why won't you shut up!"

Misha had forgotten that part of Pinsky's story. "Hey, Pinsky," he said, "why were you on Janero again?"

"Okay," Pinsky said, cracking his freckled knuckles, "so you know how there's that old fence that's falling apart there? Well, that's where I got the wood for my shop project." He grinned as though congratulating himself.

"What are you doing with old planks?"

"I was going to build a doghouse."

Misha frowned. "Why?" he asked. "You don't have a dog."

"It's what Mr. Buccigrosso assigned," Pinsky explained. "And besides, I thought maybe, if I had a doghouse, my mom would let me get a dog."

"That makes sense," Solomon said.

"But you don't have a yard," Benny pointed out.

"So?!" Pinsky replied aggressively. "You don't need a yard to have a dog. Lots of people have dogs and don't have yards. You know Jimmy?"

"Which one?" Benny asked.

"He has two dogs. Brothers. And one is giant. And he lives in an apartment."

Benny looked confused. "But where are you going to keep the doghouse?"

Misha laughed. "Oh, yeah!" He punched Pinsky in the arm.

"Ouch! Fuck!" Pinsky yelled. "That's my sore arm." He rubbed his bicep with his other hand. "Still, those schvartzes had no right to take my wood. And they had no right to hit me with it."

"No," Misha said. "You're right about that." He loosened his grip on the large branch he'd carried from the synagogue. It suddenly felt like a dead weight, an unnecessary appendage. He let it hang and dragged it along the uneven concrete until it caught a crack, then he let it fall. He had no use for the stick and forgot why he'd brought it along. His thoughts were on Operation Maccabi in '48, and what the Givati Brigade would do in his situation. He'd heard how they fought to open the Jerusalem Road so supplies could be brought to trapped Jews in the holy city. It was a fight for land, and the elite Israeli soldiers used strategy, skill, and intellect to defeat the Arabs and save Jerusalem. This felt so similar. What was to be done?

Solomon punched Benny in the arm, hissing, "Why do you always ask such stupid questions?"

Benny winced before responding, "Do you ever think about Bilaal?"

"Shut up!" Solomon shouted.

The boys crossed over onto Stanton Avenue, and immediately Misha felt different. He was agitated, nervous. He noticed himself breathing faster and wondered if it was due to fear. No, it was in a good way, he concluded, like how one feels when they are about to find a treasure hoard.

Out of familiar territory, the boys walked in silence at a fast pace, with Misha ahead, though no one was actually leading the way. It felt weird to Misha that there was no ceremony to crossing Stanton, no gate or guard. You could just do it.

Misha was counting his steps when he saw the long, lean shadows at the end of the street: a group of boys. "Look cool, guys," he commanded in a stage whisper.

As they approached the group, the boys noticed them and spread out, and Misha found his gait becoming uneven. He kept dropping down on his right foot, then compensating with his left, almost tripping forward. Then Pinsky yelled, "That's them. That's the ones who got me. Especially him, the tall one. Bunch of dirty schvartzes!"

"Will you shut up?" Misha spun to glare at Pinsky. "That's an insult, and they'll hear you."

Pinsky looked sullen. "They don't know what schvartze means. They're too stupid."

"It doesn't matter. You could call them dirty schmeckles, and they don't have to speak Yiddish to figure out it isn't a good thing."

"You have a dirty schmeckle," Solomon said to Benny, flicking his chin in the air.

With a regal bearing, Benny intoned, "My name means *The Son of Righteousness,* and I have a dirty schmeckle."

"Will you all just shut up for a second?" Misha whisper-yelled. "Just walk."

As they closed the distance, Misha's hands were cold, wet, and hot, alternating. His fingers tingled, and he was acutely aware of each and every one. How did the Israelis face danger each and every day? *Tragedy is the difference between what is and what could have been.* He mentally repeated the words.

They were close enough to the boys now to make out their wary expressions. "Hey!" Misha said loudly. "You guys beat up and stole from my friend. That wasn't right!"

The group of boys exchanged glances before one stepped forward and asked, "What? What the hell are you talking about?"

Another pointed. "No. Look. It's that boy we knocked with the wood. Remember, he cried like a little baby?"

"Oh yeah."

"Yeah!" Pinsky yelled from the back. "What the fuck?!"

"What the fuck to you!" yelled a boy from the other group.

"Come on, everyone." Misha held up his arms, like a ref holding back a boxer. "We're not here to fight. We're just here to get an apology and get back Pinsky's wood."

"Pimskee's wood?" the tall boy repeated jokingly. "What the fuck is Pimskee's wood?"

"My friend Pinsky here . . ." Misha indicated with his thumb. ". . . had his wood stolen. He needed it for a project, and we'd like it back."

"So what's Pimskee going to build with that wood, an erection?" The boys laughed.

Benny chuckled. Solomon turned and gave him furious full eyes.

Misha felt a surprising calm steal over him. "Come on, guys," he said, relaxing his shoulders. "You can't beat someone up just 'cause they cross Stanton. That's not right."

The tall boy turned serious. "Not right? Your friend there—Pimskee, or whatever you call him—was stealing my gramma's fence. He just ripped pieces down and was walking away with them. So yeah, we beat on him and took that fence back. Comin' over here and stealing my gramma's fence! You're lucky she didn't see you, or you would have got it worse."

Misha frowned and turned to Pinsky. "Is that true? Were you stealing an old lady's fence?"

Pinsky shrugged. "I mean, maybe it was once a fence. I don't know the history of the wood. But it's that old house on the corner of Janero. You know which one? It's just pieces of scrap."

"You know," Benny interjected, "if it's not keeping anything in or out, I think one could argue it was not in fact a fence."

"Fucking nerd!" Solomon shoved Benny.

"Leave him alone," Misha snapped, then turned to the Stanton boys. "We just came here to talk."

"You can't talk to these schvartzes!" Pinsky waved his palm over his face.

"What the fuck did you call us, Jew boy?"

Jew Boy. At these words, Misha felt the blood rising to his face—in anger, but also in embarrassment. He remembered a rabbi once telling him that to embarrass another for no reason was the same as killing him, because in both instances, blood filled the ears. He thought of Ze'ev Jabotinsky. The lion. An old man at synagogue had given Misha copies of Jabotinsky's speeches and essays, and Misha read and reread them, hiding them from his father. *The tragedy lives in the fact that there is a collision here between two truths. But our justice is greater.*

"Look, I think he's gonna cry," one of the boys said, pointing at Misha. "Look at his face all red."

The tall boy looked at Misha. "Get the fuck outta here."

Benny touched Misha's arm. "I think I need to pee."

"Okay," Misha said, eyes swelling, ears burning. "Okay, Benny. Let's go."

He turned and walked away, and the rest of his group followed. Misha felt the heat concentrate in his midsection, making him nauseated and light-headed. Pinsky strode up front, suddenly in the lead. Misha and Benny brought up the rear. No one spoke as they marched back to B'nai Israel.

In the small room at B'nai Israel, Richard appeared pleased. "I think we've done something really special today," he announced.

"Yes. Yes. I agree." The young rabbi again extended his hands to both sides of the table. "I knew we could get there if we all tried. If each person gave a little. And here we are. I think we've arrived at a very positive solution. And who knows . . ." The rabbi chuckled happily. ". . . we may have stumbled upon the future of Jewish education in America! Here in this little conference room, our own little Yavneh." The rabbi paused. "Principal Mazar, is there anything you'd like to add before we adjourn, as the lawyers say?"

George felt tired. The room seemed warm. He looked over at the window and saw that it was still open. Where was the air? he wondered. Where did the boys go off to?

"Principal Mazar?" the rabbi repeated. "Was there anything you wanted to say before we wrapped up?"

"Ahh, yes. No. Like you said, we've all done very good. We should all be very proud of ourselves."

JERUSALEM

1965

"Jerusalem has always been at the center of the world. On ancient maps, the world was drawn as a flower, with the continents of Europe, Africa, and Asia each an equal petal. And in the center, Jerusalem. The pistil. The nectar. In other places, it is referred to as the world's omphalos, its navel, its bellybutton, signifying a centrality both in terms of location, as the birthplace for civilization, and metaphysically, as a portal to the divine. All this points to the multifaceted nature of this city with more than seventy names—many of which, including the Hebrew one, are plural—which occupies a special sphere."

Squatting by the old Ottoman train station in the German Colony, Miriam listened closely to the speaker leading the group, but she couldn't understand. Every day she saw these large clusters of tourists and thought if she paid close enough attention, the words would make sense to her.

"The peoples here go back to time immemorial. There is no memory before Jerusalem, and all humanity reaches back to it. Every building has another building beneath it. Every stone in every old structure likely came from a previous structure. Every rock is a palimpsest. Every story first happened here. All tales of power, passion, love, betrayal, inspiration, divinity, death, and life originated in Jerusalem, only to be told anew by each generation, with different characters, in different places.

"And, speaking of places, I call your attention to that falafel stand right there. It is owned by a friend. If you get separated from the group, just find your way to Zeekee's Falafels and wait for us. Trust me, he has the best tahini. The best! You may miss quite a tour, but you won't go hungry. Okay, now let's cross the street. Try to stay together. . . ."

Miriam observed the tour participants as they walked off; they looked European in a general sense. Some French in particular. She noticed an older couple, definitely French, staring off at nothing specific—together, but each in their own world. It reminded her of the sad nice couple in Marseille and their strange and lovely French ways. Papa Louis would take her on long walks into the hidden bellies of buildings and through every alley in the city. He knew everything, and leading her down to the port, he would point in different directions to tell stories of countries that were beyond their sight. In the direction of the rock pier was a country called Mali, where they built their castles to the sky out of mud and clay. Past where the fishermen sat was a country called Italy, which has a festival where whole towns would get together and throw tomatoes at each other. Where the sun set was Spain, where they would release bulls and run from them through the streets of the city. Past Morocco was Cote d'Ivoire, where they believed babies came from heaven, and all the elders learned from what the babies saw and said. In the direction of the big boats was America, where workers were rising up against fat business owners called pigs and taking over the factories.

When Miriam would ask the direction of Israel, which her mother had talked of often, he would point at the fishermen in front of Italy. But Papa Louis would fall silent, as if sad. She asked him what happened in Israel, and he said he'd never been there and knew nothing about it. Miriam said that Israel was where she was going, and Papa Louis said he knew, but he remained quiet. Miriam still had some identification documents listing her as Perla, and each time she saw the name, she'd wonder what became of Papa Louis and Mama Juliette.

As the tour moved off, Miriam relaxed by the train station, eating sunflower seeds and spitting out the shells, unsure where to go next. She had left the Lady Davis school several days earlier, after a teacher screamed at her for being unwilling to learn new habits. The teacher told her that if she wanted to become an Israeli and work in an office, she would need to stop acting like a Jewish Arab and start acting like a Jew. She had put great emphasis on Jew.

After leaving the school, Miriam had gone first to Rabinovitch Park and gazed at the monster with three tongues. In Morocco they had stories of monsters called jinn that took the shape of people, but here they had play-grounds that took the shape of monsters. Hamifletzet was white and black, spitting up three streams of red. As Miriam tried to decide if she would re-turn to the Lady Davis school—to become a secretary and a Jew—children entered the back of the monster's head and tumbled out of the front. The school had been built in their neighborhood of Kiryat HaYovel, which had grown from an old Moroccan tent city into an area of stucco houses for new migrants. Lady Davis didn't teach all girls, but seemed to focus on Moroccan girls, turning them into secretaries, and secretaries had to act like Ashkenazim. Miriam didn't know why a dead lady from a country called Canada, whose picture was all over the school's walls, was so interested in her transformation.

Leaving the park, Miriam had started walking east, toward the valley, with no destination in mind—just knowing she didn't want to go back to the apartment or back to the school. She hadn't intended to keep going, but she'd found herself continuing on and on, sleeping under trees and in old Crusader ruins occupied by newer migrants, eating at newsstands and falafel holes, before finally, days later, arriving in the German Colony.

From the crowded train station, she could see the Old City across the emptiness of the Valley of Hinnom. It was all right there in front of her. If she closed one eye and stretched out her hand—which she'd been doing repeatedly—it seemed she could touch the Old City, but in truth it was in-accessible, beyond actual reach. Her family had gone through so much to get here—except for her father and Nissim—and it felt like they were no closer than they had been in Casablanca.

Miriam's father was still in Casablanca, still in the ground in the Jewish cemetery near their home. Her mother said he'd died of a heart attack, that he fell sick at home, that he woke up that morning with pains and they'd rushed him to the doctor and the doctor said it was natural and a tragedy. But Miriam had seen her father that morning on the streets, so she knew it was not as her mother said. She knew he'd walked on his own feet from the house that morning; she'd seen him wash his face and ears. Nissim was still in the sea off Casablanca. His body had been lost to the water, and his name lost to the air. No one ever spoke of him, and when she asked questions about Nissim, exasperation would follow, along with a series of sounds to blot out his name and memory. To speak his name was to invite the demon that pulled him into the sea.

Miriam held out her hand and followed the contours of the valley with her finger until it reached the walls of the city. It was right there, and she could see a path. She knew she couldn't go directly to the Bab al-Amud or the Mughrabi Gate, but instead would have to go to the Mandelbaum Gate—the only border crossing between Israel and the Old City of Jerusalem—but it was closed to Jews. Miriam spoke Arabic and French, however, and had an ID card identifying her as a Moroccan Christian named Perla, and she thought maybe she could find a way through.

As she finger-plotted her route, she found herself pointing at a man she knew. He was standing at the other end of the station, wearing a light coat and a small hat, both hanging off his loose body. He was smoking and talking to another man she didn't recognize, gesticulating with both hands, cigarette dangling from his lip. She'd known him from Casablanca—a friend of her father's and mother's, though he was never invited inside the house—and he, like them, had come to Israel after her father's death. Recently she'd seen him around a lot. Sometimes with her mother, out shopping and inside the apartment, the two of them alone.

The man broke away from his companion and started off in the direction of the Old City, and unthinkingly Miriam followed him. He walked confidently, cigarette leading the way and shoulders angled forward. Miriam slouched and walked slowly, acting small so she wouldn't be spotted. If she could barely see him, then he could barely see her. Those were the rules of being.

To the left was a modern city, clad in ancient stone and worn prematurely by constant dust and intermittent war. Despite the story it told the world—the name it gave itself of West Jerusalem, and the occasional aged tree beside an Ottoman arch in a crumbling building—it was not the ancient place she had heard so much about. It was newer than Casa, and whereas here all the tourists marveled at the hints of old Arabic architecture, in Casa one didn't have to search for piecemeal bits of history and identity. In her Israeli neighborhood of Kiryat HaYovel, where they'd stayed in tents until getting a tiny apartment in immigrant housing, no one even pretended it was Jerusalem. Sure, her mother called it Jerusalem, and the address of the house and school was Jerusalem, but it looked like something other, exempted as it was from the rule that houses be built of official Jerusalem stone. It was a suburb to the celestial city, adjacent to holiness, new to its history. This was where Jewish Arabs were housed until they were just Jews ready for the real Jerusalem.

To the right, on the highest hilltop, were the walls she'd heard about her entire life. They were impressive and intriguing, but she couldn't understand what was so special that people gave up their lives elsewhere to be within sight of the tall, thick barriers. The word for making the journey was Aliyah—to go up—the same word used when people were called to the Torah to make a prayer. But what were they going up to in the new Jerusalem of Kiryat HaYovel? Small, cramped homes with rats and a park housing a monster? Miriam remembered the magic of her childhood in Casa, and even the mysteries of Marseille. She could not understand the draw of Jerusalem.

Between the walls of the Old City and rising new city were the valleys. They were filled with sharp brush that obscured weaves and bundles of barbed wire. Miriam had heard rumors that there were even landmines down there, though she'd never heard one explode.

The man took a sharp left, striding away from the ridge and toward the park. Miriam sped up so she wouldn't lose him.

The neighborhood quickly shifted. Diagonal streets cut into one another at every angle, all of them lined with small shops selling jewelry and old coins and precious religious items carved from the olive wood harvested from Jerusalem's hills.

Brahm walked into a news shop. His eyes darted around, surveying the shelves, each holding cardboard boxes filled with the usual vegetables. He paused for a moment at the bags of Choco, and his teeth clenched as he thought of tearing the plastic corner in a single bite. One squeeze of the bag and the warm chocolate milk would squirt quickly into his mouth. Not now. He had things to do, and sweets could wait.

At the back corner of the shop, he finally saw what he was looking for. Brahm peered over his shoulder—a young girl, no one—and tapped the arm of the man squatting, unpacking a box. The man looked up at an angle, squinting. Brahm handed him the requisite ten lira bills, bundled tightly so only the confused Ashkenazi scientist on the outermost bill was visible. The man took the money, tucked it into his front pocket, and returned to the half-full box of food. Brahm turned to leave. As he walked out, he pocketed a packet of sunflower seeds, and seeing the girl seeing him, he gave her a wink and a nod and, with his free hand, offered her a cigarette.

* * *

Miriam was shocked. She'd been found out. Her first impulse was to freeze, like when an animal was about to attack. She clutched the nut she always carried in her pocket, rubbing its now smooth edges. Shrugging when she didn't accept the cigarette, the man kept moving, never actually stopping, and left the shop. Miriam stood there, facing where the shopkeeper was on the floor, watching out of the corner of his eye. She spun and hurried after the man—she'd remembered his name: Brahm—leaving space between them so he didn't notice her again.

Brahm turned down Shomrei Emunim. He hated the street, hated the neighborhood, hated the ultra-orthodox who populated the streets, but it was the fastest way to where he was going. The way was narrow, trash everywhere, with apartment buildings crowding in from both sides. The men were dressed in tights and big coats—all in black—yelling Yiddish back and forth. The Haredim, Brahm thought, were disgusting beasts. He flicked his half-smoked cigarette at a wall pasted over with old peeling posters, then lit a fresh one.

Miriam had never previously been to the ultra-orthodox neighborhood of Mea Shearim, but she saw no gates. Since the name meant One Hundred Gates, she'd assumed the place would be like the Old City, a fortress, only with one hundred points of entrance. She could feel the men and women staring at her, trying to push her away and out with their eyes, so she looked up as she walked and saw the barred balconies, each filled with long-haired children. Trapped in their lofty cages, the children stared blankly below at the street. Miriam wanted to free them. Let them run and play, own the streets, hide and find each other. But she didn't have time; Brahm was moving quickly.

After leaving Mea Shearim, he turned left again. Where were these hundred gates, she thought, if not at the entrance and exit to the neighborhood? Everything in Jerusalem promised, but nothing came true. All the names held the mystery of history, making the ordinary sound special, but they were empty.

When she followed Brahm into the covered part of Machaneh Yehuda, the afternoon turned to night. The air was heavier in the market, too, blood of animals mixing with the honey of baked goods and the sharpness of cooked peppers. The streets here were crowded, winding, with shadows everywhere. There in the thick tumble of commerce, it was Casablanca, if only for an instant.

Brahm turned toward a warbat stall, where large trays of sweets, cut into triangles, shone in the heat—glistening green from pistachios and golden from dough and honey. As Brahm went to the door beside the stall, he reached a long hand to grab a sticky triangle. A voice yelled out from the darkness of the stall: "Etzbaot dvash! Die!" Brahm grunted in response, opened the black door, running upstairs as the door slammed on its own behind him.

Inside the small apartment, Sharona was cooking peppers while a young boy ran in circles in the next room. Dipping a large wooden spoon in another pot, Sharona made a bowl of chraime for Brahm, the smell of fish and steam filling the small room.

"Yaakov is in the salon," Sharona said as she turned back to the stove. "And before you say again that you don't think he's yours, he's yours. I'm sick of your nonsense."

Brahm grabbed the bowl, palmed a handful of couscous, and dropped it unceremoniously in the center of the stew. He molded the combination with three fingers stained with tobacco, as if making a point, and exhaled loudly in between mouthfuls to let out the heat. After several large bites, he wiped his hand on a small torn carpet hanging by the door and lit a cigarette. Walking up behind Sharona, he pressed against her from behind.

"Nu! What are you doing? You're going to light my hair on fire!" she yelled, then muttered, barely audibly, "Disgusting beast."

Brahm took the cigarette from his mouth and pressed his groin against her backside again.

"Nu!" she repeated, exasperated. "I have to work soon. I can't now. Go out and do something. Keep yourself busy. Take Yaakov."

Brahm turned and saw the boy still spinning in circles. He replaced his cigarette and watched the movement for a moment, waiting for Yaakov to get dizzy and fall. Something wasn't right with him. He wasn't his son. Brahm was sure of it. Taking a few steps into the salon, he tapped the side of the boy's head mid-spin, and thrown off center, Yaakov tipped and then fell, tumbling onto the floor. Brahm chuckled, grunted at Sharona, and left the apartment, letting gravity take him down the steps.

* * *

Miriam squatted in the alley, distant but with a view of the black door, waiting. She was sure Brahm would exit soon. He didn't look like a man who stayed. She then saw the door open abruptly and Brahm tumble out, appearing to fall, then grabbing a warbat as if for support before regaining his feet. He'd gotten the sweet. Etzbaot dvash. Honey fingers.

Miriam chuckled, impressed.

Brahm wound through the marketplace, stopping first at an egg and chicken vendor. He grabbed three eggs, balancing them in one hand while paying the man a few coins with the other, then nestled the eggs in his coat pocket. He continued to a dairy stall and bought a small block of butter wrapped in wax paper, which he also tucked away. Though he was short flour, Miriam imagined his pockets filled with the ingredients for a cake, mixing together as he walked in the hot Jerusalem afternoon, fully baked in time for a night coffee. He next turned to a flower stall and bought a small bundle, holding them upside down as he walked away. Miriam had noticed flowers in the apartment recently. She'd asked her mother where they came from, but her mother hadn't replied, just pointed outside, where flowers grow.

Suddenly Brahm turned and walked toward Miriam. Again, she went still, assuming there would be a confrontation. He must have noticed her following him, if not from the train station, at least from the news shop, or if not from there, maybe from the warbat stall. He strode straight toward her as she stared ahead blankly, unsure what she would say if he questioned her. Maybe she would use her trick of speaking in Arabic, pretending she knew no Hebrew. But he was clearly Moroccan; it wouldn't work. No matter. Nothing could be said, no explanation given—because she had none. As she stood, trying to formulate a defense, he swept past her, glancing in her direction but not really registering her. For a second Miriam wondered how this was possible. He had winked at her before, offered her a cigarette. She had recognized him from their Kiryat HaYovel apartment, even recalling him in Morocco years earlier. How had he never really *seen* her? How had he never noticed?

Miriam broke from her momentary trance and again trailed Brahm as he retraced his previous steps, heading in the direction of Mea Shearim. He walked along Jaffa Street this time, past the Sunrise Synagogue. Stopping for a moment in front of the synagogue, he looked up at the massive sundial, and Miriam assumed he noted the time. He resumed walking at a faster pace, and she wondered where he needed to be. When Brahm cut through a narrow alley heading north, Miriam gave up trying to keep a distance. No one else was in the alley, but she felt invisible to him. Entering Mea Shearim—again Miriam noted no gate marked the entrance, but the streets were suddenly dense with people walking in twos and threes by gender— he approached a small watchmaker shop. The door was surrounded by two large window clocks, one in the shape of the sun with its rays, and one the moon. Between them stood Brahm. Beyond him Miriam saw a large, be-spectacled man look up momentarily from behind a counter, eye Brahm for two full seconds, before returning to his crooked position. Brahm disap-peared behind a curtain, giving Miriam a glimpse of ascending stone steps as he flipped the cloth aside.

She couldn't understand the pattern. A train station, the news shop, the ultra-orthodox neighborhood, the black door, the groceries and the flowers, and then the backtracking to a watch shop? The man made no sense. Was this part of a job? Had he actually seen her and been leading her around? Or was he trying to confuse another follower that she herself had not seen? Looking around carefully, Miriam couldn't remember precisely why she'd fallen in behind Brahm, but it was getting late and she still had the Old City to see.

Brahm was always surprised that the most religious neighborhoods had the best and cheapest brothels. The trick was finding them. He'd asked his associates when he first arrived in Israel, knowing Sharona did not like to talk of the business. Finally, a friend told him about the "watch shop" in Mea Shearim. The first time Brahm saw the place, he thought he was being fooled, that someone figured it was funny to send him hot to a cold spot. But when he entered, he knew; he could sense it with his entire being. He'd asked his friend why there were all the watches in the windows, and his friend said it was like the old Yiddish joke about the mohel who hung watches in his window. *Because*, the man explained in his best squeeze, *what should such a business hang in the windows?*

When Brahm arrived at the top of the steps, he saw the woman who ran the upstairs sitting on the couch knitting yarmulkes. She yelled to the hallways something about a zayan, and then added that he brought flowers. Brahm checked the eggs in his pocket, still unbroken. When a woman came out of the bedroom and looked at him, he held the flowers upright, and she waved him in.

Miriam headed east from the neighborhood. The Old City began to peek out from behind buildings and through the openings of streets. She had a plan. When she got to the city, she wanted to see the Tower of David first, then the Kotel, then the ancient market, and then go up to the Al-Aqsa Mosque, where the Temple once stood. She'd heard so many stories and myths about each of these places. At the massive squared boulders of the Kotel, you could feel the trembling of generations through the seams. At the markets, you could taste pomegranates on streets walked by Abraham and Isaac. At the Tower of David, you could sense Jewish history, a long line of kings and prophets stretching back thousands of years. And the fruit of the orchard at the Temple Mount was from the same trees that scouts plucked it from when Moshe Rabbenu sent them to describe the land for the newly freed Hebrew slaves.

The city was visible in the near distance, but inaccessible to Israelis except at one point. Everyone knew the Mandelbaum Gate. It was whispered in plans and stated as excuse, but she had never seen it depicted. She'd seen photos and drawings of the other gates—the Gate of Mercy, the Flower Gate, the Damascus Gate, the Lion Gate, the Zion Gate, the Yafo Gate, and the one she thought of most, the Maghrebi Gate, which some referred to as the Dung Gate. Each was an intricately carved ancient opening in the fortress, if one could get to them. But the Mandelbaum Gate was the key to the entirety of the Old City—the one gate that led to seven.

When Brahm left the watch shop, he felt lighter. He checked his coat pockets again. Eggs still unbroken. Butter intact. He held the flowers upside down, looked back at the watches in the window to check the time, and headed west from Mea Shearim. He took no unnecessary turns and made no unnecessary stops, but pushed through the streets as the sun started to set before him.

Miriam noticed the streets narrowing and converging, army vehicles stopped at random angles. In front of her loomed the Tower of David, and in front of it a hand-lettered sign on wooden stakes that announced in Hebrew, *Danger! Enemy territory ahead. No Passage!* Beneath it, the sign read in Arabic, *Danger! The border is ahead. No Passage.* She wondered why the difference. Turning, Miriam saw two buildings, between which seemed to be a lot of movement and people. She walked toward the seam between the structures. The road was filled with giant cement cones that rose up unnaturally from the ground. To their sides were rolls of barbed wire that looked as if they'd just been left there after someone forgot to fully unspool them. Miriam wound her way between it all. A few soldiers stood by a shack in the middle of the road, smoking and chatting, generally appearing bored. As Miriam tried to pass between them without them noticing, one turned to her, pushed his gun to his side to keep it out of the way, and said "darkon" in a tone that lacked any urgency. Miriam knew he wanted her passport. She handed him her old French identification book. He looked at the photo, held it up to her face to compare. Ten years stretched between the photo and the face, but he seemed satisfied she was a Christian named Perla. He started flipping through the pages, going forward once, backward, and then forward again. "Visa?"

"Lo," Miriam replied. "Perla."

The soldier looked at the name and laughed.

He was only a few years older than Miriam, a boy in other contexts.

"Lechi mipo," he said, with a tilt and a point of his head.

Miriam stood unmoving, unsure what to do.

The soldier, assuming she didn't understand Hebrew, held his arm up, his gun falling the length of the strap and snapping to a stop as he said in a thick Israeli accent, "Go from here! Home!"

Massouda sat at a neighbor's table, drinking a glass of hot water packed with fresh mint leaves and sugar. She sipped it slowly as the woman told her about the previous night. Massouda let her speak, never interrupting, as the neighbor conveyed that her children were donkeys—three of them, all girls—and they followed the watermelon truck around as it delivered overripe melons to each apartment in the neighborhood. At first, the woman had been content with the situation, but as the truck came by her apartment, her donkey daughters in tow, it left no melon for her. She yelled out to the truck, saying she had paid but got no fruit in return. She could not catch up with it or get its attention.

The neighbor paused her narrative and asked Massouda what she thought.

Massouda had listened to so many dreams that she'd become adept at interpreting them. She knew how to draw the future out of stories like pus from a wound. She realized that people could already see the future; they were just illiterate to its language. Massouda knew the elements and the symbols, as well as the people, and she had to be right, because she continued to be asked to read their dreams.

Massouda told her neighbor what it meant, all of it. More bad than good, if one was balancing such things. Her daughters were doomed. Her family would be cut short. Her dreams would not come to fruition. Massouda finished her tea and gestured for another glass.

Brahm walked into Massouda's unlocked apartment. He put the flowers in an old milk jug but neglected to fill it with water. He then put the butter and eggs in the sink where it was cool and looked around for the sugar. There had to be sugar if she was to bake him a cake, unless it was date cake. His mouth watering at the thought, Brahm went out to the apartment balcony and lit a cigarette. He saw a dog tied to a donkey in the courtyard and thought it the most beautiful thing he'd ever witnessed. What a friendship, Brahm thought, for good and bad. Smoke entered his eyes, and he teared up for a moment. Turning to leave, Brahm scratched himself and went down the steps into the courtyard.

The apartment was empty when Massouda came home. She entered through the kitchen and saw the flowers in the jug and eggs and butter in the sink. She pulled out the flowers, filled the jug with water and submerged the stems, then leaned in to sniff the blooms; they smelled like the market. Walking into the salon, she sucked at her teeth as if calling an unseen cat. In the corner was a small empty dish that Massouda picked up. She was happy to see it was empty, though she hadn't witnessed the food being eaten. She took the butter and eggs from the sink and placed them in the dish, uttering an inaudible prayer. She then set the dish back in the corner, where she knew the snake would look for it and find sustenance. She heard her mother's voice. She heard her grandmother's voice. She heard all her ancestors' voices in her head, telling her to feed the snake and keep it happy. *Never have an unhappy snake in your home.*

LAWRENCE

1969

Lillian had never quite come to terms with buying a house beneath a tower. The structure rose from the highest point of the hill, in a neighborhood named after it. Tower Hill overlooked the city, and Lillian worried about slippery roads in the winter. When she fretted aloud, George reminded her that she rarely drove in any season, so it wouldn't be a problem. Lillian then pointed out that if the tower fell, it would crush the house and the children. George went to the municipal archives, conducted comprehensive research on the tower, and explained that it had been in place since 1896 and had never had any structural issues. But it was like a prison camp tower, Lillian explained, with gunrests rising up its sides. And why had their families left Europe to live in the shadow of such a terrifying carceral tower? George pointed to the reservoir and suggested that bodies of water could have a calming effect. Lillian hated being told to calm down, so George chose his words carefully.

The house was centrally located for what mattered in their lives. The Jewish school where George served as principal and Lillian worked as a part-time typist was less than a mile away, and the synagogue where the family went on Shabbat was attached to the school. In the other direction, just down the hill, was Greenburg's kosher grocery, beside Marcus Miller's kosher butchery. Lillian disliked Mr. Miller and found it hard to hide her disdain. She would ask the boys to pick up meat for her, but they would jokingly call the shop *Marcus's Carcasses*, and the sound of their persistent laughter agitated her, so Lillian rarely cooked meat that did not come from a can. George noticed, but never remarked on the disappearance of fresh meat in the household.

Misha and Benny were walking home from school, pushing their way up the hill, happy to have successfully avoided walking with their brother Solomon. He'd become unbearable since his birthday was drawn on the draft lottery. Every day, he worried about a different aspect of joining the army, from the group showers to being shipped to a spot in the jungle where he'd be shot. Walking up the hill with him, as he panted and kvetched about the dangers of fighting, was hard for Misha to stomach. At one point, Benny told Solomon that *kvetch* meant *squeeze*. It angered Solomon, but now when he spoke about the war, Misha and Benny would refer to it as the Vietnam *squeeze*. They also joked that *kvetching* was whining, and wine was made by the squeeze. That's why it was called *wine*. In truth, Misha was sickened by Solomon's reaction to the draft, and his shameless fear had persuaded Misha to enlist in the Israeli Defense Forces as soon as he could—which meant as soon as he could talk to his parents about the idea.

At a tree midway up the hill, Benny and Misha stopped to look down and up. Benny continued the conversation from lower in their walk.

"I think the piece was at least well written."

"Which one? The one pro or against?"

Benny was the editor of the school newspaper and had just learned he'd been suspended from the paper for printing a debate concerning the school dress code. He'd written both pieces but was suspended for the article objecting to the dress code. Benny didn't understand how arguing against gray slacks and white shirts was so controversial and joked that *Big Pants* was trying to silence him. Misha replied that he believed they were called *Huskies*.

"Maybe," Benny proposed, "you could tell Imma and Abba about your plan to enlist in the IDF first. That might take some of the mustard off my news."

"Or I could just buy an ad in the next edition of the Lawrencian that says in big letters, NEXT WEEK'S DEBATE: VIETNAM!"

"But on our publishing schedule, that would take two weeks."

"You're right, Benny. That's impractical. I guess I should talk to them. Help bury the news of your war with the Huskies."

At home, Lillian was darting from one thing to another. Fixing the tablecloth and then shuffling in her house shoes down the hallway to the bathroom to make sure the mats and towels were properly placed. Then back to the tablecloth to make another adjustment. Still on her mental list were the windows, which needed to be cleaned and opened the right amount; the plastic on the sofa, which needed to be wiped with a warm wet cloth to remove the present streaks and leave fresh streaks of dried water; and her desk, which needed to be checked to make sure everything was in place. Chaos was always creeping in, and Lillian fought it with a constant attention to order.

When the boys arrived, she rushed to meet them because it was meat day. "Did you pick up the chicken like I asked?" she said before they'd gotten past the door.

"I thought Solomon was going to get it. He had the money, and he's the one who gets out early," Misha said.

"He didn't get anything. And he has things to worry about. You know that. I know you know that." Lillian was suddenly on the verge of tears. "And he has that girlfriend, Layla. And they may get married soon. So you know I'll have to change my name. Maybe Chemda. A mother and daughter shouldn't have the same name. It's unnatural." Lillian was tearing up.

"But Imma," Benny said, "she won't be your daughter if she marries Solomon, right? She'll be your daughter-in-law. That's different. And Layla is already a different name from Lillian."

Lillian pulled an old folded handkerchief from her sleeve. "Are you saying I'm lying?" She blew her nose loudly. "Okay, I'm lying. You're always right, and I'm always wrong."

"No, Imma. That's not what I said. . . ."

"It's not what Benny meant, Imma," Misha cut in. "But he can get that chicken now."

Misha pulled a few dollars from his pocket and pushed it into Benny's hand. "Here, go down to Marcus's Carc . . . down to Marcus's for Imma, okay?" Misha then turned to his mother. "Imma, can I help you clean?"

"Why should you want to help me? You've never helped me before. Do you think I can't do it?"

"Please, Imma. I just want to help. And maybe we can talk while we clean."

Misha walked to the table and readjusted the plastic cover over the tablecloth. Lillian rushed over to the other side of the table and yanked and shifted it back in the other direction.

"Imma, you know how Solomon might get drafted? Well, I was thinking . . ."

"No. No. He's not getting drafted. He is going to marry Layla and go to college. Become a scholar like his grandfather—you know he was the secretary to the Chafetz Chaim. He's a great scholar. When he marries Layla, I will change my name to Chemda. That's the natural order of things."

"Yes, well, I was thinking about what I should do, because even though I'm a year younger, my birthday is near Solomon's. I don't feel comfortable running away from the fight, but I don't want to fight in an unjust war like Vietnam, so I was thinking maybe I'll enlist with the IDF. . . ."

"That's fine." Lillian was shifting items beneath a clear plastic cover on her desk. Between the plastic and wood, she kept some important notes and photos, visible but untouchable. She wouldn't talk about these or respond if asked. Underneath one note, Misha could see the yellow and black of an old French armband that read JUIF, with a star around the word. Misha had tried to ask each of his parents about the star and if the armband had been theirs during the war. Each simply responded *No* before turning away.

Now Misha couldn't believe his mother had agreed so easily. "You're really okay with it?" he asked. "With me enlisting in the Israeli military?'

"Why shouldn't I be?" Lillian appeared preoccupied.

"Great," Misha began, relieved by the lack of tears or yelling. "I've been in touch with the IDF, and they want me to do an ulpan before starting, but I'm already pretty good at Hebrew, so I was thinking maybe I could just stay with Saba. I remember meeting him when I was a kid in Tsfat, and I know he's in Yavneh. . . . Do you think you could contact him and see if that would be all right?"

"Your grandfather? He's a great scholar. The secretary to the Chafetz Chaim. He has written six books on marriage and divorce. One of them has an introduction by the Chief Rabbi of Israel. Do you know how difficult that is to get? He is recognized all over the world as a great scholar."

"I've heard. But do you think it would be all right if I stayed with him when I arrive in Israel?"

"Why shouldn't it be?"

"I don't know. I just wanted to make sure. And, um, my Hebrew is pretty good, but I'll need some practice. Does he speak English at all?"

"Of course. Why shouldn't he? He was rabbi of a big synagogue in Brooklyn before making Aliyah to Eretz Yisrael."

"That's right. I always think of him as just Israeli. I forget that he's from somewhere else."

"He's the rosh yeshiva in Yavneh. *Yavneh.* You know what that means. He's a great scholar."

Suddenly Israel felt real to Misha. It had been an excuse, then an idea, a dream, then a conversation. Now it was a plan, taking shape.

Later that evening, he found his father in his usual place, sitting on the sofa reading a book. Misha knew that though his mother and father had spent time together that day, and they'd all had dinner together, she had not discussed Israel with him. His parents mostly cohabitated in silence or with his mother talking at his father's silence. His father no longer even let out occasional affirmations or grunts in response, but he paid attention. He preferred his silence and imposed it on whatever room he was in. Misha always felt bad for inflicting sound on him; each time, his father looked pained the moment someone spoke.

"Abba?"

His father glanced up from his book and said nothing, waiting.

Misha tried to make out the book's title, but he couldn't determine the language. He thought perhaps Turkish.

"Abba, I was thinking I would pack my schedule for the upcoming semesters, graduate early, and then enlist in the Israeli Defense Forces." Misha had practiced the words several times, and they came out perfectly.

His father set down the book and looked up with his whole face.

"I was just thinking that Israel needs us to fight—the true Zionists who truly care and are willing to pick up arms with their fellow Jews, arm in arm. And, you know, if I'm to fight a war, let it be a just war."

"That is an idea," his father remarked with his usual suspicion, giving nothing away.

"Imma already said yes. But, you know, I wanted to ask you about your time during World War Two. I know we've kind of talked a bit about it, not much, and since I'll be going to fight probably, I was just wondering what you did during the war. I could maybe learn from your experiences."

"Me? I worked on a rabbit farm in an area that saw no fighting. There's nothing to learn."

Misha had respect for his father, but less so every time he learned new details. How had he raised rabbits while Jews were being exterminated? Misha felt a passion to fight for Jews; why hadn't his father possessed the same passion? How was he not ashamed of what he'd done, or *hadn't done*? He said the words *rabbit farm* so casually, as if it were just a normal job in normal times.

"What did you do while you were there? Did you know how to farm rabbits?" Misha had read about Israel and the dignity of farming. It was no longer a goyische enterprise, but essential for the future of the self-sustaining Jew. Maybe his father had helped lay that groundwork.

"No. I don't know farming from fighting. I just did what was asked of me."

Silence grew between them. His father was comfortable in the silence, and Misha tried to go along, but he hated it. He tried to wait, to give his father time to ask more about his son's plans. Even if his father had never fought, Misha thought, he could at least take an interest in those willing to act. But a moment became two, became a minute that bore the weight of the moment.

"Abba, do you have any thoughts about my plans? Any advice?"

His father considered the question for another painful stretch of time. Finally, he said, "When you go to Israel, you are going to find a lot of synagogues. You may find yourself going into a variety of such synagogues, out of curiosity or to make a minyan, which is a great mitzvah. And that is fine. That is good. But never go into a mason's synagogue."

Misha frowned. "A mason's synagogue? Like stone masons?"

"A mason's synagogue. Listen to what I am saying. Do not ever step foot in one. Not even for a minute. Not even to make a minyan."

Misha thought his father was surely joking, and he tried to figure out the arcane humor. Masons worked with stones. Maybe don't get stoned; don't experiment with drugs? *Mason* meant *the dead* in Yiddish, but that was a stretch. Plus, his father never joked, and he never spoke to them in Yiddish. He said it was a dead language or a language of the dead; Misha couldn't recall the exact wording.

"Okay," he said. "No synagogues run by masons. Anything else?"

George let the question sink in, waited, and then replied, "No."

Clearly his father had nothing more to give. Perhaps he was ashamed. Misha was going to go to Israel to take risks and fight and maybe die for the Jewish cause. His father knew nothing of such things. He couldn't tell him not to go, because he couldn't even begin to imagine what being in danger or fighting might mean. And he couldn't give him advice on what to expect because this was reality, and his father lived in a world of words, of books. His father and his generation let countless Jews die and just watched, farming rabbits, pretending and submitting. What would such a man know of real struggle? Unless, of course, he read it in a book, on the sofa, in Turkish.

Misha and Benny shared a bedroom, and that night Benny asked Misha if he was really going to Israel to fight. Misha said yes, he was planning to. Benny told him he thought Misha was brave and confided that he himself would probably go to college. Benny was two years younger but had accelerated through the grades and was in the same class as Misha.

"I actually applied and got into Harvard, with a full scholarship," Benny admitted.

"That's amazing!" Misha marveled. "Especially for a Jew."

"But on my application, I put that my middle name was Shadrach. They send you a certificate when you get accepted, and now my certificate says Benjamin Shadrach Mazar."

Misha snorted. "Why Shadrach?"

"As a joke." Benny shrugged.

"But what's the joke?"

"My middle name is not Shadrach."

"No, I know," said Misha impatiently. "But why Shadrach?"

"He had two brothers, like me, one of which was named Mishael. And he was thrown into the fire but not destroyed," said Benny. "And I don't have a middle name. Solomon and you do. But me? No one could be bothered."

BEIT GUVRIN

1972

"Did you know that the Romans named this area Eleutheropolis?" Misha said to his cellmate, Sami, breaking the morning silence. "After the fall of the city during the revolt against the Romans. The City of Free Men, it means. Kind of ironic, considering our situation, huh?"

"How do you know such things?" Sami replied. He was sitting on his bunk in the stone block cell that he shared with Misha, a blanket—one Misha knew to be itchy—draped over his legs.

"I read. What else is there to do out here besides military drills?" said Misha, rising from his own bunk and walking a couple of steps toward Sami. "A couple of weeks ago I had to set up a checkpoint to find some farmer's stolen cow. I was stopping all these little Volkswagens and looking in their trunks."

"Did you find it, Oojie?" Sami asked, using the nickname Misha had been given upon arriving in Israel.

Misha had never quite understood the name, but it seemed that someone had taken the *sh* sound, turned it into a Sephardic *j* sound, and then built a name around it. He'd tried to resist, explaining that Misha was short for Mishael, so it was already a diminutive sobriquet. Then Misha had to explain what *sobriquet* meant. As a result, he became *Oojie La La* for a while, but luckily the mockery of his French fanciness had fallen away, leaving him just plain Oojie.

"Unfortunately, no," he told Sami. "The cow is still at large."

"There are things to do here besides read. You could go to the orchard with the other guys. See the girls who work there. Unload some of your hard-earned money."

"Not me," Misha said with distaste. "My commanding officer, Zazi, you know him? He said last time he went to the orchard, the whore he was with was eating sunflower seeds the whole time they were together. Then, when he was done, she remarked that he discharged more semen than she had ever seen. And Zazi was so proud, because as a whore, she had been with hundreds of guys, but he was the best."

Sami smirked. "The best? Is that what *she* said?"

"No. Not at all." Misha chuckled. "I don't know how one thing means the other."

"And Zazi, he's the one you hit?" Sami asked.

Misha's eyebrows flew up. He grinned. "You heard about that?"

"Stories like that don't stay hidden. Is it true what happened?"

"What did you hear?" Oojie asked, wondering about his legend.

"Nothing, really," Sami said with a shrug.

"Well," said Misha, leaning against the cell wall, "Zazi and I were on patrol over on the ridge, and we were taking a break. So there we are, and Zazi is doing his usual bragging, you know, about the women he has been with and how tough he is, showing his muscles. And in the distance, we see something. He tells me to look through the binoculars. So I look, and it's just an old shepherd with a small flock. An Arab shepherd. Not Druze like you, but proper Arab.

"Zazi gets real excited and picks up his rifle and says he's going to put a scare into the old Arab. I tried to joke, telling him the guy wasn't worth it, but he starts talking about how he's going to make this old schvartze dance, you know, using the Yiddish word for *black*."

"I know the word," Sami said dryly.

"Sure. Sorry."

"And did he shoot at him?" Sami asked with interest. "Was the shepherd all right?"

"Zazi picked up the gun and started looking into the scope. I was yelling at him to stop, but I think that was just getting him more excited. I could tell he was going to shoot, and from that distance, even if he wasn't trying to, he could accidentally hit the shepherd or even one of his sheep. But Zazi is a really big guy, and I couldn't just push him, you know? So I cracked him in the head with the butt of my rifle."

Sami nodded as if that confirmed what he'd heard. "And here you are." He indicated their cell with a flourish of his hand.

"Yes. Zazi got a nasty bruise and some infirmity leave. And I got twenty-one days in lockup here with you." Misha paused to allow for questions. None came. He cleared his throat. "So, what are you in for?"

"Me?" Sami widened his eyes in an expression of exaggerated innocence. "I was accused of passing gas before my commanding officer."

Misha tried to restrain his laughter. He pretended to misunderstand. "What do you mean *before*? Like *before* he passed gas?"

Sami grinned. "No, no. Before. In front of."

"Is that a violation of some rule?"

Pursing his lips like he'd tasted something sour, Sami said, "Apparently it is an old Ottoman rule the British adopted and that made its way into the IDF."

Misha shook his head, marveling. "I've never heard of such a thing."

"My commanding officer said it was a rule made by Arabs and applied to Arabs. But you know the Turks are not Arabs."

"Yeah, sure. And did you know about the rule before you . . . you know?"

"No. And I did not do it. Nor do I know who did, or even how such a determination is made. But they decided it was me, and I received thirty days as a result."

"Thirty days? For *that*?" Unthinkingly, Misha pointed toward Sami's back end. "Miriam—you know Miriam in the administrative corps? The cute Moroccan woman? I don't think she has spent a night on base in four months, and she has never been punished. And you get thirty days for farting."

Sami raised a hand in protest. "As I said, it was not . . ."

"Right. *Allegedly* farting. You have to admit that's funny."

"I admit nothing!" Sami yelled.

They both laughed.

After a moment, Misha said, "You know I wrote all over my mattress in Arabic to keep Shmuelly from stealing it while I'm in here."

"That was you?"

"Yeah." Misha was proud of this—both for being able to write in Arabic and for his ingenious plan. "Everyone is always stealing everything around here, especially Shmuelly. And he has every sexually transmitted disease imaginable. I didn't want him anywhere near my mattress."

"Yes. You wrote, *Danger, do not steal this sleep conveyance* all over it."

"Oh, you heard about it?" Oojie was again surprised at how word spread. Perhaps he really *was* a legend. "But I meant *mattress*. I thought that was the word I used."

"I heard about this," Sami said, "when I got fined for writing on a mattress. Defacing of IDF property."

"Wait, why did you get fined? It was my mattress!"

"I suppose they thought to blame the Arab for writing in Arabic."

Misha was abashed. It had never occurred to him that someone else might be blamed. "I'm . . . I'm sorry. I didn't . . ."

"Why did you write in Arabic?" Sami asked calmly, as though he'd accustomed himself to false accusations.

"I couldn't write in Hebrew, because that wouldn't mark it as someone else's property. I needed to write in a language that Shmuelly and the rest didn't know, because obviously I couldn't sign it. You know, because of the penalty for defacing army property."

"So why not write in English? No one here speaks it. You could have written Shakespeare."

"You know, that never crossed my mind. I, uh . . ."

A sergeant stepped up to the cell and said in a jeering tone, "Listen to you two fools, sitting here trading war stories like you've done something." The sergeant was tasked with checking on them, but rarely engaged them except to taunt and needle them.

"And you, Oojie, you're the biggest fool of all," he said. "You come here from America and strut around the base like you own the place. You learn Arabic and say how good and fine Arabs are and how we should get to know them. Their history. Their food. On and on.

"No offense, Sami. You're Druze. That's different. You're one of the good ones. When you're not farting in the captain's face." He laughed a mocking laugh.

"But you, Oojie. Always talking about your genius grandfather, the great rebbe." The sergeant waved his palms in the air to signify saintliness. *"Did you know that he wrote six books? And that orange grove of his: so beautiful. Such sweet smells! Like heaven on earth.*

"It was getting on my nerves, so I asked around about him—talked to some of the old timers who have been fighting since before you were born. And I found out some interesting things. You ever wonder how he got that land, that *sweet, sweet* orange grove?"

Misha wanted to answer, to snap out a retort, but realized he'd only known the land with his grandfather on it. Rav Minsky was meant for Yavneh, and it for him. Misha could not imagine it otherwise.

"No? Nothing?" the sergeant asked rhetorically. "Maybe you should ask him and tell your new friend here what you find out. Just ask him how a poor rebbe—even one with six whole books that probably made him sixty lira—gets a couple hundred acres of prime farmland near the sea. You know what, that's an order. Next time you get leave, you go to Yavneh and sit down with the great rebbe and get some answers, then you find me, and you find your friend here, and report what you learned."

With a dismissive gesture, the sergeant walked away.

"What is he talking about?" Sami asked. "What orange grove?"

Misha scowled. "He's just being a jerk."

"I don't know. He was pretty specific."

"I'm sure it's nothing," Misha said, thinking of Yavneh. When he'd first arrived in Israel, he'd spent the summer there, and he hadn't noticed anything odd. During the day, he learned at the yeshiva, watching his grandfather studying silently and teaching groups of boys. Everything the man did was intense and intentional.

Misha had also met the family who worked the land. A large Arab family that had bonfires in the evenings, sometimes grilling meat over an open flame. He'd befriended one of the daughters, Dima, who was his age and had taught him the Arabic alphabet and proper pronunciation. They'd had long talks—about his plan to go to a Hindu ashram after the military and her plan to become a nurse. Misha joked that India needed nurses, and they could go together. She replied that she liked eating meat too much to live in India. Misha told her about some of his favorite books, mostly classics, *The Odyssey, Lysistrata, Gargantua*, and she talked about erotic pre-Islamic poetry and the epic *Shahnameh*. One afternoon he'd attempted an Arabic translation of one of his favorite quotes from *Antigone* for her, and that evening, by the fire, read it aloud: *la shay' yadkhul ealam albashar bidun laena.* Dima seemed confused, either by the translation or his accent, so he repeated it in Hebrew: *shum davar atzoom lo nichnas la'olamam bnai hatmoota bli clala.* For good measure, he repeated it once more in English, where he thought it sounded best: *nothing vast enters the world of mortals without a curse.* Dima asked him what it meant and why he liked it. He explained it was like Kant's quote that *out of the crooked timber of humanity, no straight thing was ever made,* and it meant that nothing was simple or painless, and that we were fallible. That there are ghosts everywhere.

It had been a wonderful evening.

The sergeant was just bullshitting, Misha decided now. There was nothing wrong at Yavneh.

The cell was quiet again. Sami and Misha each sat on their cots, staring off toward the single window that brought in light but no air. The words of the sergeant seemed to linger, making the silence uncomfortable.

Finally, Sami spoke. "Do you know what this place used to be called?"

"Eleutheropolis. Remember? I told you."

"No, not two thousand years ago. Thirty years ago."

Misha thought for a moment. "No. I hadn't heard of . . ."

"Bayt Jibrin. You know what that means, right? You know the language?"

"Bayt. House. And Jibrin. Strong?"

"More than that. Powerful. House of the Powerful."

LAWRENCE, MA
Liebe / Lillian / Chemda (1973)

IV

TEL AVIV
Miriam / Perla (1973)
Misha / Oojie (1973)

JERUSALEM
George / Charny Jook (1973)
Liebe / Lillian / Chemda (1973)
Massouda (1973)
Miriam / Perla (1973)
Misha / Oojie (1973)

YAVNEH
Misha / Oojie (1973)
Rav Minsky (1973)

TU BISHVAT

1973

Head and shoulders wrapped in a series of shawls, Massouda rocked back and forth rapidly. One hand was clutching the Wall, as if it were propping her up and she dared not let it go for even an instant. At least twice a week, Massouda made the long uphill journey to the Wall, touched it, clutched it, kissed it with eyes closed—embracing it with everything she had. Occasionally, she would let out a shriek, a cry, a moan as the power of the Wall entered her. The other women's sounds punctuated hers, their energy in union, all pushing and being supported by this ancient limestone.

Standing beside her, Miriam was similarly covered, but looking more at her mother than the massive stones. She rarely came with her mother to the Old City, but she had today in celebration of Tu Bishvat. On the way to the city, they had passed cypress, cedar, olive, and eucalyptus, and at each tree Miriam grabbed a leaf, touched a branch, or rubbed the bark in gentle recognition.

They were standing where Moroccans had stood for centuries, in the shadow of a twice displaced quarter. On the day the Old City had been conquered in 1967, Miriam had been close by. She'd rushed through the Dung Gate and into the Maghrebi Quarter, where an ancient shantytown of Moroccans buzzed with life. Turning through the alleys of the quarter, she stopped to drink and wash her face at the fountains before arriving at the Western Wall. The alley in front of the Wall was filled with people, Moroccans and Jews and Israeli soldiers, each pressing and being pressed up against the Wall, some for the first time, and the first members of their families for generations.

Now Miriam relaxed near the same spot, in an expansive courtyard that had once bustled with her people. As soon as the city was captured, the neighborhood had been razed, bulldozed into a modern flat oblivion, to make space for the prayers. Days after the war, when Miriam had returned with her mother, excited to show her both the Wall and how she'd discovered a mini Casablanca, she found only emptiness. The courtyard where the Maghrebi Quarter had stood for centuries felt like a concrete grave, an open sore at the foot of the remaining wall of the Temple.

"Imma," Miriam said, interrupting her mother's prayers. "What about that one?" She pointed at a group of boys being bar mitzvahed in bulk. "He looks like he might make a good husband."

Massouda brought her hand over her eyes to deflect the sun. "The boy? Over there?"

"He's thirteen. He'll be a man in about fifteen minutes."

Massouda laughed despite herself, forgetting the holiness of the place. When she stopped, she replied, "But he's a voos-voos."

Miriam furrowed her brow. "A *voos-voos*? What's a *voos-voos*?"

"You know." Massouda waved a hand, trying to find words in her limited vocabulary. "The Jews from Poland. The Ashkenazim."

"Oh." Miriam pursed her lips to hide a smile. "Where did you get voos-voos?"

"That's what they're called. You know, because they're always going around saying voos this and voos that. It's Yiddish, I think."

Miriam couldn't control her laughter. "You're just making up words. They're Ashkenazim. You can't just call someone something and act like everyone knows it."

"I don't know what you're talking about," Massouda said mischievously. "But why can't you go for a franke? They're everywhere in our neighborhood."

"A franke?" Miriam repeated incredulously. "What's a franke?"

"You know. A fronk. A shluch." Massouda frowned at Miriam's confusion. "An Arab Jew. From Morocco."

"Imma!" Once more, Miriam laughed loudly. "Again, you can't just make up new words."

"These are the words I use." Massouda protested. "People understand what I'm saying. That's what's important."

"Okay." Miriam showed her palms in surrender. "But why should I go for a fronk? A shluch. How are they going to get me out of here? I want to go to Europe or America. A fronk is going to take me to Hamifletzet and tell me we're in Prague as he tries to kiss my neck like a hungry beast. Or even worse. I'll end up with an arsee parsee! You see, I can make up words too."

Massouda chuckled, delighted at the way Miriam described the world. They stood laughing among the prayers until a nearby rabbi shushed them.

"Booba," Massouda whispered the pet name she used for all her children. "Why do you want so much to move away from your family? After all we did to get here?"

Miriam moved closer to her mother and explained in a low voice, "It's not the family I want to get away from. It's Israel. I don't understand why everyone rushes over here, what they expect to find. I don't know why we came over. I liked Casablanca."

"You didn't know Casa. You were a child. After your father died, there was nothing for us there anymore."

Miriam shook her head. "We had family. I remember all my uncles and aunts and cousins on Sidi Fatah. And we had the souk and the neighborhood. And we had magic in Morocco. We abandoned our magic when we left. And we left for what? Remember how people would talk of making Aliyah, saying *Anoo aleenu artza leheevnot veleheechvot—We came to Israel to build and to be built*—like it was some kind of prayer?"

"Yes, of course. It's beautiful."

"Well, you know what the boys in the army say? *Anoo aleenu artza lidfoke et habanot ba—We came to Israel to screw the girls here.* Like it's a joke."

Massouda scowled. "That is not funny."

"No. Not at all! But it feels exactly like the difference between what we were promised and what we found."

"There is nothing in Morocco," Massouda said stubbornly. "All the family left after us. Either to come here or to Europe."

"Not all the family left. Baba is still there . . . in the ground. And Nis . . ." Miriam paused at Massouda's sharp look. "Besides," she went on. "Israel doesn't even want us, the way they treat Moroccans."

"Tfoot, Tfoot, Tfoot! What are you talking about?"

"Look where they put us, in the immigrant tents and apartments."

"But we are immigrants."

"And look what they did to the Maghrebi Quarter. This used to be a neighborhood filled with Moroccans since . . . forever. A mini Casa. And they just bulldozed it into nothing at the first opportunity."

"I'm sure Israel had a good reason. I wasn't here. Maybe it was necessary."

"And what about me?" Miriam persisted. "Why did I have to go to Marseille? The adoption."

"It was just the way it was." Massouda shrugged, but defensiveness crept into her voice as she continued. "It was the only way to do it. You know I didn't want to, but . . ."

"No, I know, Imma. That's not what I'm saying. I am not angry with you. And the French couple were very nice. But why did Israel require it?"

"It was just me and many children. It is hard for a young country to take in so many people who were not working. You have to see it from Israel's view. It wasn't because we were Moroccan."

"Pshh, of course it was. Have you been to Mea Shearim and seen the Ashkenazi families there? They were welcomed with open arms, and they each have fifteen kids. One for every month, plus a few extras for the leap years."

Massouda laughed at the description.

"I don't know who I am here," Miriam stated simply, almost mournfully, and Massouda sobered.

"Actually, I do know what I am," Miriam corrected, "but everyone acts like it's a lie."

"Miriam . . ." Massouda reached out to stroke her daughter's hand. "What are you talking about?"

"We're Moroccan. That's who we are, but here they call us Sephardi, meaning Spanish. We're not from Spain. I don't speak Spanish. I don't look Spanish. Why do they call us that?"

"History. A lot of Jews went to Morocco hundreds of years ago from Spain."

"But we didn't come from Spain. Baba was Arab, you're Amazigh, yes?

"Our family, yes. From the Atlas. But many came from Spain originally."

"I thought all Jews came from Israel originally?" Miriam argued.

"Yes, originally. But they lived in Spain."

"But they also lived in Morocco. We lived in Morocco. So why not just call us Moroccans or Arabs or Amazigh?"

"Why are you making trouble? It's just words. We're here now," Massouda said firmly. "That's what matters."

"What matters is that every day they call me something I know I'm not.

And every day they say that here is something I don't see. Some days I feel lost or crazy."

"Oh, Miriam." Massouda lowered her head as if it had suddenly become heavy.

Seeing her mother's sorrow, Miriam clasped her hand. "Imma, I'm not complaining. I just want to try somewhere new, where I feel at home. Like you did. You and Brahm can have Israel."

Massouda's head shot up. "What does Brahm have to do with it?"

"Nothing really. I'm just saying . . ."

"He had nothing to do with us making Aliyah. We barely knew him in Casa, and your father—may his memory be a blessing—did not know him at all. It was a heart attack and we had to move. . . ."

"Yes, of course," said Miriam, puzzled by her mother's sudden insistence. "What would he have to do with it?" She thought back to the last day she saw her father at the fountain.

"*Nothing.* Besides, we're going to the rabbi next week to get a divorce. Brahm's a mess."

Miriam raised an eyebrow. "Imma, you say that every few months, and then you two make up. Then you fight again and ask for a divorce again and make up before you get it. Brahm isn't going anywhere."

"He's like a tick," Massouda said. "Once he gets his head in, he sticks in."

They both laughed, and after a moment, when they'd calmed, Massouda said, "You know you're the only one I laugh with like this."

"I know."

"Not Simi or Channa or Amram or . . ."

"I know," Miriam repeated, pressing her mother's hand between both of hers.

"Anyway, let's take the shady way home. The long way. It will give us a chance to wish a happy birthday to all our favorite trees."

"Imma, you know it's not actually the birthday of the trees, right?"

"It could be. You don't know. Why are you always trying to stir up trouble? Nudnick!"

"Voos nudnick?" Miriam yelled, delighted by her mother adopting Yiddish. "You're becoming voos-voos!"

They laughed uncontrollably as they walked from the Wall, down the ramp to the gate separating the old and new Jerusalems.

PURIM

1973

Misha—or Oojie as he now thought of himself—walked into the small concrete administrative building on base in the early afternoon, when he knew it would be mostly vacant. He had to register his approved leave for two full weeks—the week before Pesach and the week of Pesach—and he didn't want anyone to overhear and give him a hard time. His plan was to go to the Dead Sea area first, then spend the second week at his grandfather's yeshiva at Yavneh.

Miriam was sitting at the intake desk of the crumbling building with two large stiff leaves wedged in her hair, protruding upward. Her face had charcoal lines drawn at angles and curves around her mouth as she chewed sunflower seeds and spat the shells into a wax-paper square beside her typewriter.

"Are you a . . . a . . . cat?" Oojie guessed as he approached her desk.

"A donkey," she replied.

"A donkey? That is a bold choice. I didn't think they were well liked in this part of the world."

"Why should I care what people like here? *I* like donkeys. And you—you decided not to get dressed up for Purim? That's boring."

"What are you talking about? I'm dressed as a soldier. See these stripes?" He held up two fingers at his shoulder. "See this hat?" He cocked his beret. "See this very serious look?" He stared intently at her face.

Miriam laughed despite herself. "You are ridiculous. Is this what happens from sitting too long in a hot tank in the Sinai?"

"Psshh. I'm barely in the tank. We keep going there on drills because the Egyptians mass on the other side of the Canal. But when we rush down there in our tanks, they've all gone home. And you know what we find at the Canal?" Oojie asked, leaning a hip against the desk.

"No." Miriam crossed her arms, resisting his familiarity. "What?"

"A unit of Egyptian soldiers playing football, barbecuing meats, and fishing all day. I thought some of our guys were lazy, but it's nothing like the Egyptians." Oojie shook his head. "We've started calling them the Vacation Unit."

"Let them have fun," Miriam declared. "I hear Sinai beaches are beautiful. Why shouldn't they enjoy them?"

"Maybe they should. Maybe they should have their commanders write a note to our commanders saying they are just going to the Canal for a tan and not to waste the petrol on driving all our tanks down. It is so dull down there in the desert, sitting in the shade cast by the tank, that I have started writing poetry." Oojie paused and swallowed. "Would you like to hear some? I know it by heart."

"No. You keep it in your heart. I'm busy now." Miriam returned to typing at her typewriter.

Oojie straightened. "Sure. Maybe later." He cleared his throat. "But really I'm here to register my leave for next month. I've been approved for two weeks." He handed Miriam the signed form.

"Ooh. Two weeks. And you say the Egyptians are always vacationing." Reading the form, she remarked, "Okay. After the first week of April, through Pesach." Miriam looked up and met his gaze. "What are your plans?"

"I was thinking of hitching a ride to the Dead Sea, Ein Gedi, Masada for the first week. I've never been. And then, for Pesach, go to my grandfather's yeshiva in Yavneh." He waited for the importance of his grandfather to register.

"You haven't been to Masada?" she huffed. "I thought all the trainees went there to run up, prove their toughness, and then scream from the top of the mountain."

"I had to get my shots the week my unit went, so I'm going now. I'm actually . . ."

"And after?" Miriam interrupted.

"After what?" Oojie said, a little taken aback by her boldness.

"After your service is over. That's soon, right? Where will you go? Or will you stay in Israel?"

Feeling unaccountably shy, he confessed, "I was thinking of going to study mysticism in an ashram in India."

"Why India?"

Again she'd asked the unexpected rather than the expected question. He enjoyed how she surprised him. "I've just always been drawn to it," he replied. "Ever since I read Hermann Hesse's *Siddhartha*. Do you know it?"

"Why not go back to America? Maybe we get married and I go with you?"

"Yeah, absolutely!" Oojie couldn't detect any joke in her tone, and he didn't convey one in response.

Miriam stamped his form. "Okay, your leave has been filed."

"And us getting married?"

"That is registered too." She smiled. "But everything is backwards on Purim. We'll see how we feel about it later."

Oojie left the building inexplicably excited. He liked Miriam, and they'd talked casually and run into each other a few times, but he didn't really know her. She had the same nervous energy he did, the same sense of homelessness, but she seemed more grounded, sure of herself. He knew her remark about marriage wasn't real, no more than his plan with his brother Benny that if neither of them had careers by thirty-five they would rebrand themselves as the Pecorino Brothers and import cheese from Sicily to Lawrence, Massachusetts. But still, it amazed him that she would mention such a thing. Because that meant that she could imagine it. And if she could imagine it, that meant that it was imaginable.

Miriam opened the drawer to file the paperwork and saw the single sheet of paper she'd avoided looking at all morning. It had come in a few hours earlier and was only a few lines long. She'd seen it quickly and put it down in the dark of the drawer. But it still sat in her mind like the shadow of a nightmare she couldn't shake.

A young boy had wandered into a military zone that had a minefield and died.

The boy was named, and she knew the name. Nissim Rasfelt. Her nephew. The firstborn son of Simi and Abraham. The first Israeli generation, born to this, their homeland. A young boy who played on his ancestral homeland and blew up. What kind of land ate its own? The funeral would be delayed—would not take place later in the day as usual, but in a few days—because the blood and all parts of the body had to be carefully collected. The tombstone would read Nissim Rasfelt. The name her mother yelled at Simi for choosing, arguing the name was blessed and should never be used—it was too crowded already. But Simi insisted, saying she had a claim to it too. The quarrel ended in the usual way, each blotting out the words of the other for fear that they would be heard and invite the evil eye. The disagreement didn't conclude but rather was wiped from the record due to its sensitive subject, and both Massouda and Simi had been left feeling as strongly about the matter as when they'd started.

Staring ahead blankly, Miriam wondered if she could really live with Oojie. He was funny, in that voos-voos way. And he was smart, like a scientist. But he could also be annoying—more like a voos-voos than a man. He was American, however, which was most important. It meant he had access to the world. He was in Israel because he wanted to be for as long as he wanted to be, and when his service was over, he could go anywhere. They could leave together, return to his native land and watch the American workers rise up against the pigs and take the factories.

Beyond the administrative building, Oojie saw Sami smoking and waved at him.

Sami gave a half wave in return, then looked down at the ground.

Oojie had thought, locked up together, they'd become friends, but things had been weird between them ever since the sergeant had taunted him about Yavneh. He'd wanted to talk to his grandfather afterward, but the constant deployments to the desert made that difficult. He couldn't understand why his commanders kept getting sucked into the trap every time Egypt moved a muscle. Egypt was just pretending, playing. From what he'd witnessed in the desert and read in the international press, the Egyptian soldiers were lazy and unmotivated. And why shouldn't they be? Their cause was unjust. It was simple: Egypt wouldn't attack because it couldn't attack. Israel was stronger and smarter in '48 and '67, and it had only improved since then. It had promised to create the new Jew, and it had delivered in spades. Israel had unleashed the strength of the Jew that had lain dormant for two thousand years, and Egypt and the world knew the Arabs were no match. Oojie hoped his commanding officers would recognize that soon so he could cease the endless Sinai runs, though the deployments did give him material to write home about.

Sami looked down as quickly as he could when Oojie waved. Oojie seemed like a nice enough guy—certainly much nicer than the other Israeli soldiers—but something about him bothered Sami. At first, he thought it was the way Oojie didn't turn away to give him privacy when they shared a cell, but then he realized it was more. It was the way the American looked at him even off the toilet. The way he practiced Arabic with him, Oojie's little quirks that always invaded his space. Even the way he was too nice to him. It made Sami feel like an object. He would see Oojie writing in a little notebook and imagine him drawing pictures of Sami, and writing home with pride that he had an Arab friend. It was best to look down. Best to not engage. Best to deal with the Israeli soldiers he understood.

PESACH

1973

Oojie was sitting in a chair in his grandfather's study, sunburned and in pain from his week in the Judean Desert. At the Dead Sea he'd floated and covered himself in mud at its banks as his skin turned brown. He'd hiked into Ein Gedi and eaten dates directly from the tree and washed the stickiness off under the clean waters of the mountainous falls. He'd climbed Masada and seen the storied spot where his ancestors held their final battle against their Roman oppressors. The Temple had been destroyed, Jerusalem ransacked, and all that remained were the fierce Jewish warriors on the mount. The thousand of them fought off the Romans for years as the enemy built a ramp closer and closer to the top. And when the Romans were about to penetrate the last fortress, the warriors killed themselves, choosing death on their terms. They did it so Jews would be remembered with honor, not as slouching helplessly to their own demise, and he felt that power.

As Oojie walked the edges of their settlement and looked down at the vast desert below, he imagined being there, under attack at the last holdout of the Jewish fighter. He wondered if he would've had the courage to take his own life for his people, for posterity, so that successive generations would know that there was a better path than offering your wrists to your captors.

After Masada, Oojie returned to the Dead Sea with a sharper perspective. He'd floated and stared into the searing sun through closed eyelids until he saw spots and his skin turned from brown to red. He hitchhiked his way to Yavneh for Pesach, sitting in the back seat of a small Volkswagen, his arms and legs, by then a peeling pink, in close contact with the passengers to his left and right. The coolness of their skin felt good initially, but when they shifted and bodies separated, it was all fire again.

When Oojie had imagined Pesach, he'd pictured himself studying at the yeshiva with its sages, but instead he found himself in the dark study, alone, avoiding the brightness outside. He'd spent the day pulling books off shelves at random, trying to interest himself in the various mystical and legal texts, but they all seemed so tedious, focused on pointless minutiae. He tried reminding himself that Rabbi Yosef Karo, one of the great mystical Kabbalists, also wrote the authoritative *Shulchan Aruch*, which dealt with such mundane matters as the proper way to wash one's hands and tie one's shoes—the universe in a grain of sand. When that didn't work, he started snooping through his grandfather's things. He opened folders and found typed divorce decrees and handwritten drafts. He opened notebooks and found jotted thoughts and letters in his grandfather's script. And then he opened an olive wood box, which also had notes and letters, but written in another's handwriting. And then another's handwriting. And another's. In English and Yiddish and Hebrew, the letters all had dates, some going back decades. And each letter began the same way, addressed to someone specific that the writer seemed to love—*Dearest Hannah, Dear Yisrael, My Dear Booba, Dear Imma*. All letters were addressed to someone, of course, but these greetings and opening sentences felt weighty somehow. Most began with an apology for what the writer was about to say, what they were about to do, what the reader would find beside the letter, likely before the letter was read. They attempted to make sense of the senseless, absolved the reader of any responsibility or guilt, and requested as much in return. One after another, they conveyed immense sadness, despair, regret, guilt. Who were these people, Oojie wondered? And why did his grandfather have so many letters that were not addressed to him? One spoke of losing his job and putting the family deep in debt. One spoke of a shameful visit to a prostitute, where the writer caught an aggressive venereal disease. One spoke of the writer's mother, spoke *to* his mother, and of eating mushrooms to join her in heaven.

Oojie spread the letters out on the desk, dozens of them, and examined the names mentioned. They had a familiar ring—Ashkenazi names that he'd grown up with, that filled their synagogues and Jewish schools. He thought he knew one, but no, maybe not. Maybe it was just a common name. Weissman, Grosstein, Kleinman, Schwartzman.

He'd put together that these were suicide notes, but not why his grandfather had them all, stored away, where the families couldn't access the raw truths, their shared histories and most important moments. It felt unseemly that he'd taken them, kept them hidden in . . . what, a box of curiosities? While dozens of families didn't know what happened to their loved ones.

Disgusted, Oojie pulled the letters together, pushed them back in the box, shut the lid, and returned it to its place.

He felt agitated. The week in the desert had physically tested him, and his time among the ghosts at Masada confirmed his growing belief that one should never compromise one's values. His skin burned and itched, crisping up and peeling off his body. Oojie thought about the ten plagues of Egypt, which would soon be recounted over a meal. At each plague's mention, they would dip a finger in the wine to remember. Blood. Frogs. Lice. Flies. Cow pestilence. Boils. Hail. Locusts. Darkness. And the killing of firstborn children. They crowded out other concerns. Oojie had so many things he needed to talk to his grandfather about, but he didn't know how. He'd spoken and studied with his grandfather-the-rabbi, but he'd never simply talked to him. It was always about the Torah, the Talmud, the Midrash. That his grandfather was a great rabbi was never questioned, but Oojie knew little about his past and nothing about the man.

Knowing he had to find a way to broach the topics that concerned him, Oojie waited for his grandfather to return from the yeshiva. He waited in the study during the day, and when the sun set he waited outside. The breeze off the ocean felt cool, winding through the citrus grove and returning with the smell of salt and flowers.

When Rav Minsky arrived home, the sky had at least three stars, usually a marker of the beginning of a holiday. Oojie saw he was deep in thought, muttering to himself as he walked toward the house. Rav Minsky didn't see his grandson sitting in the dark until Oojie called out to him.

Oojie had so many questions—about the land, and now also about the letters—but decided to start with the ones he'd had the longest.

"Saba," he began as the old man approached. "I don't believe I was ever told. Can I ask how you ended up here?"

His grandfather seemed surprised by the question, and also impatient, clearly in a rush to do something in the house, but as was customary when an inquiry was put to him, he paused, thought for a moment, and answered. "This is Yavneh."

"No, I know," Oojie said, striving for patience himself. "But how did you end up here?"

Another long pause. "I came to Yavneh to build the yeshiva."

Oojie could most often hear the Brooklyn cast to Rav Minsky's Ashkenazi accent when his grandfather made a point in English. "Of course. But I am wondering how you specifically ended up *here*." Oojie felt that his emphasis made it as clear as it could be.

Rav Minsky frowned. "Who else should have ended up here?"

Hiding frustration, Oojie tried another way. "Perhaps I'm not asking correctly. You lived in Brooklyn before making Aliyah, right? And when you made Aliyah to Israel, you arrived here in Yavneh. And you got all this land and this grove?"

His grandfather looked around, as though this should be obvious. "Yes?"

"How?" Oojie paused. "How was that possible?"

"With Hashem, all things are possible." Rav Minsky replied, pinching his fingers as he invoked God's name.

"Yes, of course. But . . ." Oojie searched for a polite way to frame the question. "How did you afford it? As a rabbi and a scholar?"

His grandfather was silent a moment, as if waiting to hear the end of the question. Finally, he spoke slowly and deliberately. "The land was empty and was being offered to a rabbi who would establish a yeshiva and save Yavneh and its sages."

"But . . ."

Rav Minsky interrupted. "There was no money involved."

Oojie gestured around them. "And . . . what of these trees? The orange trees. I've heard from Dima and her cousins that they've been here for generations."

"Yes, most of them."

"Then how could it have been empty?" Oojie prodded. "Who tended to the trees?"

Rav Minsky shrugged. "I do not know. Perhaps it was Arabs. They have served as caretakers of the land."

Oojie cocked his head. "Then how could it be free? Wouldn't they need to be paid for it?"

"One should not trouble oneself with such questions." His grandfather slashed a hand through the air. "Hashem gave this land to Avraham and the Jews. Everything else is silliness."

"But . . ."

"Misha . . . Oojie, we have to prepare for Pesach. We have other things to think about."

Rav Minsky proceeded into the house, but Oojie stayed outside under the stars, pondering his grandfather's answers. They didn't sound right. The box of letters. The land. His sergeant's mocking. What did others know that he didn't? What was his grandfather hiding?

When Oojie had first arrived in Israel, he'd met someone who edited copy for the *Jerusalem Post*. Sitting there in the dark, Oojie resolved to call him and ask for articles about Yavneh—also Yibna, as the Arabs called it— from the Mandate years until 1967.

After Pesach.

LAG BAOMER
1973

On the edges of the orange grove was the home of the Arab family who worked the land at Yavneh. Small and built of stone in the Arabic style, the house was referred to as *old*, meaning from before the current century, before the current country, a remnant from old Palestine.

There was little casual conversation at the yeshiva or his grandfather's house; if it wasn't about the Talmud or Midrash, it was barely discussed— so Oojie had begun wandering over to the stone house some evenings to eat outside with Dima and her family. At his grandfather's, Oojie found the food of Poland, the Ashkenazi food he'd grown up with in Pittsburgh and Lawrence. It made him feel heavy. He'd come to Israel to eat something different, to *be* different. At Dima's, they grilled meats and peppers over an open flame, made enormous dishes in giant pots, and used spices that smelled as if they'd come from the land they sat on. It excited him. At the yeshiva, when he mentioned his dinners at the stone house, the rabbis remarked that his grandfather had never charged the family rent for staying there, affirming that his grandfather was a great and generous man.

Oojie had walked over this evening hoping to find only Dima. His friend at the *Jerusalem Post* had researched Rav Minsky's land, and Oojie felt compelled to tell her what he'd found. It was the truth, and as difficult as it may be to hear, he believed those affected by it were entitled to it.

At the stone house, he found the entire family outside, finished eating and now arguing and laughing. The bonfire providing light as well as heat, Oojie was readily seen, so he joined them, not wishing to be rude. As they told stories, he listened, occasionally turning to Dima for translation. They remarked upon Oojie's sudden beard, with Dima's father saying he finally looked like a man. When the family began to drift away, Oojie asked Dima if she would go for a walk, and she agreed.

The stroll through the trees at night was quiet, and might have been peaceful if Oojie hadn't had something heavy to share. After a few minutes, when they were beyond earshot of the house, he broke the unbearable silence.

"Dima, do you know how you and your family ended up here?"

Dima looked surprised by the question. "This is our home."

"No." Oojie tried to clarify. "Sure, but when did your family come here?"

"I don't know," Dima replied slowly, cocking her head in the direction of the land. "We've always been here."

"Well, that's not exactly tr . . ." Oojie stopped himself, realizing that was a conversation for another time. "So your family has been here for a long time? Is that what you're saying?"

"What's the point of this?"

Shoving his hands into his pockets, Oojie took a deep breath, then said, "I found out something about your family, and I think you should know it. I would want to know if it were my family."

Squinting at him, Dima asked, "What are you talking about?"

Oojie stroked his beard in the manner of his grandfather, slow and thorough. "Well, I was talking to my friend Sami at the base. I've told you about him. And a sergeant who was listening tipped me off to . . . well, no. He didn't really tip me off. That would indicate he was acting in good faith. He more . . . mocked me. But anyhow, he told me something was off about this orange grove. At first, I didn't believe him because he's kind of a weirdo. Like one time I was talking to someone and I referred to the sergeant as *bachor*—you know, Hebrew for *young man*—and he overhears and turns around and says, *I'm on to you and your plans*. We ask what he's talking about, and he says that he knows we're planning on raping him. We were shocked. But he insists he heard us whispering *bachore*—*in the hole*. Now, I know that the two words sound kind of alike, but how he arrived at that is truly bizarre. I mean . . ."

"Oojie," Dima interrupted. "What are you talking about?"

"Sorry." Oojie gave his head a quick shake, as if to clear it. "I was just trying to say that at first I assumed the sergeant was just messing with me. A lot of the guys at the base joke around, even when it's not funny. But then

I came here—you know, when I was really sunburned—and I found this box of letters my grandfather had."

Dima frowned. "And these letters are about my family?"

"No. But they made me realize he keeps a lot of secrets. Problematic secrets. Just like the rest of my family. And that he's not altogether truthful, and that his image and the stories about him may not be totally accurate. So I asked a friend at the newspaper to do a little digging about this property. And what he found shocked me."

"Okay," Dima said, still looking dubious.

Oojie took a paper from his pocket with dates and notes scribbled on it. "So," he began, "on November 20, 1947—mind you, this is before my grandfather even came to Israel—a group of men from the Stern Gang, which was one of the Jewish militias at the time, came to this grove because they believed a family—your family—had informed the British about their secret training camp nearby. They came before dawn and woke everyone up. They then called out five men by name, probably from the house that you live in now. They chose five because a week prior, the British had raided the Stern Gang's camp and killed five members. So the militia members gathered the five men—members of your family, I don't know the relationship—and opened fire on them with machine guns. They did this in front of the other members of the family as both revenge and a warning about talking to the British. Four of them died on the spot, and the fifth died later. I think they were then buried somewhere on this land."

Oojie's friend hadn't relayed that last detail, but ever since he'd heard the story, Oojie had felt their presence here. He was sure their graves were near.

For a long moment, Dima stood staring at Oojie—actually, through Oojie. She'd placed her inner palm at her forehead and was picking at her scalp.

"Do you need a hug?" Oojie asked, leaning in to embrace her.

"No!" Dima stepped back, stopping him with an open palm. "I don't understand. Are you certain that happened here?" She pointed at the ground. "To my family?"

"Yes. I was very specific with my friend at the *Jerusalem Post*. And even my sergeant, who's a bit of a friar, knew about it."

Dima shook her head. "But how have I never heard about this? That was just thirty-five years ago. Someone would have said something."

"Honestly, I don't know. If your family is anything like mine, it's all ghost stories and silence."

"Why are you telling me about this?"

"I just . . ." Oojie inhaled deeply and exhaled fully. ". . . thought you should know. I'd want to know if I were you."

"Okay." Dima turned away. "I have to go home now. I need to think about this."

"I understand," said Oojie, trying to sound soothing. "I'll be here another day before I have to go back to base. Can we talk tomorrow? I hate to leave things like this."

"Okay," Dima said, though he sensed she wasn't really listening. She turned in the direction of the stone house.

As she walked away, Oojie recalled he'd intended to frame the story, to put what he'd learned in context. "I think we have to remember," he added loudly, "that history is to blame here."

He struck out in the other direction, blood rushing through his arms and face, but he felt light, unburdened. Though it was difficult, it was important to bring the truth to light. There was so much ignorance and injustice. Oojie recalled the words of Louis Brandeis—the first Jew on the Supreme Court—that sunlight is the best disinfectant. Everything should be brought out into the sun. Enough shadows and myths; people should know the raw truth. Oojie was slightly bothered that Dima hadn't thanked him. She'd just walked away. Of course what he'd imparted had been hard for her, but finding out about her family and sharing it had been equally hard for him, and it felt like she hadn't recognized that. Hopefully when they talked the next day, she'd thank him.

SHAVUOT

1973

Despite their best efforts, Oojie and Miriam had fallen asleep on the early morning bus ride to Jerusalem. They wore their uniforms, Uzis—with spare clips taped to the sides—slung over their shoulders and resting between their knees, so they could ride for free. The gentle swaying of the bus as it wound up and down hills, along with the early summer heat trapped inside, had rocked them to sleep. The last thing Oojie said before drifting off—as he shifted his gun from a pinch point on his inner thigh—was that Uzi would have been a nice name for a baby, but it had probably been ruined. Miriam laughed before resting her head on his epaulettes and covering her eyes with her beret.

The driver woke them after the bus had almost entirely emptied, joking that he hoped the Arabs didn't attack while our brave soldiers dreamed. Miriam didn't acknowledge the comment, but Oojie, scratching his increasingly itchy beard, gave the driver his coldest stare.

Outside the station, the sun was rising. In this light, over the uniform stone of every building, Jerusalem truly felt like a golden city. The song "Yerushalayim Shel Zahav" came to Oojie's mind. He started humming, recalling the verse, *But as I come to sing to you today, and to adorn crowns to you, I am the smallest of the youngest of your children. . . .*

Miriam's laughter made Oojie realize he was singing out loud. He had another poem he'd written for her. He'd give it to her later, maybe in the evening. She acted as if she didn't like his poems, asked him to stop his American romantic nonsense, but his annoying her with his eccentricities, and her laughing and telling him *enough*, had become part of their interplay.

Oojie wanted to go to the Old City and the Wall while it was still early and quiet. He speculated they'd hear the cock crow, and he would betray Miriam. She clearly didn't understand the reference but shot the joke down before it took on a life of its own. They walked toward the Old City by way of the Damascus Gate, passing through the Arab neighborhoods of East Jerusalem. Miriam stopped at a street vendor and bought a Ka'ak al-Quds bread for them to share. Oojie joked that since Jews and Arabs had independently invented the bagel, maybe this circular bread could be the basis of a peace deal. Miriam told him that he had a surprising number of sesame seeds throughout his beard.

From the Damascus Gate, they passed all the shuttered stalls. The streets were limited to cats and children, each of which occasionally ran through the alleys, making tight corners, and disappeared. When the two of them turned left, the magnificence of the last remaining Temple wall stood before them. Oojie had hoped the rising sun would bathe the Western Wall in radiance, but he had miscalculated the geography. The Wall was the western wall of the Temple, which meant that as one approached it from the west, the rising sun's rays hit the gold-clad Dome of the Rock on the Haram al-Sharif, which glowed while the Western Wall cast a shadow that enveloped much of the Old City.

Oojie and Miriam split up, going to opposite sides of the mechitzah separating the sexes. They each approached the Wall slowly, touched it with their right hands, said the Shema Yisrael prayer, and then tucked a small folded prewritten note in its great cracks.

When they reunited beyond the mechitzah, Oojie asked with a grin, "What's it like on the women's side?"

"Small," Miriam responded.

They exited the Old City through the Jaffa Gate, heading west for the long walk to Kiryat HaYovel. Oojie was excited to meet Miriam's family, but a little nervous about whether they'd accept him. He asked question after question about their traditions, etiquette, and what to say to each individual member. She said he'd be fine, but told him not to lend money to Brahm, even if Brahm cornered him. Not to boast of good things or it would invite the evil eye. Not mention bad things or it might invite the jinn. And not to bring up Simi's Nissim, who had recently died from a land mine. Oojie wanted to express his condolences, to articulate that his memory should be a blessing, but Miriam explained that his funeral had happened, and "now we don't talk about him with words."

As they walked, the city came to life around them, people and cars filling the streets. They heard the soft call of white-spectacled bulbuls in the trees, and Oojie thought to joke about *bulbul* also meaning *penis* in Hebrew but decided against it, leaning into the comfortable quiet.

As they got closer to Miriam's house, she remarked, "Jerusalem is actually not such a bad city."

Oojie agreed.

"Are you still thinking about that nonsense of going to India?" asked Miriam.

"No," Oojie said, and before following up with a joke about souring on Indian food, he closed his mouth.

"Some days, I can actually imagine staying here," Miriam said.

"Me too," said Oojie. "Maybe we could stay together?"

"Let's see how things go with my family today," Miriam said.

They both laughed.

When they entered the neighborhood, Miriam asked if Oojie first wanted a tour around the area. He said yes, and she took him to the Lady Davis School, her favorite newsstand, and then the monster in the park. They sat together on a bench and watched the children roll out of the monster's mouth, screaming and laughing as they tumbled to the ground.

"Do you want to guess what their names are by how they look?" Oojie asked.

"Yes." Miriam pointed toward a small child. "That one with the cauliflower nose, he's named Uzi."

TISHA B'AV

1973

The room smelled sour. No one had eaten or drunk anything since the previous day, and though it was hot, their bodies had stopped producing sweat. Everyone at the yeshiva rocked and prayed, working out the nervous energy produced from fasting and the sadness produced by remembrance. The history of calamities spanning all of Judaism was compressed into this day, the ninth day of the month of Av.

Oojie was in the room with the boys—under thirteen, not yet men—because it was where his grandfather taught of the meaning of Tisha B'Av. At their age, according to the terms of the law, the boys didn't have to fast, but still they all did so out of devotion. Oojie was there to listen to Rav Minsky's teachings, but also to find a moment to talk with his grandfather.

He'd gone in the morning to see Dima—they'd not spoken since their walk together—but he couldn't find her. When he'd knocked on the door of the house, no one answered. The surrounding area was unusually quiet—it felt empty—and Oojie wanted to ask his grandfather if he knew where the family was working.

Rav Minsky was seated at the middle of a table teaching the children about the history and meaning of the holiday. He spoke softly, in his customary manner, but his tone conveyed more passion than usual.

"We all know what happened on Tisha B'Av in Jerusalem. That is always the focus of the story. But it is important to widen one's perspective and consider all of Eretz Yisrael on this day of mourning." Rav Minsky spread his arms out, almost touching two of the yeshiva boys. "The two temples were destroyed on this same day six hundred years apart in Jerusalem, but we here are sitting on the land of Judaism's rebirth. Here in Yavneh.

"When the Romans had Jerusalem surrounded, there was a great famine within the city walls, and the Jews were dying while the second Temple risked destruction. Yet out at Masada, a group of biryonim zealots had conquered Herod's palace on the plateau, which it is said contained an endless supply of food. For a while, it looked like the future of Judaism was high on that peak in the desert. Judaism began and grew from one family over generations, and perhaps those at Masada would repeat this beginning.

"But the brother-in-law of one of the leaders of the biryonim was Rabban Yochanan Ben Zakkai, whom you may know as the Ribaz. He knew that something had to be done, but he also knew that if he was seen opposing the biryonim, they would kill him.

"So he spread a rumor among his students that he was gravely ill. And his students spread it throughout the city, and suddenly there was great concern for the great Ribaz. He then had a further rumor spread that he had died. This was so that he could escape from the walled city, past the biryonim and the Romans. He hid in a coffin, and his loyal students served as the pallbearers, carrying his coffin out of the city for burial.

"The Ribaz had his coffin carried straight to the Roman camp. When the coffin came by the Roman general, the Ribaz emerged alive, and said, 'Peace be upon you, king.' The general was taken aback, saying that he was the general, not the king, and such disrespect toward the emperor was punishable by death. The Ribaz replied that the prophets had foretold the Temple would fall to a king, and since the city and Temple were on the verge of falling to the general, the general would surely soon be a king.

"As they were speaking, an imperial messenger entered the tent and announced that the emperor of Rome had died, and the senators had proclaimed the general the new emperor of the Roman Empire. The general had to leave for his coronation, but he told the Ribaz that because of his prophecy, which had proven true, the new emperor would grant him one request. The Ribaz responded immediately and said, 'Spare me Yavneh and its sages.'

"Pay attention that he did not ask for the emperor to spare Jerusalem or the Temple. Why? Because that was not Hashem's plan. The Ribaz knew that Judaism must continue in a new direction.

"The new emperor granted the wish, and at Yavneh, the sages set out to find a way to continue Judaism without the Temple. So many of the commandments and rituals demanded a Temple, and it was not clear how Judaism would survive without it. But through study and debate, the sages at Yavneh found a way forward. And this way has carried us for two thousand years. It is precisely what we do here each day, unchanged in essence.

"Now, not far from here, in the mountains of the Judaean Desert, is Masada. It is where the biryonim took shelter while fighting the Romans. While their brothers and sisters starved in Jerusalem, they had unlimited food. But of course, the Romans attacked. For years, the Romans constructed a massive ramp up to the plateau. And on the eve of the final attack, the biryonim at Masada killed themselves. Despite the prohibitions against suicide, they took their own lives rather than risk being killed or enslaved by the Romans.

"On Tisha B'Av, we are reminded of Yavneh and Masada, two vastly different approaches to tragedy. Yavneh was a compromise, a way to recognize the reality of Hashem's plan and find a path for our covenant to survive in the wilderness. Masada appeared as strength, but was actually weakness. It did not care for the community or the future. It refused compromise and chose death, and it is not the symbol we should embrace. On Tisha B'Av, as we fast and mourn, every generation must choose between Yavneh and Masada. Even this generation."

As Rav Minsky finished speaking, it was as if the story had left his body. It was shocking to watch him return to his natural state and quickly begin mumbling a prayer in a meditative murmur. Before he could settle into the prayer, Oojie jumped up and sat in the empty seat directly beside him.

"Saba, that was very interesting. I was just at Masada a few months ago, and I'd never thought of Masada and Yavneh in conversation."

Rav Minsky nodded and continued to murmur to himself.

"Saba," Oojie began again. "I'm sorry to bring this up today, but have you seen the Arab family that tends the land? I looked for them but couldn't find them."

"I do not know where they are," Rav Minsky replied with apparent indifference.

Oojie could suddenly smell the hot, rancid breath of his fasting grandfather. It was in these moments Oojie remembered that, even if Rav Minsky was a gaon with an eye to the heavens, he was also an old man. "You haven't seen them around?" he persisted.

"No. Not in several months."

"Several months?" Oojie repeated incredulously. "Do you know what happened?"

His grandfather remained expressionless. "We had to let them go."

"What?" Oojie realized he'd spoken too loudly and lowered his voice. "Why?"

"There was a rumor going around that their family had been murdered and buried by Jews during the war. It was no longer safe to have them around."

Heat washed over Oojie, more painful than any sunburn. "I don't . . . I told Dima about that. I don't understand."

Finally, Rav Minsky exhibited an emotion. Puzzlement. "Why would you do such a thing?"

"Well, because it's the truth," Oojie said, feeling equally defensive and anguished. "Members of the Stern Gang did it. They killed five members of her family in retaliation for talking to the British."

"You were misinformed," his grandfather said.

Oojie sharply shook his head. "No. I checked with the newspaper archives. With a friend at the *Jerusalem Post*."

"I know the event to which you are referring. I heard about it when I first arrived in Israel. It did not happen here."

"I don't understand."

"There was a tragedy that took place not far from here, at a citrus grove closer to Ra'anana. And that was with the Shubaki clan, not the Arab family that worked here."

Oojie felt sick. "Okay, so I was wrong. Can Dima and her family come back then? If it's not true, I don't understand why you fired them and kicked them out of their home."

His grandfather put his arms on the table, as if teaching again. "Because they believed it. And what would they do with that belief? They would surely act against us. They would surely take revenge. It is only natural. I had to get rid of them before they attacked us. As the Talmud commands, *If someone comes planning to kill you, you should rise and kill first.* It was necessary."

"No!" Oojie knew he was being too loud, but he no longer cared if he made a scene. "Couldn't you have explained? That it was an incorrect rumor?"

His grandfather became still more calm. "What do you think caused the pogroms and blood libels against us for centuries? Do you think we really made our matzah from the blood of their babies? The goyim will never care about our truth. They can't understand it, so it's better not to waste one's time with it. Besides, what is the truth I should have tried to convey here?"

"That I was wrong! And they should disregard it. I can take the blame."

"If I told them it was not here where their family was murdered, but another citrus grove close by, and it was not their uncles, but rather their cousins, do you think that would make a difference? How could I expect them to work for me, and allow us to live here in peace, knowing such things?"

The heat had made its way into Oojie's eyes. They felt swollen. His vision blurred. "I still think something . . . I think we can figure it out. There has to be a way."

"Oojie," his grandfather intoned, "today is Tisha B'Av. It is our day of mourning, and we have no space to mourn for others. Our tragedy goes back thousands of years. Our tragedy is deeper than theirs."

Rav Minsky lowered his head and began mumbling his prayer again.

Oojie had to get out of that room. He ran outside and took several deep breaths to calm down. He needed to find Dima to explain what had happened, but he had no idea where she might be. He thought back to what he knew of her and recalled she'd told him about family who lived in the next village over.

Oojie ran in the direction of the village. It wasn't that far, but seemed to take forever because he had to stop and breathe every few minutes, the fasting having made him lightheaded.

When he arrived at the cluster of homes, he ran up its primary street, looking frantically for Dima. At each intersection, he stopped, doubling over to pant and look both ways. Until suddenly, she was there. Sitting in a white plastic chair, outside a small house, smoking. She wasn't doing anything, just sitting and staring off, holding a cigarette and looking surprisingly calm. Maybe she wasn't upset with him. Maybe everything would be all right.

"Dima!" Oojie called out as he ran toward her.

She looked over and saw Oojie and said nothing.

"I'm sorry," Oojie said, out of breath as he rocked to a stop in front of her. "I just ran here and I've been fasting since yesterday. I'll need a minute." Again Oojie doubled over. He could smell the smoke from her cigarette and felt nauseous.

"What are you doing here, Oojie?" she said tonelessly.

"I just heard what happened to you and your family. I can't believe it. I ran right over. I'm so glad I found you."

"No. Not here in this village. *Here*," she said with emphasis. "What are you doing here in Israel?"

Oojie shook his head. "I'm here in the army. You know that."

"Then go be in the army." Dima waved as if to dismiss him.

"But I needed to check on you. To make sure everything was okay."

Dima finished her cigarette and stamped it out on the ground. "Nothing is okay. Why should it be? But it is not your problem. Just go."

"I made a mistake, Dima. I didn't mean for any of this to happen. I can get my grandfather to reconsider. I'm sure of it. He's a good man."

"It doesn't matter," Dima said. "This was always going to happen."

"But I think I can fix it," Oojie protested.

"Why did you tell me?" For the first time since he'd run up, Dima held his gaze. "What did you hope would come out of it?"

"I don't know," said Oojie. "I just thought you should know."

"And then what?" she pressed.

He shrugged. "And then once you knew, you'd forget about it."

She scoffed. "That makes no sense."

"Well, I mean, it did to me. You have a right to know about your history, your family, your past, right? But also you need to get on with things as they are. So you then need to forget."

"But I already didn't know. What's the point of making it more complicated and painful to get to the same point?"

"Not knowing and forgetting aren't the same," Oojie argued. "Forgetting and not remembering aren't the same. Does that make sense?"

"No."

"It's like if you and a good friend, or maybe your mother or father, don't agree on a very important thing. That happens. You've had big fights, and every time you talk about it, you disagree more. So what do you do? Do you keep arguing every time you see them and waste all your time fighting? Or do you forget about it and move on?"

"That's a terrible example," Dima said testily. "That's not forgetting, just thinking about something else for a bit."

"Maybe it's a problem of translation. How about this. Think of Sunnis and Shia and the deep disagreements . . ."

Dima held up a hand. "No." She lowered her hand slowly. "Oojie, I don't know what is this game that you're playing. You can't be on both sides here. You can't be neutral. Trying to fix everything."

"It's not a game," he insisted. "I want to help."

Dima stood. "You left your home to play soldier in another country. So go! Play soldier."

"I know you're angry," said Ooojie, "but this is my country too."

"Okay, then." Dima nodded sharply. "You've chosen a side. Now leave us alone."

"What are you talking about? I haven't chosen a side!"

"Oojie." She sighed. "Who do you think they're training you to shoot with that gun you carry?"

Oojie wanted to argue that he was learning Arabic, that he had Arab friends, but he felt so lightheaded.

"Dima," he pleaded. "I know this is my fault for having bad information. I shouldn't have said anything. But let me at least try to fix it."

"What *fix it*? There's nothing to fix. We were the last Arab family on that land. We used to have neighbors. It was never going to last."

Oojie was having trouble finding the words, but he knew they existed. In Hebrew or English or Arabic. The fast was to blame. He felt nauseous. The glare of the sun was attacking his eyes, and he needed to sit, maybe to sleep.

"Dima, I don't feel well. It's the fast. Can I come back tomorrow and talk to you about this? Please?"

"Please don't," Dima responded, then turned and walked into the house, shutting the door.

Oojie moved slowly in the direction of the setting sun, determined to return tomorrow, to figure things out. He couldn't understand how after decades, everything could turn sour in an instant. How had his grandfather just disposed of them? And how had Dima just disposed of him? The sun was blinding, so he looked down. To get his mind off his nausea, he starting counting the rocks, alternating between English, Hebrew, and Arabic words for the numbers. He stared at his feet as they kicked up dust and knocked pebbles away. Left foot, right foot, left foot, right foot. He found himself thinking of food and getting hungry. He remembered hearing from someone in his tank unit that the Egyptian soldiers couldn't tell their left from their right, so they were given a potato for their left hands and an apple for their right hands. And their sergeants would call out *potato, apple, potato, apple, potato, apple* as a cadence. Oojie looked down and thought of the Sinai and moved his feet. He imagined boots shuffling in the sand. *Potato, apple, albatatis, tufaah, Potato. Albatatis. Apple. Tufaah.*

ROSH HASHANA

1973

"I'm sorry about the movie," Oojie said to his parents and cousin as they exited the Esther Cinema onto Dizengoff Square. "It's supposed to be a great theater, but I guess there are always technical difficulties."

"What are you talking about?" his cousin Gila shot back. "That was a wonderful movie. As good as anything in Hollywood. And that was some theater!" She looked back and blew it a kiss.

"The projector broke before the final scene," Oojie said dryly. "We don't know how it ended."

"Of course we do," Gila said. "The note the Israeli prisoner gave the Syrian guard didn't have the military information he promised. It was blank. But by then he had his freedom, and he tricked the Syrian, ran across the border, and went home."

"How did you get that?" Oojie asked his cousin, who was considering making Aliyah to Israel. "The movie cut out just as he handed the guard the coordinates."

Gila tapped her temple. "You have to understand that we'll always outsmart the Arabs," she said. "They're pretty stupid."

"Gila!" George snapped quietly. "That's not nice."

"What?" Chemda interjected. "Let the girl speak her mind. She has a right."

"Have I told you about the Egyptian soldiers in the Sinai?" Oojie asked. "They are the laziest soldiers I've ever seen. Sitting around all day, fishing in the Canal. I don't know what they think they're going to catch."

Oojie turned to his father. "Abba, I heard a joke in the tank corps I think you might like: Do you know how Nasser got his name? Gamel Abdel heard Israeli jets were coming, so he jumped into the Suez Canal and came out nasser."

George smiled.

"I don't get it," Gila announced.

"*Nas* is Yiddish for *wet*. So nasser. He came out wetter."

Gila laughed loudly. "Oh, that's a good one."

Oojie pointed to the square in front of them. "You see the Bauhaus design. It is all over Tel Aviv and is some of the best architecture in the world. Even the Europeans say so."

"That's wonderful, boychik." Chemda touched Oojie's cheek. "My god, I can't believe how big and strong you've gotten here."

"Imma." Oojie batted away the compliment. His mother kept talking about how he looked just like a soldier, and though he liked it, he felt it best to pretend he didn't. "We'll head down to Rothschild Boulevard, where you'll really see a lot more architecture."

As they turned along Dizengoff Square, they saw a protestor standing on a box, holding a placard that read *Zionism = Racism*. In front of him a small group of men had gathered, and the man in front yelled at the protestor, "Go wave your sign at the Arabs in their countries. They're the racists and antisemites."

The man on the box shot back, "Israel is a colonialist oppressor."

"Nonsense! Israel wants peace."

"Yeah," the protestor sneered. "They want a *piece* of Jordan and a *piece* of Egypt and a *piece* of Syria. . . ."

The man in front cut him off. "And a piece of my schmeckel!"

The crowd on the square squealed with laughter.

"Oojie, what is this?" his mother asked.

"Nothing, Imma. Just a guy who's anti-Israel stirring up trouble. But it's a democracy, so this stuff happens. Freedom of speech. And they mean well, but if it was up to them, we'd give away half of Israel, the Old City. The country would be dwarfed. *We'd* be dwarfs."

"Zay kenen farbrenen," Chemda said, staring at the man with the placard.

"What does that mean?" Gila asked Oojie.

"*They can be burnt.* It's what Imma says about anyone who is anti-Israel."

Gila laughed.

* * *

On Rothschild, Oojie pointed out each white rounded balcony and building line to show the beauty of the Bauhaus boulevard. He told his family about all the ways Tel Aviv was growing and modernizing. New roads, new trains; there was even a new central bus station under construction that was going to be the most efficient in the world once it was finished. His parents listened intently, his father nodding slightly as he soaked it in, while his mother kept commenting how amazing it was that he was now a true Israeli. Oojie loved hearing it and told them they'd eat lunch at a falafel stand that he felt was the best in the city.

When they all sat, Oojie asked how their stay in Yavneh had been so far. They said it was excellent. George remarked that he particularly liked the early morning walks from the stone guest house to the yeshiva. Very peaceful.

Oojie had initially been shocked to learn that they were staying in the old stone house, but decided upon reflection that it was better someone should stay there than it remain empty.

Gila announced she'd found something in the house that she was excited to take back as a souvenir. She pulled a giant key from her purse.

"Look at this thing. It's enormous." She placed it next to her food. "It's literally bigger than my falafel."

"Is that . . ." Oojie started, ". . . isn't that the key to the house? Is it okay to just take it?"

"Yeah, your grandfather said it was okay. They never lock the door anyway. It's so safe here. But look at this thing. It's ridiculous. Why should a key be this big? How do you even put it in your pocket?" Gila laughed. "I think I'll hang it on the wall of my apartment. Remind me of this wonderful trip. It's silly, but it's also kind of cool."

Obviously uninterested in the key, Chemda spoke up. "You said we might meet your new friend, Miriam."

Oojie shook his head. "It doesn't look like that's going to happen. She's getting ready for a little vacation in the Sinai."

"Does she not want to meet us? Why shouldn't she want to meet us?" Chemda pulled out a used tissue to wipe the tears that suddenly appeared.

"Of course she does," Oojie placated. "*She does.* She just can't this visit. But hopefully soon."

"But you two might get married?"

"Imma!" Oojie found his neck heating. "I don't know. Maybe. Who knows?"

"So I might have black grandchildren?"

"What?" Shock and displeasure at his mother's question mingled. "Why should they be black?" he said, his tone unintentionally harsh.

"You said she was African," Chemda shot back. "Why are you saying I'm lying?" She grabbed the tissue in anticipation of fresh tears.

"She's Moroccan!"

"And that's in Africa," sniffed Chemda. "I wasn't lying."

"Moroccans aren't black," Oojie ground out. "And even if they were, why should it matter?"

"It doesn't. Don't get upset," Chemda said. Then added, "But I have seen black Moroccans."

"Imma!"

George cleared his throat. "If you get married," he began, "you'll stay in Israel?"

Turning to his father in relief, Oojie replied, "Maybe. I don't know."

"What would you do here? Go to university?" Gila asked.

"He'll become what Israel needs," Chemda answered for Oojie.

"I was thinking of maybe going into psychology," Oojie said.

"Israel doesn't need psychologists," Chemda declared. "Become an engineer. Israel needs engineers."

"We'll see." Oojie looked around for something uniquely Israeli to point at to change the subject.

EREV YOM KIPPUR

1973

Oojie stood at the outdoor central bus station, watching the shawarma sellers, discount shoe vendors, and prostitutes, all within a few meters of one another. He marveled at the diversity of the market and wondered what brought all these trades together. Flesh, he decided. They were all selling flesh of some sort: cooked, cured, and fresh.

The buses crawled along the tight streets and idled loudly, adding a layer of exhaust to the already complex smells of the space. How did buses fit into the flesh theory? Oojie pondered.

He was waiting for Miriam, who was stopping off en route to the Sinai. Tel Aviv wasn't really on her way, but she said it was, and stuck by the fiction. Oojie shouldn't really be meeting her since he was now a corporal and she was a private, and she wasn't technically on leave, but he couldn't resist seeing her off on her trip, and he secretly planned to ask her to marry him upon her return.

Miriam's plan was to take the bus to Eilat, cross the border, then hitchhike down the eastern side of the Sinai to Dahab, then to Sharm el-Sheikh, before hitchhiking up the west to Port Said. She'd been told by Papa Louis, her adoptive father from her childhood stint in France, that one could see the Canal best from its mouth, which he had described to her as one of the grandest things man had ever built. Also, she didn't want to spend Yom Kippur in Jerusalem with her family and hoped the desert would provide a respite from the heaviness of it all.

While waiting for her bus to arrive, Oojie considered the upcoming holiday. He liked Yom Kippur, the ending of a cycle and a wiping clean of the slate. The year had been hard, but he was feeling hopeful, and he liked the formality of a new beginning that Yom Kippur promised. Atonement. He would fast and pray and cleanse himself of all the past year's worries. And the day after Yom Kippur brought with it a blank slate filled with fresh promise.

Oojie started feeling a little nauseated and decided to move from his spot near the underground toilets. As he made his way to the end of the street, he saw Miriam against the wall, sitting atop her olive-green duffel. When she saw Oojie approach, she stood and they hugged hello. She explained the bus had arrived early, and Oojie asked about the ride from Jerusalem. She said it was fine, short.

"I might visit the city on my way back to Yavneh," Oojie said. "I like it more and more each time I go. It's really growing on me."

"A city growing on top of someone?" Miriam said, pretending to inspect him for debris.

Ooojie chuckled. "I could even imagine living there one day," he said, watching her carefully. "Could you?"

She made a face, but not of disgust, more of resignation or acceptance. Oojie had learned to take such faces as good signs and not to push for the answer he wanted.

"Are you excited for your trip?" he asked, moving closer to casually brush her arm.

"I am," Miriam said, giving him a playful hip bump to let him know she was aware of what he was doing. "But I'm tired. I didn't sleep much. Brahm came home drunk and stumbling, rooting around the house for drink or money." She rolled her eyes.

"If you'd ever spend a night on the base, you wouldn't have to deal with Brahm," he teased.

Miriam didn't disagree. She didn't laugh either.

"Will you be fasting?" Oojie asked.

"Probably not," Miriam said. "Not in the desert."

From her expression, Oojie knew the real answer was definitely not.

As the bus to Eilat lurched forward and Miriam reached for her duffel, Oojie pulled out a small notebook from his pocket.

"I wrote you a poem."

"Another one?" Miriam said, smiling.

"Of course. Can I read it to you? It's not long."

Miriam looked around at the crowded, noisy streets and the people moving toward the doors of the bus. "Not now. Give it to me, and I'll read it while I ride."

"Can I at least read you the end?" Oojie pouted.

"Sure," Miriam said with a laugh.

Oojie opened the notebook and read slowly:

The gazelles turn to the night;
Happy and contented;
The harvest has ended;
The summer is gone.

"How do I know those lines?" Miriam asked, smiling.

"From the Book of Prophets," Oojie said, pleased she recognized them. "The last two lines are Jeremiah."

"But there's more, right? Another line that comes after? A different one?"

"Yes," said Oojie. "But I think it ends better this way."

EPILOGUE

Yom Kippur, 1973

Chemda dug deep in the back of the corner cabinet of the kitchen and withdrew a small satchel of Chanukah gelt. She pulled at a large chocolate coin, carefully removed the golden wrapper, and shoved the whole piece in her mouth. As she chewed it, she began unwrapping the next one. With some chocolate still in her mouth, she ate the second piece. Chemda then pulled out two more coins and held them in one hand, while the other hand pushed the bag back into the recesses of the cabinet, where no one would find it. Chemda fingered the grooves on the two coins, marveling at how they felt like quarters and half dollars, before peeling them both and pushing them whole into her mouth.

Chemda rushed to throw away all evidence of the chocolate so no one would know she'd eaten it, though no one knew of the existence of the chocolate, so no one would know anyway.

The house was empty. George and Benny were at synagogue for Yom Kippur, which this day fell on Shabbat, making it doubly special. Yom Tov upon Yom Tov; Shabbat shabbaton upon Shabbat. They left the house early at Chemda's urging so they could make sure to have seats for the long day of praying and rocking and fasting. She had her transistor radio on in her pocket, with a single monaural earphone in her ear and the volume turned as high as it could go, so she'd likely sounded as if she were yelling as she told them to go quickly.

The radio was set to news, with occasional weather, but Chemda noticed little of it. It was just noise—people speaking loudly in the background— that kept her mind at peace. She heard something was going on in the schools and that it might rain during the week, both stated with the same level of urgency.

Chemda went to the various bedrooms and looked around, counting the beds. Confused, she returned to the dining room and then the space outside her kitchen. Walking over to her desk, she leaned over to pull up the glass topper. The earphone cord got stuck at the corner and ripped out of her ear, catching her earring. She laid the glass back down and tried to untangle the cord from her earring. Holding her tongue against her teeth in concentration, she could taste smears of chocolate mixed with remnants of pink lipstick. She twisted and pulled until the pieces came apart, then quickly pushed the earphone deep into her ear with an emphatic digit. Chemda heard the tones of an urgent bulletin, but noticed the glass on her desk was now askew.

War has broken out in the Middle East as Egypt and Syria have launched a brazen surprise attack against Israel. Experts are saying that . . .

She lifted the glass, propped it against the wall, and pulled up the out-of-time desk calendar beneath it, revealing a hidden assortment of photos and papers. In her ear she heard the words *missiles* and *tanks* and *Suez Canal*, but they were just words. Numbers were mentioned.

Forty-eight, fifty-six, sixty-seven, six days, two weeks, over a year, experts believe . . .

Chemda sat for a moment, letting herself be stationary when no one was at home. She picked up a black-and-white photo from its spot beneath the calendar. The family in Stawsk in front of the Great Synagogue, everyone dressed well, everyone there. The trees appeared gray, but she remembered the day and remembered they were very green.

One expert believes this will be over in days. It is always an air war over there. That is what we learned in '67. And the Mossad is the best in the world. That is just a fact.

Another photo of two blurs in the forest. She and her sister running free and fast, bodies obscured by the light, the camera not able to catch the movement, but still she could make out the smiles. Beside it were a few leaves from that forest that she had tucked into a book and smuggled to America. They were impossible to pick up, too desiccated and delicate to hold their shape if she did so.

Stuck to a leaf was a page from Rav Minsky's first book, which she had typed and proofed for her father. At the last instant, she had pulled the folio from the manuscript so the final draft would be incomplete. Not whole by one. She had told him it must have fallen out, been lost, reshuffled. Accidents happen, things beyond our control. He was uncharacteristically furious, his life's work—a book reimagining biblical mysticism that conceived of a universe—now deficient due to random chance. A book now with a hole in it. Forever damaged. As he yelled at her, she'd thumbed the folded page in her inner pocket.

A torn felt star, yellow, with black wavy script spelling *Juif.*

The real wild card is the Soviets . . .

An article from the *Jewish Daily Forward* announcing the new chief rabbi of the Brooklyn synagogue upon Rav Minsky's move to Yavneh. The rabbi's son, from Stawsk, no longer a boy, but with a full evident beard. The eyes seemed sinister in newsprint as he looked straight out from the page, as though challenging the reader. He was a scholar, the article read, from a long and honorable line of rabbis. Unbroken and therefore important. He had a wife at home and five children, all daughters. This threatened to disrupt the lineage. Chemda had never read past the description of the children, their names and ages listed, frozen in time.

A small card with the Kaddish on it, handwritten with a quill, and at the bottom a name. Devorah. A bee. The first and only time she'd ever written it, just in case the Kaddish needed to be said. From *dever,* a *thing* or a *word.*

Lines of tanks have been seen in the north and south, with most appearing to be Egyptian and Syrian. Israel is having trouble calling up its soldiers and reservists because of the day of fast. We're told there are no radio broadcasts today due to the holiday, and it's not clear how a mass mobilization will be facilitated. We are hearing reports of high casualties suffered in Israel, and small contingents of soldiers are trying to repel the . . .

Sick of the tone of the news broadcast, Chemda pulled the radio from her pocket and rolled the dial until she heard another voice.

Today in Lawrence it will be a high of seventy-two degrees with low barometric pressure. Tomorrow there is a ninety-six percent chance of rain for most of the day. At the tone, the time will be 10:15 a.m.

A long beep.

Today in Lawrence it will be a high of seventy-two degrees with low barometric pressure. Tomorrow there is a ninety-six percent chance of rain for most of the day. At the tone, the time will be 10:16 a.m.

Chemda shuffled to her bedroom closet and pulled out a plastic head covering. She wrapped it around her head so as not to forget it. "I'll go out tomorrow," she said aloud to the room, "to do the shopping. Sunday, yes, but with rain, fewer people."

The weather announcement repeated itself. The plastic on her head reminded Chemda to clean the bathroom. As she shuffled toward the bath, she stopped and changed direction. The kitchen. There was something there she needed. In a minute.

On her way, she thought of the Ne'ila at the end of Yom Kippur. The ark open as the prayer to close the gates of heaven and inscribe the book of life is repeated. She intoned the words of the Shema three times as required, thinking of the meaning—of begging God to hear the people of Israel as they proclaim that God is one. And then, as the gates close, hope for the future, for the next time the book of life opens. Then in the kitchen, the hidden chocolate. Time to finish the hidden chocolate. She could get more at the market tomorrow. When her family returned from synagogue, she would greet them with the final statement of Yom Kippur. Chemda said it aloud now: "L'Shana Haba'ah B'Yerushalayim." She repeated it in her mind, to remember to say it later. *L'Shana Haba'ah B'Yerushalayim.* Moist chocolate staining her teeth and lips, chocolate sauce mixed with pink lipstick. A third time as an incantation. *L'Shana Haba'ah B'Yerushalayim. Next Year in Jerusalem.*

ACKNOWLEDGMENTS

Thank you: to my family, living and not, who entrusted me with pieces of their stories. With special gratitude to Abba, perhaps the only person in the family unafraid and willing to discuss the past when asked, and Imma, who filled every story with magic. To my wife, Danielle, who believes in my work more than anyone else, who reads every first and last draft, and makes sure I have no excuse not to write. And to my son, Mardoche, whose first year of life coincided with the writing of this book, and whose unique ability to sleep in any position at any time, made the writing of it possible. And to my editor, Nicola Mason, whose care and commitment made the final draft infinitely better than the initial draft she was given. I am indebted to the team at Acre Books, who put such care into this book: Barbara Bourgoyne, Sarah Haak, and Michael Alessi. Thank you to the sensitivity readers from the Jewish and Muslim communities who carefully reviewed the manuscript and provided me with important feedback.

Thank you also to all the readers who read earlier drafts or excerpts and provided me their thoughts: Caroline Picard, Terry Duvall, Kjerstin Pugh, Paulina Nassar, Chris Natali, Jason Bacasa, Sam Marvit, Jennifer Wood, Maia Ipp, Caleb Tankersley, Kumari Devarajan, Michelle Fredette, Kristen Arnett, Meghana Mysore, Melanie Hoekstra, T.J. Baker, Elizabeth and Pat Donohue, Mat Daly, Ronna Wineberg, and Anne Elizabeth Moore. And thank you to William, for forcefully convincing me to turn from writing non-fiction to fiction.

Thank you to the Mesa Refuge for providing me time and space to first outline this project, and to Tin House for providing a welcoming space to workshop it.

This book was largely written between 2020 and 2022. I could not have imagined that it would be released as Israel was committing a genocide against Palestinians in Gaza. I condemn the genocide and continued occupation, and stand in solidarity with Palestinians in their continued struggle for freedom, dignity, and equality.

REFERENCES

This is not a bibliography to better understand the history of Israel or Palestine. Those exist elsewhere, and I encourage the reader to seek them out, especially those that maximize Palestinian voices, which are too often silenced and ignored. This book is about the creation of Israel's mythologies and the ways they grew out of family stories and self-identities. It is about the stories that Israel and diaspora Jews tell themselves, a reinforcing narrative that has grown over the last century. As a result, many of the sources consulted are deeply flawed. They are mythologies masked as neutral historical or scholarly works. They served to inform me and remind me of the stories Jews grow up with, internalize, and rarely question. These sources' true teaching lies not in the content conveyed, but in the provenance, evolution, and acceptance of the narratives within them.

Furthermore, this is an incomplete list of works referenced, because a comprehensive list would be impossible. What went into this book includes a lifetime of family stories and tales that cannot be cited and whose veracity cannot be proven. Indeed, to try to do so would miss the mark. This is a work of fiction, and what is important is that these stories were told and believed, not that they were completely accurate. Additionally, as I was writing this novel, I never expected to include a reference section, so I did not keep close track of sources. This is my attempt to reconstruct some of those used.

Ali, Taha Muhammad, *So What: New and Selected Poems, 1971–2005*, trans. Peter Cole, Yahya Hijazi, Gabriel Levin (2006).

Arab Higher Commission for Palestine at U.N.O., *Jewish Atrocities in the Holy Land* (1948). (Memorandum.)

Bachman, Jeffrey S., ed., *Cultural Genocide: Law, Politics, and Global Manifestations*, (2019).

Bar-Itzhak, Haya, and Aliza Shenhar, *Jewish Moroccan Folk Narratives from Israel* (1993). (A fascinating book that contains transcriptions of Jewish Moroccan folk stories. Though there were some I had not previously heard, many were familiar from my grandmother and aunts.)

Begin, Menachem, *The Revolt: Story of the Irgun* (1951). (Written by Israel's sixth Prime Minister and former head of the Zionist paramilitary organization, the Irgun, Begin recounts the guerilla warfare and terrorism that they engaged in before and during Israel's independence.)

Benson, Susan, *Counter Cultures: Saleswomen, Managers, and Customers in American Department Stores, 1890–1940* (1987).

Benvenisti, Meron, *Sacred Landscape: The Buried History of the Holy Land Since 1948*, trans. Maxine Kaufman-Lacusta (2000). (One of the few books that examines in depth how Israel systematically renamed Palestinian villages, towns, cities, and landmarks as a way of erasing their history and culture.)

Blum, Howard, *The Eve of Destruction: The Untold Story of the Yom Kippur War* (2004).

Calhoun, Ricky-Dale, "Arming David: The Haganah's Illegal Arms Procurement Network in the United States, 1945–1949," *Journal of Palestine Studies*, Vol. 36, No. 4 (Summer 2007).

Chauncey, George, *Gay New York: Gender, Urban Culture, and the Making of the Gay Male World 1890–1940* (1994).

Ehrenreich, Ben, *The Way to the Spring: Life and Death in Palestine* (2017).

Elon, Amos, *The Israelis: Founders and Sons* (1971). (Tells the familiar Israeli narrative of Jews taming a wilderness and occupying an empty land. Though historically inaccurate, this type of mythology is one that many Jews have grown up with and internalized.)

Hankin, Saul, *Brothers and Sisters of Work and Need: The Bundist Newspaper Unzer Tsayt and Its Role in New York City, 1941–1944* (2013). (Dissertation.)

Harkabi, Yehoshafat, *Arab Attitudes to Israel*, trans. Misha Louvish (1972).

Harkabi, Yehoshafat, *Israel's Fateful Hour* (1988).

Hayoun, Massoud, *When We Were Arabs: A Jewish Family's Forgotten History* (2019).

Hazkani, Shay, *Dear Palestine: A Social History of the 1948 War* (2021). (Analyzing soldiers' letters during the 1948 war, the author shows how soldiers were indoctrinated in ideologies and mythologies that have come to define Israel.)

Hewitt, Nicolas, *Wicked City: The Many Cultures of Marseille* (2019).

Khalidi, Rashid, *The Hundred Years' War on Palestine* (2020).

Khalidi, Walid, *All That Remains: The Palestinian Villages Occupied and Depopulated by Israel in 1948* (1992).

Maarouf, Mohammed, *Jinn Eviction as a Discourse of Power: A Multidisciplinary Approach to Moroccan Magical Beliefs and Practices* (2007).

Magnes, Judah, *Dissenter in Zion: From the Writings of Judah L. Magnes* (1982). (The writings and letters of an important anti-Zionist who was prescient in his warnings.)

Montefiore, Simon Sebag, *Jerusalem: The Biography* (2012). (This book tells the story of the multiple peoples that have lived in the contested city over thousands of years.)

Morris, Benny, *1948* (2009). (Though the author provides a corrective to the mythology Israel has propounded about its founding and history by analyzing declassified military sources, his conclusions are deeply problematic.)

Morris, Benny, *Righteous Victims* (2001).

Pappe, Ilan, *The Ethnic Cleansing of Palestine* (2007).

Peteet, Julie, "Words As Interventions: Naming in the Palestine–Israel Conflict," *Third World Quarterly,* Vol. 26, No. 1 (2005).

Pinsker, Leon, *Auto-Emancipation* (1882). (One of the earliest Zionist tracts, this text links antisemitism to the fear of ghosts.)

Renan, Ernest, "What Is a Nation?" transcription of a conference presentation delivered at the Sorbonne on March 11, 1882, in Ernest Renan, *Qu'est-ce qu'une nation?* (Renan discusses how an essential quality for a nation to exist is to learn how to forget.)

Said, Edward, *Orientalism* (1978).

Said, Edward, *Out of Place* (1999).

Said, Edward, *The Question of Palestine* (1979).

Sand, Shlomo, *The Invention of the Land of Israel* (2012). (A useful book that shows much of the history and narrative foundational to Zionism has been a modern invention.)

Segev, Tom, *One Palestine, Complete: Jews and Arabs under the British Mandate* (1999).

Shammas, Anton, "Torture into Affidavit, Dispossession into Poetry: On Translating Palestinian Pain," *Critical Inquiry* (Autumn 2017).

Shehadeh, Raja, *Palestinian Walks: Forays into a Vanishing Landscape* (2008).

Slucki, David, *The International Jewish Labor Bund after 1945* (2012). (The Jewish Labor Bund represented an often-forgotten voice of anti-Zionism in Jewish thought.)

Van Creveld, Martin, *The Land of Blood and Honey* (2010). (The book repeats the familiar one-sided shallow history of Israel–Palestine.)

*

Cohen, Benjamin, ed., *The Illustrated Guide & Hand-book of Israel* (1960). (It was extremely difficult to find maps and descriptions of Jerusalem pre-1967, so I relied in part on old guidebooks.)

Fodor's Guide to Israel, 1967–1968 (1967).

The Guide to Israel, Seventh Edition (1964).

Hoade, Fr. Eugene, *Guide to the Holy Land*, 4th Ed. (1962).

Hoade, Fr. Eugene, *Jerusalem and Its Environs* (1959).

Israel: Complete Illustrated Vacation Guidebook (1963).

Mann, Peggy, *Israel in Pictures* (1965).